PATRICIA WENTWORTH

Born in Mussoorie, India, in 1878, Patricia Wentworth was the daughter of an English general. Educated in England, she returned to India, where she began to write and was first published. She married, but in 1906 was left a widow with four children, and returned again to England where she resumed her writing, this time to earn a living for herself and her family. She married again in 1920 and lived in Surrey until her death in 1961.

Miss Wentworth's early works were mainly historical fiction, and her first mystery, published in 1923, was *The Astonishing Adventure of Jane Smith*. In 1928 she wrote *Grey Mask* and gave birth to her most enduring creation, Miss Maud Silver.

POISON IN THE PEN

Patricia Wentworth

HarperPaperbacks
A Division of HarperCollinsPublishers

This is a work of fiction. The characters, incidents, and dialogues are products of the author's imagination and are not to be construed as real. Any resemblance to actual events or persons, living or dead, is entirely coincidental.

HarperPaperbacks *A Division of* HarperCollins*Publishers*
10 East 53rd Street, New York, N.Y. 10022

A hardcover edition of this book was originally published in 1955 by J. B. Lippincott Company.

Cover illustration by Paul Cox

First HarperPaperbacks printing: August 1996

Printed in the United States of America

HarperPaperbacks and colophon are trademarks of HarperCollins*Publishers*

10 9 8 7 6 5 4 3 2 1

CHAPTER 1

Miss Silver looked across the tea-tray a good deal in the manner of the affectionate aunt who entertains a deserving nephew, but the young man who leaned forward to take the cup of tea which she had just poured out for him was not really related to her in any way. He was, in fact, Detective Inspector Frank Abbott of Scotland Yard, enjoying a Sunday afternoon off duty and very much at his ease. It would have been difficult to guess his profession. He might have been in the Army, the Navy or the Foreign Office, he might have been at the Bar. For the rest, he wore discreet and beautiful clothes of a most admirable cut, and his tall, slim figure accommodated itself with the ease of long custom to the largest of Miss Silver's curly walnut chairs, whose spreading laps and carved encircling arms were so much more comfortable than they looked. The cool light eyes set in a pale irregular face softened noticeably as they rested upon his hostess. He admired her—his own word would have been revered. She entertained, she amused, she instructed, she provided his sense of humour with unfailing food, but even in his most irreverent moments he never ceased to feel a profound respect for her.

She smiled at him now and enquired whether he had enjoyed his leave.

"You were staying in Ledshire, were you not, for at least part of the time? The cards you sent me revived quite a number of memories. The one of the Market Place at Ledlington—"

He laughed.

"The view of Sir Albert's trousers is superb, isn't it?"

Since the statue of Sir Albert Dawnish which dominates the square is known to be one of England's leading eyesores, Miss Silver did not encourage this frivolity. She remarked instead that the Dawnish Quick Cash Stores had become a national institution, and that Ledlington, and in fact the whole county, had benefited by Sir Albert's generous disposal of his wealth. After which she returned to the question of his holiday.

"Did you see anything of the Marches?"

"I was invited to a cocktail party. The cousins I was staying with were going. I saw the Chief Constable, the beautiful Rietta, and the son and heir. And the infant daughter. It was being handed round with the drinks. A pleasant gurgling child. It stuck a fist in my eye and said 'Goo!'."

Miss Silver beamed.

"They are so delighted to have a little girl. Only children are a great mistake. Were you staying with cousins all the time?"

He reached for one of Emma's scones, feather light and sinfully enriched with both butter and honey.

"Cousins? Yes—but not the same ones all the time. I always forget just how many children my great-grandfather had, but I believe I am as well provided with relations as any man in England, to say nothing of the Scotch and Irish branches and a few adventurous spirits who have scattered themselves over the Commonwealth and the United States. As they are all very matey and hospitable, I need never pay an hotel bill, and holidays come cheap. I did three separate lots this time and finished up with Joyce Rodney, who is really only a step-cousin but we used to be rather friends."

He put down his cup and Miss Silver filled it again. She said, "Yes?" in a mildly interrogative tone, and he laughed.

" 'Yes' it is, though I don't know how you spotted it. But then I never do. As a matter of fact Joyce was worried, and I would rather like to talk the business over with you." He took a sandwich and dismissed her murmured "If you think that she would not mind" with a quick "No, no, she will be only too glad. She isn't used to anything of the sort, and it is getting her down."

She sat back in the chair which was the feminine counterpart of his own and waited. He thought what strange stories this tranquil room had heard. The Victorian pictures on the walls—*Hope, The Black Brunswicker, The Soul's Awakening,* the old-fashioned furniture, reproduced the atmosphere of an older and less hurried day before the aeroplane brought the countries of the world so close together that they must either learn to live together in peace or rush upon some final conflagration. Carpet and curtains repeated as nearly as possible the colour and pattern of those which had originally companioned the furniture, their predominant shade a cheerful peacock-blue, modified in the carpet by wreaths of pink and yellow flowers. The workmanlike writing-table and the numerous photographs with which mantelpiece, bookcases and occasional tables were crowded testified to the profession which had provided this modest comfort. There had been a time when Miss Silver had engaged in what she always alluded to as the scholastic profession, when she had in fact been a private governess with no other expectation than that of spending her life in other people's houses until such time as she retired on what must perforce have been very meagre savings. That the way should have opened for her to become a private enquiry agent she regarded as providential. She became known to an increasing circle, she earned a sufficient income, she had her flat, her comforts, her attached housekeeper Emma Meadows. She had a great many devoted friends. The photographs in frames of silver, of plush, of silver filagree on plush, testified to this. Many frightened people had sat where Frank Abbott was sitting now. Strange stories had been stammered out in this quiet room, and in the upshot virtue had been vindicated, crime exposed and justice done in the manner of the Victorian tract. Always conscious of these things, Frank found them very much in evidence as he said,

"Joyce has recently gone to live at Tilling Green. She lost her husband out in the Middle East—he was working for one of the big oil companies. There is a delicate child and no money. She has no near relations of her own, and she went to Tilling because Jack Rodney had an elderly cousin there who offered her a home."

Miss Silver said, "Yes?" again.

"She wrote very kindly—Joyce said it was like a gift from heaven. She couldn't take a job unless it was something she could do at home, because the child needed great care. Miss Wayne offered a home and a small salary in return for duties about the house. I gather she does a pretty full day's work—hens to feed, cooking, and all the rest of it—but she doesn't complain about anything so long as it's all right for the child."

Miss Silver, having finished her tea, picked up a brightly flowered knitting-bag and extracted from it four needles from which depended about an inch of what was intended to be a child's jumper in a pleasing shade of blue. Her niece Ethel Burkett's little Josephine would be seven in a month's time, and the garment was part of the twin set which had been planned as a birthday gift. She could always knit and listen at the same time, her hands held low in her lap, the needles moving rhythmically and at great speed. She said now in her pleasant voice,

"And there is something wrong?"

He nodded.

"She has been getting anonymous letters."

"My dear Frank!"

"It is always unpleasant, and of course no one knows better than you that it can be a symptom of something very nasty indeed."

"What are the letters about?"

He lifted a hand and let it fall again.

"She has torn them up—the usual instinct to get rid of something horrid."

"But I suppose she would have given you some idea of the contents?"

"One of them was about her husband. He died rather suddenly—heat-stroke, I think. The letter suggested that it wasn't a natural death. There have been two of them. The second went on to accuse her of having come to Tilling to 'catch another man.'"

Miss Silver permitted herself to say "Dear me!" and added, "Has she confided in Miss Wayne?"

"She hasn't told anyone—except me. You know what those poison-pen letters are—very unpleasant. Miss Wayne is a prim, mousey little thing who couldn't say boo to a goose. There was an elder sister who died some months ago. I gather it was she who invited Joyce to come to Willow Cottage. She was the elder and always took the lead in everything. As far as the village is concerned, she will go on being Miss Wayne to the end of the chapter, and the other little creature will continue to be Miss Renie."

Miss Silver coughed.

"Is there someone who dislikes Mrs. Rodney, or who has any reason to resent her presence in Tilling?"

"I can't imagine why anyone should dislike Joyce. She is one of those pleasant girls—nice to look at without being a beauty, intelligent without being a brain. In fact there are no extremes—nothing to rouse up the sort of enmity which the letters suggest. People are usually sorry for a young widow. She doesn't make a parade of her mourning, but she was very fond of her husband and she is devoted to the little boy. Miss Wayne has lived there a long time and knows everyone in the neighbourhood. Joyce says they have all been very kind."

Miss Silver's gaze rested upon him mildly.

"You say Miss Wayne does not know about these letters?"

"Oh, no. She is a timid person—it would alarm and distress her very much."

"Has Mrs. Rodney any suspicions?"

"None whatever."

"And you yourself?"

His colourless eyebrows rose.

"I was there for four days. I was taken to a jumble sale at the village hall. I attended morning service on the Sunday, and was afterwards introduced to several people whom I had missed at the sale. We were invited to tea at the Manor. I have no reason to suspect the parson, the verger, or any of the estimable middle-aged and elderly ladies who assist them to run the parish. In fact I have no reason to suspect anyone—how should I have?"

She continued to look at him in a thoughtful manner.

"These things do not always depend upon reason."

His eyes displayed a sardonic gleam.

"Woman's intuition? I'm afraid I can't compete. I don't know the exact figures for the current year, but speaking generally, there are about two million more women than men in the country. Terrifying to reflect that they are all at it day in, day out, exercising this formidable gift!"

Miss Silver considered that he was not really providing her with very much in the way of information. She said in a meditative voice,

"A jumble sale—the Sunday morning congregation—the Manor—that would cover a good deal of ground in a village. What is the family at the Manor?"

He gave her an appreciative glance.

"As you say, quite a lot of ground. The Manor is an old one, and the family has been there a long time. The name used to be Deverell, but somewhere in the last century the male line died out altogether and a Repton came in through a marriage with the heiress. He refused to change his name, so they have gone on being Reptons. They were very nicely to do until the property got split up again about thirty years ago, when the direct line ended with a woman who got all the money and the place went to a male cousin who is the present incumbent. He is Colonel Roger Repton. He is pretty hard up, and he is guardian—the heiress having died—to her daughter, a girl called Valentine Grey, who has come in for the family fortune. Attractive creature fluttering on the edge of matrimony with one Gilbert Earle, a chap in the Foreign Office who will probably be the next Lord Brangston and would certainly be able to do with the money, since the present man has a string of five daughters to provide for. He called them after flowers, and I gather they neither marry nor work for a living. I have met them in my time, sitting out whilst other girls danced. To the best of my recollection they are called Violet, Daffodil, Rosemary, Daphne and Artemisia."

The last name elicited a mild protest.

"My dear Frank!"

"Cross my heart ma'am, they call her Artie—I swear it!"

She drew on the blue ball.

"Let us return to Tilling Green."

"By all means. There are also living at the Manor Colonel Roger's sister, Miss Maggie Repton, the kind of sister who clings to the place where she was born and brought up because it has simply never occurred to her to go anywhere or do anything. She does keep house with a good deal of inefficiency, because young Mrs. Repton won't do it at all."

"There is a young Mrs. Repton?"

"There is indeed—the decorative Scilla! One of the things I haven't discovered is whether she spells it like the flower, or in the classical manner like Scylla and Charybdis. You see, quite a lot might depend on that."

Miss Silver saw, but she made no comment. He continued.

"Roger was considered to have made a fool of himself when he married her. She is definitely not what you would expect to find in Tilling Green, and she makes no secret of the fact that the country bores her and she yearns for town. I imagine she didn't know how little money there was going to be—especially when Valentine got married."

"That will make a difference?"

"Oh, yes. I understand that she contributes very handsomely to the expenses."

Miss Silver went on knitting.

"Just why are you telling me all this?" she said.

He smiled with a spice of malice.

"Don't I always tell you everything?"

"Not unless you have a reason for doing so."

"Perhaps I wanted to talk it out for my own benefit. Putting things into words straightens them out, and—you are always stimulating!"

She said, "I am wondering why you have described the household at the Manor whilst leaving the jumble sale and the congregation undescribed."

"One can't describe everyone."

"But you began with the Manor."

If he hesitated, it was only for a moment.

"It was probably because one of the letters mentioned Gilbert Earle."

"What did it say?"

"I didn't see it—I told you that. Joyce didn't keep either of them. But as far as my information goes it accused her of trying to attract him—throwing herself at his head, that sort of thing, only I gather in rather more unvarnished language. The anonymous letter writer doesn't generally worry about keeping the party clean."

"And does Mrs. Rodney know Mr. Earle well?"

"She knows him. He's down there constantly at weekends. But as a matter of fact she met him abroad some years ago when she was first married. They have friends and acquaintances in common. He has occasionally seen her home from the Manor or after some village do. There is nothing in it or ever has been, I am sure about that."

"Would Miss Valentine Grey be equally sure? Or young Mrs. Repton?"

He laughed.

"I don't know about Scilla Repton, but I don't think Valentine is in the least likely to object to Gilbert seeing other people home. There doesn't seem to be a general impression that she is head over ears in love with him.

There was someone else—the parson's nephew, one of here to-day and gone tomorrow type. He and Valentine were pretty thick. And then he just vanished from the scene. Didn't come, didn't write, and Gilbert Earle began to make the running. Now she is going to marry him. Joyce says her heart isn't in it."

"Are they friends?"

"Yes, I think they are—" He hesitated. "Joyce hasn't a great deal of time, you know. What with running the house, taking the child to kindergarten and fetching him again, well—"

Miss Silver murmured agreement.

"I am glad to hear that the little boy is well enough to go to school."

"Yes, Joyce is very happy about it. He seems to have taken quite a turn. It is so good for him to be with other children."

She made no comment upon this. After a moment she enquired,

"Do you know whether anyone else in Tilling has received an anonymous letter?"

He appeared faintly startled.

"Why do you ask that?"

"My dear Frank, you must surely see that it is a most important point. Such letters are you describe are instigated by a desire for power, or by either a personal or a general spite. If the motive is a personal one it may wear itself out or at any rate go no farther, but if it proceeds from a desire for power or from a general spite there is no saying where it will stop or how much mischief it may do."

He said briefly, "That's what worries me."

"Mrs. Rodney has not thought of taking the matter to the police?"

He pushed back his chair.

"She wouldn't hear of it. It would be very much resented in the village. I think it might make her position there impossible. Everyone has been very friendly, and the child is getting on so well." He got up and put down his cup. "I don't know why I bothered you about it. It will probably all fizzle out."

CHAPTER 2

Of the two newspapers subscribed to by Miss Silver it was her habit to peruse the lighter and more pictorial at breakfast, reserving the solid fare provided by the *Times* for a later and more leisured hour. It was about ten days after Frank Abbott had tea with her that her eye was caught by a headline which displayed the name of Tilling Green:

INQUEST AT TILLING GREEN

She had often noticed how singularly an unfamiliar name, once noted, is apt to recur. She read the paragraph with interest. A young woman had been found drowned in a stretch of ornamental water belonging to the grounds of the Manor House. Her name was Doris Pell, and she neither resided at the Manor nor was employed there. She lived with an aunt, and they carried on a business as dressmakers in a small way. The evidence reported her as having been greatly distressed by the receipt of anonymous letters accusing her of immorality, an accusation for which, the Coroner stated, there was no foundation—she was a perfectly respectable girl. The police were pursuing enquiries as to the authorship of the letters.

Miss Silver laid down the paper. A lamentable waste of a young life. She contrasted, not for the first time, the extreme courage and tenacity of purpose with which trouble is encountered in one case, and the ease with which it is succumbed to in another. Since this dead girl had apparently had the support of innocence, why had she put up no fight? The light that beats upon a village is of course sufficiently unsparing—white is white, and black is black, and a character once lost or even breathed upon will continue to be doubted indefinitely. But youth should possess some spring, some power of recovery, some ability to make a new beginning. Her thoughts remained saddened for some time.

It was not until later in the day when she was dealing with her correspondence that the matter was once more brought to her attention. She was engaged with a letter from her niece Ethel Burkett. Raising, as it did, the question of Ethel's sister Gladys, whose by no means harmonious relations with her husband Andrew Robinson were a perennial source of anxiety, it was affording her grave reason for thought.

"Dear Auntie," Ethel wrote, "I do not know whether Gladys has written to you, and I hate to trouble you with her affairs, but I really do think you have more influence with her than anyone else. A separation from Andrew would be *fatal*. He has been most tolerant and long-suffering and he has a horror of any scandal, but I have a feeling that if she were to go so far as to leave him, he would not readily take her back."

It was at this point, and while Miss Silver was reflecting upon just how far a selfish and headstrong young woman was likely to go in the process of cutting off her nose to spite her own face, that the telephone bell rang. She picked up the receiver and heard Frank Abbott say,

"Hullo! Is that you?"

Having been reassured upon this point, he continued.

"Then may I come and see you? . . . Thank you. I'll be right along."

She had no more than time to write what might be called an interim letter to Ethel setting out the view that Gladys, having no money of her own and being notoriously averse from anything in the nature of work, would, in her opinion, hesitate to separate herself from Andrew's very comfortable income, when the door opened and Emma announced,

"Mr. Frank—"

She was, as always, affectionately pleased to see him, and he on his side as affectionately at home.

When Miss Silver had settled herself in her chair and taken up her usual knitting, he said,

"Well, I don't know whether you can guess what has brought me."

She inclined her head.

"I have seen the paragraph about an inquest at Tilling Green."

"Stupid, damnable affair. More damnable than stupid, I should say. What gets into any human being to make him—or her—set out to poison and destroy. Do you know, I met this girl when I was down there. She had come in to do some needlework for Miss Wayne. She was a sensitive, shy creature—coloured up to the roots of her hair when I spoke to her. Joyce had been good to her, and the girl obviously adored her."

Miss Silver had seldom seen him with his surface cynicism so completely broken through. The drawl was gone from his voice and the chill from his glance. She said with a good deal of warmth,

"My dear Frank—"

He nodded.

"I am a fool, but it has got me on the raw. She was

such an inoffensive creature—plain, simple, kindly. And someone could take pleasure in destroying her!"

She knitted thoughtfully.

"Is there any suspicion of foul play?"

"Not in the technical sense. The law does not call that sort of thing murder. There seems no reason to doubt that she jumped into the lake and drowned herself—'Whilst the balance of her mind was disturbed!' That, as you will have seen, was the verdict. She had taken some work up to the Manor. They say she seemed as usual." His shoulder jerked. "You may have noticed that people always do say that kind of thing when anything like this happens! There is a place where the drive crosses an ornamental stream. The stream passes under a bridge and falls over rocks to this lake they speak of. She must have jumped over the low parapet on the lake side and hit her head. After which she drowned. As the verdict says, she was off her balance, and the thing that drove her off her balance is patent. That is what I have come to see you about."

The blue frill which depended from the needles was lengthening. Miss Silver said,

"Yes?"

He spoke with a return to his usual manner,

"You see, we've been asked to send someone down there. I don't know whether you remember, but about five years ago there was a very nasty outbreak of this sort of thing about ten miles away at Little Poynton. They had a couple of suicides there and a lot of other trouble, and it was never satisfactorily cleared up. They ended by calling in the Yard. March has been on to us officially about this Tilling business. It seems that several people have had letters. He has got hold of two. One was posted in London. It is one of the most recent and may provide a clue. After all, only a small number of Tilling people can have been in Kensington on the day when the letter was posted there."

Miss Silver made a slight negative gesture.

"I do not feel that a hardened writer of anonymous letters would provide so obvious a clue."

"I don't know—everyone slips up sometimes. Anyhow it's all the clue there is. The paper is cheap block stuff—ruled. Envelope rather better. Writing big and thick, clumsy ill-formed letters—the experts say left-handed. A sprinkling of spelling mistakes—probably deliberate. No fingerprints except what you would expect—branch office—postman—recipient. All very helpful!" He leaned forward suddenly. "Now what March suggests is that you go down there with the official blessing and do your stuff. The Chief thinks it is a good idea, and I am here to find out if you will take it on."

She knitted in silence for a little, and then said,

"I do not, unfortunately, know anyone in the vicinity. It would be of no use for me to go down unless my visit could be contrived to appear a natural one."

"The Miss Waynes occasionally took in a paying guest. One of them was a Miss Cutler, now living in Chiswick. It could be arranged for you to meet her in a casual manner, after which it would be child's play to induce her to recommend a country lodging. You could then write to Miss Wayne and enquire whether she would be prepared to take you in."

After a moment she said,

"Miss Wayne is not to know?"

"No one is to know, except Joyce. Miss Wayne least of all. She is constitutionally timid and would never have a happy moment if she thought she had a detective in the house."

She looked at him gravely.

"I do not know. I do not like the idea of my hostess being in ignorance. It is in fact repugnant."

"My dear ma'am, if your advent is to be broadcast!" Her glance reproved him.

"It would be a grave responsibility for Mrs. Rodney. Is she prepared to undertake it?"

"She rang me up this morning from a call-box in Ledlington. She is very much worried, very much upset about Doris Pell, very much afraid that there may be further trouble. I had talked to her about you when she first told me about the letters. She asked me if you could not come down, and suggested this paying guest business. It seems Miss Wayne had been speaking about Miss Cutler and saying she really thought she must repeat what had been a very pleasant experience. So you see, it would be quite easy."

She drew upon her ball of wool.

"Perhaps. But I would prefer that she should receive at the very least some hint that my visit was a professional one."

He said, "Impossible!" and then relaxed into a laugh.

"The fact is she has one of those tongues which never really stops. You know—the gentle trickle just going on and on. She wouldn't mean to give anything away—she probably wouldn't know she was doing it—but you can't talk all the time and be safe with a secret. Joyce said it would be hopeless, and that she really would be frightened to death. She is terrified already about the letters—gets up in the night to see that the doors are locked, doesn't like being left alone in the house, all that sort of thing. Joyce says she will jump at having an extra person there. And you know, you couldn't really do better. She has a cottage on the edge of the Green—neighbours to right and to left of her, the village shop within a stone's throw, the entrance to the Manor just on the other side of the Green, and church and parsonage beyond. When I tell you that the chief village busybody, a Miss Eccles, lives next door on the one side, and the chief village mystery on the other, you will realize that you simply can't refuse such a marvellous opportunity."

"And pray who or what is the chief village mystery?"

"He is a gentleman of the name of Barton, a quiet, harmless old boy who keeps cats and doesn't invite any of the ladies to tea. He doesn't even have a woman to do for him, so naturally there is a general feeling that he must have something to conceal. He does his own cooking and cleaning, if any, and he keeps his door locked, which is a thing even Miss Wayne hasn't done until lately."

In the course of her professional career Miss Silver had frequently been obliged to embark upon a course of action to which as a private gentlewoman she would not have committed herself. She began to consider the desirability of making Miss Cutler's acquaintance.

CHAPTER 3

Elderly ladies cannot easily be hurried. It took a little time to contrive the kind of approach which Miss Cutler would consider to be pleasant and natural. A mutual friend, or someone who could play that part—a drawing-room humming with conversation, tea-cups poised and cake and biscuits in circulation—in such a setting it was easy enough to talk of country holidays, to mention Ledshire, and to be immediately the recipient of Miss Cutler's interested comments upon the shocking fatality which had so recently taken place at Tilling Green—"Where I stayed, I actually stayed, Miss Silver, only just a year ago."

"Indeed?"

Miss Cutler nodded vigorously. She had a bony intelligent face and hair which had shaded from red to so very pale a gold that it might almost have been taken for grey. It still curled, and she had long ago given up any attempt to control its exuberance.

"Oh, yes," she said, "I was there for three months with the Miss Waynes at Willow Cottage. That poor girl who committed suicide made me a couple of blouses. Such a nice quiet creature—I was quite dreadfully shocked."

Miss Silver heard all about the Miss Waynes.

"You have never been back again?"

"Well, no. Miss Esther died—very suddenly, poor thing. Though I'm sure I don't know why one should be sorry for people who die suddenly. It is unpleasant for their families of course, but much happier for them. Anyhow it must have been a great shock for Miss Renie. She depended on her for everything. Really quite painful to see a grown woman so subservient. I hear she has a widowed niece living with her now."

"And does she still take in guests?"

"I really don't know. They were not at all well off, and if the niece is dependent . . . I have sometimes thought of going down again, but I don't know what the housekeeping would be like now, unless the niece does it. Miss Renie was *not* a good cook! On the other hand, there was a very pleasant social circle at Tilling Green. Horrid for them all having this poison-pen business. And just as that charming girl at the Manor is getting married! There was another young man on the tapis when I was down there. She wasn't engaged to him, but they all thought she was going to be. He was the parson's nephew, Jason Leigh. Such an odd name—and rather an odd young man. Anyhow nothing came of it, and she is marrying the other one next week, I believe. I made friends with a Miss Eccles when I was down there, and she wrote and told me. We still correspond occasionally." She went on talking about Tilling Green and the people whom she had met there. "Colonel Repton at the Manor, married to quite a young wife—very pretty, but not very popular. The people bore her, and they don't like it. . . . Valentine Grey has a lot of money. Gilbert Earle, the man she is marrying, is the heir to a title. . . . Miss Eccles says Colonel Repton will be put to it to go on living at the Manor without the allowance which her trustees have been paying him while she lives there. She is herself some kind of distant connection of the family, so I suppose she knows. She says they are having a rehearsal of the wedding ceremony. I don't know that I care about the idea. I know it is very generally done, but it seems to me to detract from the sacred nature of the occasion. I may be wrong, but that is how it seems to me." Miss Cutler's loud, decided voice continued with hardly a break, but she contrived to make a very good tea.

Miss Silver was, of course, the perfect listener. She was interested, she was agreeable. When encouragement seemed desirable she supplied it. By the time she left she had quite a clear picture of Tilling Green and its inhabitants, together with a number of unrelated details which she memorized without effort and which she could rely upon herself to reproduce at will. She went home and wrote a letter which she addressed to Miss Wayne, Willow Cottage, Tilling Green, Ledshire. It began:

"Dear Madam
        "An acquaintance of mine, Miss Cutler, has

told me of the very pleasant holiday she spent with
you some time ago. I am encouraged to write and
ask you whether you would consider allowing me
to come to you as a paying guest for a short time.
The quiet surroundings of a village . . ."

To this letter she presently received the reply which she
expected. Miss Wayne would be very pleased. She was
sure that any friend of Miss Cutler's . . . She had lost her
dear sister of whom Miss Cutler would doubtless have
spoken, but she and her niece would do their best to
make a guest's stay pleasant. She was writing to thank
Miss Cutler for the recommendation. As to terms, everything kept going up so. She felt obliged to charge a
little more than they had asked a year ago. . . .

The small spidery writing ran on to a signature which
could just be identified as Irene Wayne.

CHAPTER 4

Miss Silver found herself
delighted with Willow Cottage. Tilling Green was a
charming little place, far enough from Ledlington not to
have been spoiled but within sufficiently easy reach by
bus. It had a fourteenth-century church with some interesting tombstones and brasses, the fine old Manor
house, and two or three really charming half-timbered
cottages. Willow Cottage was of course of a later date,
which she considered preferable from the point of view
of a residence. Old cottages were doubtless picturesque,
but they were sadly apt to have uncomfortably steep
stairs and low ceilings, to say nothing of out-of-date
sanitary arrangements and a shortage of hot water. Wil-

low Cottage had a nice little modern bathroom which, as Miss Wayne informed her, had taken the place of an early Victorian conservatory.

"We found it full of ferns when we bought the cottage—it is thirty years ago now—and it made the dining-room so damp. My sister decided immediately that it must go. She was a wonderful person, Miss Silver. She always made up her mind about things at once. The moment she saw that fernery she said that it must go. Now I am quite different. I am afraid I see so many *difficulties*. I said, 'Oh, Esther!'—that was my sister's name—and she said, 'Well, what are you oh'ing about?' It was very stupid of me of course, but I couldn't help thinking how inconvenient it would be to go through the dining-room if one wanted to take a bath, but she pointed out that mealtimes would quite naturally be different from bathtimes, and that if one had a tendency to be late in the morning it would help one to overcome it. And so it actually did. I found that I was able to get up quite half an hour earlier without it being any trouble at all. It only needed a little perseverance."

Without thinking its situation ideal, Miss Silver was in no frame of mind to cavil at it. There might so easily have been no bathroom at all, and she was delighted with her bedroom, one of the two which looked towards the front of the house and provided that view across the Green towards the Manor gates and the neighbouring church described by Frank Abbott.

Miss Wayne informed her that there was to be a wedding at the Manor within the next day or two.

"Really Tilling Green will be quite gay—a rehearsal for the wedding on Wednesday and a party at the Manor in the evening. It is giving them a great deal of work—Colonel and Mrs. Repton and his sister. It is she who really does the housekeeping—young Mrs. Repton doesn't take much interest. Joyce and I are not invited, but as I said to her, 'My dear, we really can't expect it. Of course I have known them for thirty years, and you and Valentine have been friendly—and we could have got Jessie Peck in to be with David—but as we were not asked, there is no more to be said about it. You must remember that we are not relations.' I must say I shouldn't myself consider Mettie Eccles or Connie Brooke to be anything more than connections. My dear sister always thought it absurd to use the word relation for anyone farther away than a second cousin."

Miss Silver checked this dissertation with a question.

"And the bride? She is a young relative of Colonel Repton's, I think you said? You have known her for some time?"

"Oh dear me, yes—from a child—Valentine Grey. The wedding is on Thursday afternoon. Such a charming girl, and the bridegroom is so very goodlooking. Of course one didn't quite expect—but people very seldom marry their first love, do they?"

Miss Silver turned an interested ear.

"Very seldom indeed, I should think."

"How kind of you," said Miss Wayne in her small earnest voice. She proceeded in a burst of confidence. "I do really mean it, because I was just thinking that perhaps it was an unkind thing to say, and one doesn't like to feel one has been unkind."

Miss Silver smiled.

"It is, I think, a question of fact. Characters develop and tastes change. Someone who would be congenial as a companion at seventeen or eighteen years of age might no longer be so in five or six years' time."

Miss Wayne continued to gaze. She was a little mousey creature with a tendency to turn pink about the eyes and nose when moved or distressed. She blinked and said,

"How well you put it. I shouldn't like to have felt that I had been unkind. Valentine is such a charming girl, and no one has heard anything of Jason Leigh for a very long time. I asked his uncle about him the other day—he is our Vicar's nephew, you know—and he said, 'Oh, he never writes.' 'Oh!' I said. 'Oh dear, Mr. Martin, that is very sad for you, isn't it?' But he said he didn't think it was, because young men liked to be off 'adventuring.' Don't you think that was a very *curious* word for him to use?"

Miss Silver enquired what Mr. Leigh's profession might be.

"Oh, he *writes*," said Miss Wayne vaguely. "Rather odd sort of books, I think. My niece tells me they are clever—but then if you are not clever yourself you like something simpler, don't you think? A nice love story with a happy ending, if you know what I mean. Of course I can't help taking an interest in dear Valentine and hoping that she will be very happy indeed. I think I told you they are having a rehearsal of the ceremony on Wednesday afternoon. Would it interest you to slip into the church and watch? I have never seen a wedding rehearsal, and there cannot be anything private about it, can there? Of course Joyce and I have been asked to the wedding, and if the Reptons see you with us on Wednesday, I expect they will ask you too. After all, one more can make very little difference—there are always some people who cannot come. I know for a fact that Janet Grant, who is a very old friend, will not be able to be there because the rather tiresome sister-in-law who is always getting ill has had one of her attacks, and that means Janet having to go all the way down into Kent. Esther used to say—my dear sister, you know—she used to say that Jessica wouldn't get ill nearly so often if she hadn't been allowed to count on Janet running down there every time her finger ached. But of course one mustn't be unkind about it, and no one knows better than I do how terrible it is to be *lonely*. Jessica didn't marry, you see, and she doesn't get on with Janet's husband, Major Grant—such a nice man, but rather a sharp temper. So it is all rather sad. Now my dear sister and I, there was never a word between us all the years we lived together. But then it is generally men who make the trouble, is it not?"

It was this identical theme which was occupying Mrs. Needham who had kept house for the Rev. Thomas Martin at the Parsonage across the Green for almost as long as he had been there himself. If he ever looked back to the days before her coming, it was with a heartfelt shudder. A wife in failing health, a succession of well-meaning but incompetent "helps," the shock of Christina's death and his own conviction that the failure of their marriage must somehow have been his fault and his alone—these were not things upon which any man would choose to dwell. At his darkest hour Mrs. Needham had walked in, sent undoubtedly from heaven by way of a Ledlington registry office, and she had been there ever since—large, strong, imperturbable, a good cook, an excellent housekeeper, a wonderful manager. She had, in fact, so many virtues that the absence of just one might be considered to weigh lightly in the scales. She was kind, she was clean, she was honest, she had every domestic quality, but she had a tongue which practically never stopped. There had been moments when Tommy Martin had felt that he couldn't bear it. It was at these moments that he allowed himself to look back, and he never had to look for long. In time he developed a way of life in which she learned to play her part. When he went into the study and shut the door he was not to be disturbed. For the rest, he could bear with her and in case of need withdraw his attention to a point at which he really hardly knew whether she was talking or not.

At the moment when Miss Wayne was deprecating the trouble-making proclivities of men—in which connection she would certainly have used a capital—Mrs. Needham was enlarging upon the same topic to a visitor of her own, Mrs. Emmott, the Verger's wife, a thin lugubrious woman whom no one had ever seen out of black. They were enjoying a nice cup of tea and some of Mrs. Needham's featherlight scones. Mrs. Emmott had just remarked that there was no smoke without some fire, and Mrs. Needham was agreeing heartily.

"That's just what I said, my dear. Show me a bit of trouble, and ten to one there'll be a man somewhere behind it. Not that I'd believe anything wrong about poor Doris, for I wouldn't, but if there wasn't a man in it somewhere, why did she go and drown herself? Girls don't, not except there's a reason for it."

"I can't say there's anyone ever saw her with a fellow," said Mrs. Emmott in a resigned voice.

They had already been talking about Doris Pell for the best part of half an hour. Mrs. Needham was ready to go on to someone else. She said,

"Oh, well—" And then, "There's more goes on than meets the eye. Now only last night—but there, perhaps I didn't ought to say anything."

Mrs. Emmott gazed at her.

"Then you shouldn't have brought it up."

"Well, perhaps I shouldn't. Not that it was anything really, and if I don't tell you, you'll go thinking all round it and about, when it was only Connie Brooke that rang up, wanting to see Mr. Martin when he was out."

"And what's wrong about that?"

"I didn't say there was anything wrong, only she was crying, that's all."

"Maybe she's got a cold."

Mrs. Needham shook her head.

"There's a difference between a girl that's got a cold and a girl that's been crying her eyes out. 'Oh, is he in?' she said, and I said, 'Well, no, he isn't. He's gone over to Ledlington to one of those meetings about the Orphanage, and he said he'd stay to supper with the Reverend Craddock. Friends at College they were, and he's ever such a nice gentleman.' So she said, 'Oh dear, oh dear!' and I could tell by her voice she was crying again. And just then who should come in but Mr. Martin himself. It seems Mr. Craddock had been called out to someone that was taken ill, so he had come home for his supper after all. I gave him the telephone and I told him who it was, and before I had time to go a step I could hear her say, 'Oh, Tommy darling, can I come and see you? I don't know what to do!' You know how all these young ones call him Tommy."

Mrs. Emmott looked down her nose.

"It didn't ought to be allowed," she said. And then with melancholy interest, "Did she come?"

Mrs. Needham was pouring herself another cup of tea. She nodded.

"Oh, yes, she came. And I was right about the crying—her eyes were all bulged up with it. And she didn't go away any happier neither, for I was coming through from the kitchen with his supper-tray when they come out of the study. I stood back, as it were, and they didn't see me. And he was saying, 'Well, my dear, you had better think it over. I can't tell you what you ought to do, because I don't know what it is that you've got on your mind. But if it is really anything to do with those horrible letters, then I think you may have a duty.' "

"Well, I never! And what did she say to that?"

Mrs. Needham leaned forward in the chair which she filled with amplitude. She had a lot of strong dark hair only lightly sprinkled with grey. Her eyes were brown and soft, and she had cheeks like rosy apples. She dropped her voice and said,

"She began to cry again. I stood just where I was with the tray, and I couldn't help but hear. Mr. Martin, he said, 'Oh, my dear child, don't! That handkerchief's nothing but a rag. Here, take mine.' And she sobbing and saying, 'Oh, poor Doris—I don't know what I ought to do—but once I've said it I can't take it back, can I?' And he said, 'No, you can't, so you'd better go back and think it over.' And with that he'd got the door open, and if you ask me, he was glad to be rid of her. For they take advantage of him, indeed they do—coming here at all hours and never thinking whether it's his supper-time or not!"

When they had finished their tea Mrs. Emmott went on down to the village shop, where she picked up a tin of Irish steak which her friend Mrs. Gurney had been keeping for her. They had a comfortable melancholy conversation, in the course of which Mrs. Emmott passed on what Mrs. Needham had been telling her, with some additions of her own.

Later that evening Mrs. Gurney told Jessie Peck, who was a cousin of hers, and Jessie Peck told her sister-in-law who worked Tuesdays and Thursdays for Miss Eccles and Wednesdays and Fridays for Miss Wayne. Just how many people the sister-in-law told cannot be estimated. Her name was Hilda Price, and she was a strong persevering talker. Within twenty-four hours most people in Tilling Green were aware that Connie

Brooke had something on her mind. She knew who had written the anonymous letters. . . . She knew something about the death of Doris Pell. . . . She couldn't make up her mind whether she ought to tell what she knew. . . .

CHAPTER 5

It did not take Miss Silver long to discover that Miss Wayne really did very seldom stop talking. If her visit had been, as it was supposed to be, of a private nature, this might have proved trying, but in the circumstances it was extremely helpful. After even a short time in the house she found herself in possession of the life histories of nearly everyone in Tilling Green—their faults, their failings, the tragedies which here and there had broken the even tenor of village life—wartime losses, post-war changes—the births, the marriages, the deaths, and the departures, were displayed rather after the manner of a jigsaw puzzle. There was a fact here, a conjecture there, a sigh over some dereliction, a tear for someone missed, a speculation as to what can have occasioned some regrettable incident— Why after thirty years had the Farmers suddenly gone away?—Why had Lily Everett broken off her engagement to John Drew?—What was the real reason why Andrew Stone had gone to Australia?

Miss Silver sat knitting whilst the trickle of talk went on. The flow increased noticeably when the question of Miss Renie's mysterious next-door neighbor came up.

"Such an extraordinary person. My dear sister was very loth to think ill of anyone, but as she often said, why should you lock your doors and shut your windows and never let anyone inside your house if you haven't got something to hide? The Vicar says it is because he doesn't like women. But how often has he got in himself—that is what I should like to know. And with the door of Gale's Cottage round at the side—such a very odd place to have a door, only some of those old cottages do—you can't help seeing who comes out and who goes in."

Miss Silver's interest was really very flattering.

"Mr. Barton lives there quite alone?"

"Oh, quite—unless you are going to count the cats."

"He has cats?"

Miss Renie threw up her hands.

"Seven of them! Quite insanitary—I don't suppose the house is ever cleaned! And such great raw-boned creatures—quite savage-looking! And all with Bible names—really quite profane!"

A little way back from the fire, young Mrs. Rodney was putting a patch on a small pair of grey flannel shorts. "David does go through them now that he is getting stronger," she said in her pleasant voice.

Miss Silver smiled at her kindly.

"That must be a great comfort to you," she said.

Miss Renie was spreading out the cards for a game of patience, using a board covered with green baize balanced precariously upon a three-legged stool ornamented with poker-work. She looked puzzled.

"Because he wears out his clothes?" she enquired.

Joyce Rodney laughed.

"Because he is so much stronger, and that makes him wear them out."

"Oh, I see—" But she still looked puzzled. "Yes, I do see. And he *is* stronger, but there are so many things that can happen to a child, and one can't help feeling anxious, can one? Now there was poor Mrs. Pavey—she lost six. You can see all their names on the stone in the churchyard, and a place left for her own, poor thing."

The slight tightening of a muscle at the corner of Joyce Rodney's mouth did not escape Miss Silver. She hastened to remark that little David had a very brown and wholesome look. When they were alone together later on Joyce said,

"There is really no need to worry about David now, I am thankful to say. Aunt Renie is so kind, but she is inclined to be over anxious and to take a gloomy view. She has never had any responsibilities, because Aunt Esther did everything, so she gets nervous. Only I wish she wouldn't tell stories about people who had dozens of children and didn't know how to look after them properly. It's stupid to mind, but I can't help it."

Miss Silver rested her knitting in her lap.

"Mrs. Rodney—"

"Oh, please call me Joyce—everyone does."

Miss Silver coughed.

"In a little while perhaps, if my visit is prolonged. At this juncture I think it would be imprudent to strike too intimate a note."

"Oh—"

"It would be better if we are a little formal. What I was about to say was that Miss Wayne has talked very freely about a number of things that have happened in Tilling Green over a considerable period of time, yet she has not mentioned the death of Doris Pell or the fact that an inquest attributed that death to suicide."

"It upset her terribly."

"And you think she cannot bear to speak of it?"

"She was very much upset. Unfortunately Miss Eccles came in with the news and wouldn't stop talking about it. I really thought Aunt Renie was going to faint. You haven't met Miss Eccles yet, but she is one of those people who must know everything and then hurry on to tell somebody else. I suppose it is leading rather a dull life and not having any private affairs of her own. Anything in the least out of the way is something to talk about. But Aunt Renie and I were really fond of Doris. She was quite a clever dressmaker. She made the dress Aunt Renie is wearing, and she copied a coat and skirt for me. We were both too much shocked by her death to think of it as news."

Miss Wayne returning to the room at this moment, the subject would have been dropped if she herself had not said in a small shaky voice,

"Oh, my dear, were you talking about poor Doris?" She turned to Miss Silver. "Such a painful subject—but you must have read about it in the papers. We went to the funeral of course. Poor Miss Pell was terribly overcome—she is the aunt, you know, and she had brought Doris up. The whole village was there, and the flowers were lovely." She dabbed her eyes and the tip of a reddened nose. "You can understand how we feel about it. But I did not intend to sadden you with our troubles. Joyce should not have spoken of it. We must talk about something more cheerful. Valentine Grey's wedding—now that would be the thing!" She addressed her niece. "I was telling Miss Silver about the rehearsal tomorrow afternoon. I thought we could just slip in at the back and see how it went without being in anybody's way. Mettie Eccles rang up—rather waste of a telephone call, as she is our next-door neighbour, but she is a little extravagant about things like that, and they do mount up. But on the other hand, when you are busy it does save time if you can just have a call instead of going out of one house and into another and perhaps getting caught up in quite a long conversation. . . . Dear me, where was I?"

Joyce looked up smiling.

"Mettie Eccles had rung you up—"

"Oh, yes—of course—how stupid of me! Esther always said I let my thoughts wander too much. Yes, Mettie rang up, and she said that Lexie Merridew isn't very well. She is one of Valentine Grey's bridesmaids, and it will be quite terribly disappointing if she cannot be at the wedding. Mettie said her dress is here, because Valentine was giving the bridesmaids their dresses. They are from Elise in Ledlington. And if Lexie really can't come, Valentine was wondering about having Connie instead." She directed a flurry of explanation at Miss Silver. "That is Connie Brooke. She and a friend keep the little kindergarten school that David goes to. So many business men who work in Ledlington have bought or built houses in this direction that there is quite an opening. Penelope Marsh comes over from Lower Tilling, but Connie has the last house on the Green. She used to live there with her mother, who was related to the Reptons, and now it comes in very nicely for the school and so convenient for David. Connie won't look so well in the dress as Lexie would have done—such a pretty girl! And poor Connie—but there, we must not be unkind, must we? And she is just about the same size, so the dress will fit."

CHAPTER 6

The rehearsal was at half past three. Walking across the Green, Miss Silver was regaled with information about the Vicar, the Rev. Thomas Martin—"A widower—his wife died thirty years ago, and he has never married again. Such a pity! It must be so lonely for him." The parsonage—"Much,

much too big of course. Everyone is very fond of him, but I do not think it is suitable for the young people to call him Tommy. It shocked my sister very much. She quite took him to task about it—she was so strong-minded. He only laughed, but she did not consider it a laughing matter. And he is so untidy in his dress—it is really a great pity."

They were not so very far back in the church after all, Miss Wayne moving forward three times until they could have a really good view of the chancel, already decorated with greenery and pots of lilies. The scent was strong upon the chilly air. There were hours of daylight left, but even in high summer it would be dark under these grey arches. For the wedding tomorrow all the lights would be on, but now the body of the church was in shadow.

Miss Silver was glad of her winter coat. She never went down into the country without providing herself against the exigencies of the English weather. She wore her second-best hat, black felt with a ruching of violet ribbon. For the wedding itself she would assume her best headgear, quite newly purchased and of a shape considered by her niece Ethel Burkett to make a most becoming change. It was of black velvet trimmed with three pompons, one black, one grey, and one purple. At the moment it reposed in the bottom drawer of the bow-fronted chest in Miss Wayne's spare room, very carefully covered with tissue paper, together with a new pair of grey kid gloves and a woven scarf of grey and lavender silk.

On her way up the church Miss Mettie Eccles had paused beside them. She imparted the news that Valentine's friend, Lexie Merridew, who was to have been chief bridesmaid, really had failed at the last minute. "Some childish complaint—so very inconvenient. Really these things should be got over before a girl is grown up. They have had to ask Connie to take her place. Not really suitable, but the dress will fit, and of course she is thrilled." She went on her way with her usual air of being in a hurry. Miss Silver received the impression that it would be impossible for the rehearsal to proceed without her, and that if it had been handed over to her to run, Lexie Merridew would have been wearing her own dress and there would have been no question of the bridegroom not having arrived in plenty of time. Disgraceful, really disgraceful, that he should be late, and that they should have had to begin without him.

As it was, everything that could go wrong did seem to have gone wrong. Miss Eccles said so in one of those pointed, piercing whispers which can be relied upon to carry into the farthest corner. It certainly reached Colonel Repton standing at the chancel steps. Connie Brooke, deputizing for the bridesmaid who had so inopportunely developed German measles, saw him look over his shoulder with one of those frowns which had always frightened her. Whether the whisper reached Valentine Grey or not it was really quite impossible to tell. She stood beside the cousin who was her guardian, very tall and straight and pale, with her chin lifted and her eyes on the old jewelled glass in the east window. It made the chancel dark, but the colours were lovely. And it had been old already when Giles Deverell had it taken down piece by piece and buried it to save it from Cromwell's men.

Valentine looked at the crimson and violet and sapphire above the altar. The chancel was darkening already, but the colours were bright against the autumn light outside. Her own dress was dark. A dark blue, but it looked black down here in the shadows. She thought, "There are things that you can save if you bury them deep enough," and heard Maggie Repton say for perhaps the twentieth time, "Oh dear, oh dear, whatever can have kept him?" She did not have to turn her head to be aware of Aunt Maggie sitting in the front pew on the bride's side of the aisle, fidgeting with her prayerbook, her gloves, the long cut-steel chain which was looped twice about her neck and was constantly getting too tight and having to be eased.

Mettie Eccles in the pew behind had all she could do not to put out a restraining hand. Maggie always did lose her head when anything happened. And what an odd pair she and Scilla Repton made. No one who didn't know would have taken them for sisters-in-law. But then Roger Repton had made a perfect fool of himself by marrying a girl who was less than half his age. Miss Eccles had had plenty to say about it at the time, and she had plenty to say about it still.

"It's not as if it was just the difference in their ages. One must be broad-minded, and I have known some really quite successful marriages where the man was a good deal the elder. It doesn't always answer of course, but I would be the first to admit that it can be quite successful. Only no one can possibly pretend that Scilla Repton is a domestic type. Far from it. I don't suppose she is prepared to do a hand's turn in the house, and like everyone else they are terribly understaffed—daily girls from the village. And how much of that will they be able to afford once Valentine has gone? It's really no use pretending we don't all know that it is only her money that has made it possible for Roger to hang on at the Manor."

And now—how much longer *would* they be able to hang on? Every fibre of Mettie Eccles' slim body quivered with impatience to know the answer to that. And not to that only. She was so constituted that ignorance upon any point, so far from being bliss, was really a minor form of torture. She was at this moment quite devoured with curiosity as to why the bridegroom had not turned up. They were going on with the rehearsal without him. Why? One would have thought that they would have waited for more than the ten minutes or so which was all that Roger Repton had conceded. Did they know that it would be no use to wait? But in that case there must have been some message—a wire, a telephone call. But no, there had been no sign of any such thing. Valentine had not been out of her sight for a moment. And nor had Roger, or Maggie, or Scilla. There had been no message. Gilbert Earle was quite definitely and inexplicably absent from his wedding rehearsal. He and his best man were to have driven down from town. They had rooms booked at the George. They were dining at the Manor. The wedding was set for half past two next day. And no sign of Gilbert Earle.

Scilla Repton turned her graceful neck and said in her languid voice,

"Bear up, Maggie. It will be all right on the night."

Maggie Repton pulled on the steel chain. She had a dreadful feeling that she might be going to burst into tears at any moment, and Roger would be quite dreadfully angry if she did. She met Scilla's amused glance with a frightened one and said with a catch in her breath,

"Oh, do you think so?"

"My dear, of course! You don't suppose he's got stage fright and is backing out, do you?"

There was amusement, even enjoyment behind the words. Mettie Eccles was perfectly aware of it. Not at all the way to talk in church. And not the way to dress either—she felt no doubt about that. She did not approve of people being casual, though as it was only a rehearsal and not the wedding itself, Maggie really needn't have put on her purple. She knew for certain that it was what she was going to wear at the wedding. She was having a new hat, but definitely nothing more. The purple should have been kept for tomorrow. Now she herself was wearing just what she always wore at a week-day service. Not in any sense of the word a wedding garment, but perfectly suited to one of the minor church occasions. If Maggie was too dressed up, Scilla, she considered, had gone to the opposite extreme—a tweed skirt, a scarlet cardigan, a black beret pulled on over shining golden hair, a scarf with all the colours of the rainbow. Not suitable—not suitable at all! And Connie copying her in that absurd way! Someone ought to speak to her about it. She would make a point of doing so herself. Scilla's clothes cost money. A skirt run up at home and a badly knitted jumper were not going to turn poor Connie Brooke into either a beauty or a fashion-plate. To the end of the chapter she would go on being a washed-out copy of somebody else, with her colourless hair, her pale round face, and the poking figure which she really might have done something about if she could ever have remembered to hold herself up.

Miss Eccles felt justifiably pleased with her own neat, upright carriage, in fact with her whole appearance. She might be fifty-five, but she had a complexion, and there was no more than a sprinkling of grey to soften the waves of her hair. Her eyes were still quite startlingly bright and blue. She really had every reason to be pleased with herself.

No one could have felt less pleased with herself than Connie Brooke. If things had been different, it would have been wonderful to be Valentine's bridesmaid. She had never dreamed of such a thing—how could she? It was only the chance of Lexie Merridew going down with German measles and the dress fitting her. It would have been marvellous if only—if only—

That sick feeling came up in her throat again. It would be awful if she were to be sick in church. She couldn't be sick with Mrs. Repton looking on. If only she knew what to do—Tommy had been sweet, but he hadn't told her what to do. She had meant to tell him everything, but when it came to the point she couldn't do it. Suppose he didn't believe her. There were times when she couldn't believe herself. She didn't know what to do.

Up at the chancel steps the Reverend Thomas Martin, a large untidy man in the bulging garments familiar to everyone in the village as the more elderly of his two known suits, was understood to say that he thought that would do nicely—very nicely indeed. Since he used a subterranean whisper, no one could be quite sure of the words. He beamed upon Valentine in very much the same way as he had done at her christening, and added more or less audibly,

"You won't care to be walking up to the altar rails by yourself, so that's about as far as we can go. He'll be turning up any time now, and you'll be laughing at whatever it is that has kept him. Anyhow it's all quite foolproof, my dear, so you needn't fret yourself. I've married too many couples to let either of you put a foot wrong, so never give it another thought."

She had seldom felt less like laughing. There was a numbness in her mind. Her thoughts were dark, and cold, and still. Only every now and then there were flashes of light, of pain, of something that was terribly like hope. It couldn't be hope. Tommy was smiling like an india rubber gargoyle. He was a kind old pet and she loved him, but he saw too much. She didn't want him to be sorry for her. She smiled back at him and said in quite a natural voice,

"Oh, yes, it will be all right."

Roger Repton swung round with a gruff "Well, that's done! Ridiculous rubbish if you ask me! Modern craze! Wedding's quite bad enough without dragging everyone through a rehearsal first!"

The two bridesmaids moved apart, Connie awkward and abstracted, Daphne Hollis pretty and poised.

Valentine said, "Thank you so much, Tommy darling," and turned from the chancel. When she took that step tomorrow she would be Gilbert's wife, she would be Mrs. Gilbert Earle. Unless—

There was one of those flashes in the darkness of her mind. It came and went, and the numbness closed down again. The door at the end of the church was pushed open and Gilbert Earle came in. His fair hair was ruffled, there was a smear of mud on his cheek, and a three-cornered tear half way down his left sleeve. He wore a charming rueful expression, and it was plain that he expected a general indulgence. Miss Eccles declared afterwards that he was limping a little, but no one else appeared to have noticed the fact. He came straight to Valentine and said in his agreeable voice,

"Darling, you'll have to forgive me. John tried to take the hedge into Plowden's field. He'll be coming along as soon as they've patched him up a bit. I, as you can see, am only the worse for a little mud."

CHAPTER 7

The old rooms at the Manor lighted up well. The dining-room with its panelled walls and its portraits, its draw-table and its high-backed chairs, the drawing-room with its French carpet and the brocaded curtains which might look shabby in the daytime but whose ageing beauty preserved a lamp-lit splendour. Fifty years before their tints of peach and gold would have been repeated in the coverings of chairs and couches, but to-day the patched remnants were hidden under loose chintz covers too often cleaned to do more than hint that they had once displayed pale wreaths of flowers. There were portraits here too—a charming graceful creature with a look of Valentine, Lady Adela Repton in the dress she had worn at the famous Waterloo ball—her husband Ambrose, shot down by the Duke's side next day and painted with an empty sleeve pinned up where the arm had been. He had a lean face and an irked, angry look.

Roger Repton resembled him strongly, even to the expression. It was Scilla's idea to give this party, and in the two years that they had been married it had been borne in upon him that when Scilla wanted anything he might just as well let her have it and be done with it. But that wasn't to say that he was prepared to look as if he was enjoying himself, because he wasn't. The house was upside down, and there had been that damned silly business of the rehearsal in the afternoon. He wanted to sit down peaceably by the fire and read the *Times,* and if he went to sleep it wouldn't be anybody's business. Instead of which, here was this damned party. A fuss on the wedding-day he was prepared for. Weddings were damned uncomfortable things, but he knew what was the proper thing to do and he was prepared to go through with it. It was this thing of having a dinner-party the night before that got him. The bridegroom should be entertaining his bachelor friends, and the bride should be getting her beauty-sleep. Val looked as if she needed it. She was like a ghost in that pale green floating thing. He frowned at Lady Mallett, and discovered her to be saying just that.

"Valentine looks like a ghost."

Since it was his habit to contradict her, he did it now.

"I can't think why you should say so!"

"Can't you?" She chuckled. "Hating all this, aren't you? Scilla's idea of course, and very nice too! What's all this about Gilbert's friend having driven them both into a ditch?"

"You've got it wrong! It wasn't a ditch, it was the hedge into Plowden's field!"

"Had they been celebrating?"

"Not noticeably."

"Well, he must be a shocking bad driver! It was he who was driving—not Gilbert? Because if it was Gilbert, I should advise Valentine to break it off! You can't go marrying a man who drives you into ditches!"

"I told you it wasn't a ditch!"

She gave her rolling laugh.

"What's the odds? Here, what's the matter with Valentine—stage fright? I remember I nearly ran away the day before I married Tim. I must go over and cheer her up. Or is it you who want it more than she does? As I said, you're hating it all like poison, aren't you? The fuss and the bother—and Val going off—I don't suppose you're feeling too cheerful about that, are you? You'll miss her in more ways than one, I expect."

Her grandmother had been a Repton and she ranked as a cousin. If she didn't mind what she said, it was astonishing how often other people didn't mind it either. Her large dark eyes held an unfailing interest in her neighbours' affairs. She dispensed kindness, interference, and unwanted advice in a prodigal manner. Her massive form, clad in the roughest of tweeds, was to be seen at every local gathering. Her husband's long purse was at the disposal of every good work. Tonight she was handsomely upholstered in crimson brocade, with an extensive and rather dirty diamond and ruby necklace reposing on a bosom well calculated to sustain it. Large solitaire diamond earrings dazzled on either side of her ruddy cheeks. Her white hair rose above them in an imposing pile. Her small and quite undistinguished-looking husband had made an enormous fortune out of a chain of grocery stores.

Roger Repton said, "Yes." It was no good getting annoyed with Nora Mallett. She said what she wanted to say, and no one could stop her. If she wanted to talk about his financial position, she would. She was doing it now.

"Eleanor did you pretty well in her will, didn't she! Six hundred a year until Val was eighteen, and another two hundred after that as long as she made her home here! Poor Eleanor—what a mess she made of her life marrying that man Grey! Anyone could see with half an eye that he was after the money. You know, I always thought she had a bit of a soft spot for you. Of course you were first cousins and all that, but nobody thought anything of their marrying in Victorian times—in fact it was quite the thing to do when the estate went in the male line and there were only daughters."

"My dear Nora, Eleanor and I were not Victorians."

"Much better if you had been—you would almost certainly have married."

He said abruptly, "Well, we didn't, and that's that!"

"And more's the pity. Such a shame for you to come in for the Manor without the money to keep it up properly. Stupid things those old entails. Much better really for Valentine to have come in for the place and have done with it. With the money she had from her mother, everything would have been easy enough." She became aware of his lowering look and added, "Well, well, I daresay it's all for the best if one only knew it, so cheer up!"

"I can't see that there's very much to cheer up about."

She laughed.

"Wait till the champagne has been round!"

She moved away and left him thinking morosely. Champagne two days running! And the one thing he wouldn't do was to offer cheap wine to a guest. He wished the whole thing over and done with. But there would still be the bills to come in.

Mettie Eccles came up in a purposeful manner. She wore the black dress which had figured at every evening party for the last ten years, but she had a long floating scarf of bright blue that matched her eyes, and she seemed, as always, very much pleased with herself. Her looks went darting here and there, taking everything in, approving, criticizing.

"What is Gilbert Earle doing here? He ought to be having a party of his own in town, then he wouldn't have been run into a hedge by—what's the man's name—John Addingley. I hear he's got three stitches in his lip—the Addingley man, not Gilbert—and he couldn't have been any beauty to start with. What is he—something in the Foreign Office like Gilbert? They used to go in for looks and manners, but now they only need to have brains. So dull! But Gilbert hasn't done so badly. I suppose he has the brains, and he certainly has the looks. Between you and me, Roger, isn't he just a bit too goodlooking? I suppose Valentine doesn't think so. Or does she? If she does, she is about the only woman he knows who would rather have him plain. Of course it makes a difference when you are considering a man as a husband."

He said stiffly, "I don't really know what you mean."

Her eyes were brightly blue.

"Nonsense, my dear man! You know as well as I do! He would be the answer to any maiden's prayer, only it doesn't always work out in the domestic circle. I suppose the money is all tied up?"

"Naturally. Really, Mettie—"

She nodded.

"Yes, yes, I know—most improper to speak of it! But what's the good of being old friends if you can't? And whilst we are being indiscreet you might just as well tell me why Valentine looks—"

"My dear Mettie, I haven't the slightest intention of telling you anything! Not that there is anything to tell. Valentine has been run off her legs. She is tired out and no wonder."

"Oh, well, if that is all—Brides ought to look their best but they very seldom do. Gilbert seems devoted enough. He's got rather a knack of it, hasn't he? Too charming to too many people. But I suppose with Valentine it's the real thing, so all the others will be thinking how lucky she is. And of course he will be the next Lord Brangston. Too tiresome for the poor people having all those daughters, but very nice for Valentine. Not that a title does you much good nowadays, but it's decorative and she can afford to keep it up."

Gilbert Earle had crossed the room to where Valentine stood with John Addingley, a tall hatchet-faced young man with a strip of plaster crossing his upper lip. Valentine stood between them. She had used rather a delicate lipstick, because when she tried the brighter shade it made her look too pale. She had put a little colour on her cheeks, and it looked all right upstairs, but when she caught a glimpse of herself in one of the long mirrors between the windows down here she could see that it stood out on the smooth white skin like a stain.

Gilbert said, "Am I allowed to take you in?" and she smiled a little and said, "Yes, I think so. We are only waiting for Scilla. It's shocking of her to be late, but she always is." Her voice was sweet and quiet. It sounded as if she was too tired to raise it or to accent the words. There was no feeling behind them.

In the pause that followed Maggie Repton was heard to say, "Oh, dear—" and Sir Timothy Mallet took out his watch and looked at it.

Then the door opened and Scilla Repton came in in a gold dress with the least possible amount of top to it. Arms, shoulders, and breast were as white as milk. Her hair was golden under the light. She came in without hurry and stood a moment, smiling, before she said in her languid voice,

"Oh, you're all here. And I'm late again—how dreadful of me! Maggie, who do I go in with? Is it the bridegroom, or Sir Tim—I can't remember."

Gilbert met her eyes with a laughing look.

"Oh, not with me, I'm afraid. Valentine and I are on show as a pair tonight—aren't we, darling?"

Valentine said gravely,

"I suppose we are." There was a faint note of surprise in her voice, as if it had only just struck her. And it was true. They were on show like exhibits in a glass case with all the lights turned on so that everyone might see. But after tomorrow they would be alone. A stab of fear went through her, a sense of the irrevocable.

Scilla was smiling, her head a little tilted back, her lashes drooped.

"Oh, no," she said, "—have a heart! After all, you'll

be going off together for the rest of your lives. It's our turn tonight. Val can do her best to soothe Roger's lacerated feelings, and you, darling, are coming in with me, so that is all about it."

CHAPTER 8

The evening was over and quite a number of people were glad of it. Connie Brooke was one of them. It ought to have been a wonderful party, the sort of thing to remember and look back on when times were dull. And she had had a lovely dress to wear too, one that Scilla Repton had given her, almost new and just the pale blue she liked best. Penny Marsh thought it made her look too pale—"run-in-the-wash" was what she had really said. But everyone knew that fair girls could wear blue, and it would have been quite all right if she hadn't been so upset and cried so much. Her skin showed it terribly when she cried, and her eyelids were still hot and swollen. She had hoped no one would notice it.

But Cousin Maggie had. She had come right up to her in the drawing-room after dinner and asked in her fidgeting sort of way whether there was anything the matter. It was kind,but it made her want to cry again. And of course she had recognised the dress—"I suppose Scilla gave it to you. But really, my dear, the colour—rather trying! Perhaps you haven't been sleeping."

"No, Cousin Maggie, I haven't been sleeping."

"Oh, well, you shouldn't let it go on. Nora Mallett was quite concerned. She said you looked as if you hadn't slept for a week! And I said I would give you some of my tablets—very good ones which Dr. Porteous gave me two years ago when I was staying with my cousin Annie Pedlar. They were wonderful! And you do feel so much better about everything when you've had a good night's sleep."

Well, of course they both knew that she had been dreadfully upset two years ago about Cousin Roger's marriage. As if anything more wonderful could have happened! There they were, two dull elderly people, and Scilla—wonderful, beautiful Scilla—had been willing to come and live with them. She let her thoughts dwell on how marvellous it would be to live in the same house as Scilla and see her every day.

As she walked home across the Green with Mettie Eccles she kept on trying to think about Scilla—how lovely she had looked in that golden dress. She was much, much more beautiful than Valentine. Talk about looking pale—Valentine had looked like a ghost, everyone was saying so. Why should she be pale? She was the bride, tomorrow was her wedding day, she had everything that a girl could possibly want. Her own unhappiness came up in her throat and wouldn't be swallowed down. She wondered if Cousin Maggie's tablets would really make her sleep. It would be wonderful if they did. She would have to dissolve them—she had *never* been able to swallow anything like a pill. . . .

Miss Mettie was saying, "You don't look fit for anything, Connie. You had better have something hot and get to bed as quickly as you can."

"Oh, yes. I left my cocoa all ready on the stove—I shall have to heat it up. And Cousin Maggie gave me her tablets, so I shall be sure to sleep."

Mettie Eccles said sharply, "I thought you couldn't swallow a tablet. I remember your mother saying so."

"I'll dissolve them in my cocoa."

"Goodness—they'll taste nasty! But of course you

don't taste things, do you? Why can't you just swallow them?"

Connie said weakly, "I don't know—I can't."

She did hope Miss Mettie wasn't going to argue with her about it. She didn't feel like arguing with anyone tonight. It would be easier to try and swallow the tablets, but if she did she would be certain to choke.

Mettie Eccles went on about it all across the Green. "How many tablets did she give you? How many did she tell you to take?"

"I don't think she said. I expect it will be on the bottle."

"Well, I shouldn't take more than one if I were you. It isn't as though you were used to things like that."

They said good-night at Miss Eccles' gate and Connie went on alone. It was a great relief to be alone. She didn't want to have to think any more, or to talk, or to answer any more questions. She only wanted to have her hot drink, and to lie down in her bed and go to sleep.

She always left a light burning when she was out. She didn't like the feeling of coming into a dark house. She unlocked the door, and there was the light waiting for her. When she had locked it again she went through to the kitchen. Her cocoa stood ready on the oil stove in an enamelled saucepan. She lit one of the burners, put the pan on to heat, and went upstairs. Now that the eveing was over she was so tired that she could hardly drag one foot after another, but she hung the pale blue dress away, in what had been her mother's room, before she went down for the cocoa. She took Cousin Maggie's tablets with her. She thought she would have slept without them, but she wanted to make sure. When she had drunk the cocoa she washed cup and saucepan out at the sink, put out the light downstairs, and went up to bed. It would be lovely to have a real long sleep.

CHAPTER 9

All over Tilling Green there were houses where people were going to bed or were already there and asleep. At the Manor Roger Repton gave something between a yawn and a sigh of relief as he laid down keys and money on his dressing-table and took off his white tie. By this time tomorrow the whole damned fuss would be over. What was the good of worrying? Pity you couldn't always help it. Valentine was bound to marry some time, and how could you tell how any marriage would turn out? Take his own—He shied away from that. No good thinking about things that didn't bear thinking about—Get back to Valentine. There was no reason why it shouldn't turn out all right for her. Gilbert wasn't the first young fellow to play about a bit before he settled down. And the money was tied up all right—no playing ducks and drakes with it. There had been enough of that with poor Eleanor and that fellow Grey. Pretty, fragile creature Eleanor. The going had been too tough for her, and she had just given up. He wondered how it would have been if they had married. Everyone said it wouldn't do, so he went off to the East and she married Grey. But not at once, not for quite a long time. And Grey was a rotter. Stupid affair the whole thing. But Valentine would be all right with Gilbert. They were going to miss her, and—they were going to miss the money. He began to think about how badly they were going to miss the money.

His sister Maggie thought the evening hadn't gone so badly after all. Mrs. Glazier was a really good cook, and everything had been very nice. Of course they would probably not be able to go on having her after this—or would they? Roger always did talk as if they were all going to the workhouse next week. Papa did too. They didn't call them workhouses now, but the principle remained the same. If you hadn't enough money you had to keep on thinking about it, and that was so very tiresome. It was a pity that Valentine was getting married. Marriages didn't always turn out the way you thought they would. She might be very unhappy, as her mother had been. She might have wished she had stayed as she was. Gilbert was a very goodlooking young man, and some day he would have a title, because poor Lady Brangston had gone on having daughters, so he would be Lord Brangston when his old cousin died. There wouldn't be any money, but Valentine had enough for two. Charming young men didn't always make the best husbands. She would have liked to get married when she was a girl, but nobody asked her. And perhaps it was safer not to have a husband at all than to have one who turned out badly like Valentine's father who had broken poor Eleanor's heart and spent quite a lot of her money.

She took off the amethyst necklace which had been her mother's and put it away. The stones were a lovely colour and it was a handsome necklace. She could remember her mother wearing it with a dress of lilac satin cut low upon the shoulders and trimmed with a lace bertha. Women had good shoulders then. Mamma's had been very smooth and white. The necklace had looked very well. Her own neck was too thin for it. She put it away with a sigh, lifting the three trays of an old-fashioned jewel-case and laying it out carefully on the padded satin at the bottom. The folded piece of paper was on the next tray. Only a little piece of it showed under a heavy bracelet set with carbuncles. She put out her hand to the torn edge of the paper and drew it back again, but in the end she lifted the bracelet and unfolded the crumpled sheet. Someone had written on it, the letters clumsily formed, the lines slanting awry.

After a time she folded it again and put it back with the bracelet to hold it down. Then she replaced the other two trays and locked the box and put away the key.

Valentine Grey slipped out of her pale green dress. Mettie Eccles had said to her, "You shouldn't be wearing green, you know. It's unlucky." She stood with the pale floating cloud of it in her hand and thought from what long, long, long-ago ages these superstitions came down. Green was the colour of the Little People—the fairies. They couldn't bear you to wear it, especially on a Friday, because Friday was the day of the Redemption and they had no part in it—

She hung up the dress and went to the dressing-table to take off her pearls and lay them down. Her hand went up to the clasp and dropped again. There was a letter fastened to the pin-cushion with the brooch she had worn that afternoon, a little diamond feather, very light and sparkling. The envelope was the sort they sell with Christmas cards. It was very tightly stuck. The writing was large, and thick, and awkward. She didn't know it at all. She picked it up, tore it open, and discovered another envelope inside, a small grey one. There was no writing on it.

There was nothing to frighten her, but a pulse beat in her throat. There was nothing to be afraid of, but her hand had begun to shake. Out of the grey envelope there came a scrap of paper. Words had been pencilled on it in a hand she knew:

"The old place. I'll wait till twelve. If you don't come, I'll be ringing the front door bell at nine o'clock."

There was no signature, but she did not need one. The least scrawled word that Jason ever wrote was signature enough. Sense, memory, feeling, shut her in with the sole thought, *"He's here."*

It was at its first impact pure release and joy. It was as if she had grown wings and could fly to her own place of heart's desire. And then she was jerked back without escape, because it was all too late. He had gone away, and she had not known whether he was dead or alive. There are a thousand deaths for the one you love, and in every hour one of those deaths could fall. You could not go on like that, never knowing, never hearing. It wasn't possible. She was marrying Gilbert Earle tomorrow. Anger flowed in where the joy had been. Did Jason really think he could throw her down and pick her up again just as he chose? Did he think that his world would stand still while he left it to go adventuring? The word came to her with the very sound of his voice. She let herself listen for a moment. A small flame of anger came up in her. "He that will not when he may—" She had been willing enough, and he had gone away without a word. She found that she was holding the paper so tightly that it hurt.

And then suddenly she was tearing it into shreds and scattering them from the window. The anger in her burned for an outlet. Since he had set time and place for them to meet, she would go, and for once, just for once, everything should be clear between them. Let him look at what he had done, let him watch the smoke of the burning and see the utter destruction. And then nothing more.

She took off the long, full petticoat which she had worn under her green dress and put on a dark skirt and jumper. She took off her pale green shoes with the crystal buckles and put on low-heeled shoes with a strap. She tied a dark scarf over her head and slipped into a short, loose coat.

When she opened her door, the passage was empty before her. She came out upon the landing. The hall lay shadowy below. A small low-powered bulb burned there. There is always something dreamlike about being alone in a sleeping house. The daily maids had gone home hours ago. Mrs. Glazier, who was the gardener's wife, had gone back to their cottage. Somewhere on the floor from which she had come Scilla and Roger and Maggie would be sleeping—they were all tired enough. Scilla had hardly waited to say good-night before she went yawning to her room.

As Valentine crossed the hall, the feeling of emptiness and silence came up about her. It was like going down into a swimming-pool and feeling the water rise about your waist, your throat, your chin. Now it had closed over her. She walked in it, leaving the light farther and farther behind until she came to the drawing-room door.

When she had turned the handle and passed within, there was no more light. She closed the door without latching it, took out the little torch which she had slipped into the pocket of her coat, and switched it on. A narrow beam straggled into the darkness, showing chairs, tables, couches—shapes half guessed at in some uncharted place. She came to the pale curtains and slipped between the middle pair. The other two windows had cushioned seats behind the old brocade, but this one was a door, like the one in Scilla's sitting-room which lay beyond. As she came out upon the terrace she switched off the torch. She would not need it again. Her feet had taken the way too often for that, by day, by dusk, and in the dark. And tonight it was not really dark at all—low clouds with the moon behind them and everything dimmed but visible.

She went to the end of the terrace and down the steps.

A lawn sloped gently, edged with trees. Presently there was a path which went away to the left and wandered among them. There were shadows that came and went as a light breeze moved the branches overhead. The trees thinned away. Here the ground rose to a viewpoint where a great, great-grandfather had set one of those formal summerhouses which the early Victorians called a gazebo. She climbed to it by a path which was overgrown with grass. As she came to the top, something moved in the shadowed doorway. She stood still, her heart knocking against her side.

There were two wooden steps up into the gazebo. Jason Leigh came down them and dropped his hands upon her shoulders. It was all so easy, so familiar, so near the pattern of what had been that she did not feel it strange. The months between were gone and the gap had closed. They were Jason and Valentine, and they were together. They stood like that without moving until he said,

"So you've come. Just as well. I meant what I said about coming up to beat on the front door if you didn't. Well, now we'd better sit down and talk. The steps will do."

He let go of her and they sat, as they had done so many times before. If the moon had been out, they would have seen the slope of the Tilling woods, the Green like an irregular triangle with its bordering of houses, and the trickle of the Till going down through the meadows to join the Lede. There were no lights in any of the houses, but the outline of the Green was visible and the black mass of the church. Nearer still a faint mist brooded above the lake where Doris Pell had drowned.

Neither of them spoke for a time. Valentine had come here to be angry, to beat herself against the thing in him that could love her and leave her, which could go away but could not stay away. But now that they were here together she could not do it. If he came he came, and if he went he went. There was **no**thing she could do about it. Only how could she marry Gilbert Earle when she felt as if she were married already to Jason? What was marriage? It wasn't just the words which Tommy would say over her and Gilbert tomorrow. It wasn't just the physical bond, the physical sharing. For some people it might be that, but not for her. She felt with a deep inner knowledge that she would never be Gilbert's wife. And if they had never kissed, never touched, and were never to touch or kiss again, the bond that was between Jason and herself was something that would never change or break.

Out of the darkness at her side he said,

"What are you going to do?"

"I don't know—"

He laughed.

"A bit eleventh-hour, isn't it?"

He heard her take her breath.

"Why did you go away?"

There was a movement as if his shoulder had lifted and dropped again. The gesture came up out of the past, as dearly familiar as the tough lean body, the dark hair, the slant of his brows, the mobile mouth, the swift change of expression from grave to gay. He said,

"Needs must when the devil drives."

"Jason, why did you go?"

"My darling sweet, there is only one answer to 'Why?' and that is 'Because.'"

"Meaning you are not going to tell me?"

He nodded.

"Got it in one."

She said in a low shaken voice,

"Why did you come back?"

"About time I did, wasn't it?"

After a little she said, "No." And then, "If you hadn't come—"

"You would have married Gilbert and everything would have been all right?"

She took another of those long sighing breaths.

"No. There isn't any way out."

In her own mind she thought, "I'm in a trap. I can't marry Gilbert. I can't break it off. Not now. Not like this."

The church clock began to strike. The twelve strokes fell upon the air with a mellow sound. Jason said,

"Well, darling, it is your wedding day. What does it feel like?"

She put the flat of her palm upon the step between them and pushed herself up. She felt as if the weight was too much for her to lift. But she was no sooner on her feet than he pulled her down again.

"No good running away from it, Val. You know you can't marry him."

Having pulled her down, he let go of her at once.

Her voice sounded lost as she said,

"I must."

"You know perfectly well that you can't! I'm not doing anything to influence you. I haven't touched you, I haven't kissed you, I'm not making any impassioned appeals. I'm just asking you what you expect to happen if you go through with this marriage. Who do you think is going to get anything out of it? If you're thinking of Gilbert, I can imagine pleasanter things than finding yourself landed with a reluctant girl who is in love with somebody else. If you are thinking of me, I can assure you that I shall get anything you may suppose me to have deserved. And if you are thinking of yourself—well, I should recommend you to think again."

She did not feel that she had anything to think with. She put her face down into her hands and leaned forward until they rested upon her knees. She had no thoughts, only feelings. In retrospect, the lonely ache when he was gone. Now and here, Jason so near that her least, slightest movement would bridge the space between them. In the future beyond these passing hours of darkness a nothingness, a blank in which she could conceive of neither thought nor action.

Time went by. He did not move or speak, but if they had been locked in one another's arms, she could not have been more aware of him. In the end she lifted her face a little and said in a weeping voice,

"Why—did—you—go?"

He gave that half shrug again. This time it was followed by words.

"I had something to attend to."

She went on as if he had not spoken, or as if she had not heard.

"You came to meet me here. You didn't say that you were going away. You kissed me, and you went. You didn't write. You didn't come—" Her breath failed and the words with it.

He said, "It was tough for you. I always told you loving me was going to be tough."

She got her breath again.

"People can't just go away like that. And come back. And find that nothing has changed. If you are too unhappy you just can't go on."

He said without impatience,

"You knew I came, and went, and didn't write."

Again she went on as if she hadn't heard him.

"I got a letter. Someone wrote it, but I don't know

who it was. It said there was a girl, and that was why you went."

"I can't tell you why I went. There wasn't any girl."

"There were three letters altogether. They were—*nasty*—as if slugs had crawled on them."

"Anonymous letters are apt to be like that. You could have had more sense than to believe what they said."

Her head came up.

"I didn't! Jason, I didn't! But the slime got on to everything."

He said with something that wasn't quite a laugh,

"Try yellow soap and a nailbrush!" Then, with an abrupt change of manner, "Val, wake up! You can either believe in me or not believe in me. Whichever you do, you've got to do it blind. Your anonymous letter writer didn't produce any evidence, I take it. Well, I'm not producing any either. If you believe in me you believe in me, and that's that. If you don't believe in me, we make a clean cut here and now, and I wish you joy. As I remarked a little while ago, it is your wedding day. Or not, as the case may be."

She cried out at that.

"You haven't even said you love me!"

His voice did not change.

"If you don't know that without being told, there aren't enough words in the language to get it across."

And all at once she did know it—deeply, surely, and with certainty. He had gone away and said nothing. He had come back, and he would say nothing still. Perhaps the same thing would happen again. Perhaps it would happen many times. Perhaps she wouldn't be able to bear it—she didn't know. But she did know that he loved her, and because of that she couldn't marry Gilbert Earle. She got to her feet and stood there below the wooden steps, looking up at him as he rose too.

"I must go. It won't be my wedding day, Jason."

She went down the hill alone, as she had come. She knew what she was going to do, but she did not in the least know how she was going to do it. They had parted without a kiss, without a touch. What was between them was much stronger than kisses or the touch of the flesh, and she had so nearly betrayed it. She was like the sleep-walker who awakes suddenly on the sheer edge of some frightful fall. Another step and her foot would have been over the edge. The space of a few hours and she would have been Gilbert's wife. Everything in her shuddered, and then sprang up exulting because she had waked in time.

She came on to the terrace and back through the door which she had left ajar. As she passed between the folds of pale brocade and drew them close behind her, the darkness in the room was like a solid wall. She couldn't see to take a single step, she couldn't see her hand before her face. She turned her head a little to the right and saw, cutting the darkness, one bright streak. The door into Scilla's sitting-room was ajar and there was a light there.

She moved towards it without thought or plan. It drew her and she went towards it. When she was about a yard away she stopped, because someone was speaking, there in the lighted room. It was Gilbert Earle, and what he said was, "Scilla, what is the use?"

And Scilla laughed.

It was a slow, lazy laugh. She said,

"Darling, I wasn't really thinking about things being useful."

They must have been very close together. The two voices came from the same place. If they were not in one another's arms, the voices would not sound so close. He said with a kind of groan,

"We've been over it all before."

"And you wouldn't face it." There was a light flavour of contempt in her voice.

He sounded as if he had drawn back a little.

"We always knew it couldn't last."

"You always meant to eat your cake and have it, didn't you, darling? In fact, to put it bluntly, you always meant to have Valentine's money."

"I'm very fond of her."

"But just a little fonder of the money."

"You've no right to say a thing like that! I couldn't afford to marry a girl who hadn't something of her own."

"You couldn't afford to marry me?"

"My dear girl, there's no question of my marrying you."

She said quite softly and sweetly,

"Roger would divorce me—if he knew."

It had all passed too quickly for Valentine's thought to take hold of it. There was a shattering sense of shock. She turned round and groped her way towards the other door. Her outstretched hands touched nothing until she came to it. She had made no sound, and she had not stumbled.

She passed through the hall and up the stairs to her own room.

CHAPTER 10

After Miss Silver had brushed her hair and arranged it for the night, plaiting and controlling it with a stronger net than the one which she used by day, it was her invariable practice to read a chapter from the Bible before putting out the light and composing herself to sleep. Tonight, sitting up in her warm blue dressing-gown with the hand-made crochet trimming which had already done good service upon two earlier gowns, she read with edification in the book of Proverbs and the sixth chapter. Passing from a recommendation to avoid becoming surety for a stranger and the advice given to the sluggard to consider the industry of the ant, in both of which she wholeheartedly concurred, she came to the description of the man who sowed discord, and the inclusion amongst things hated by the Lord of—

"A lying tongue, and hands that shed innocent blood,

An heart that deviseth wicked imaginations, feet that be swift in running to mischief,

A false witness that speaketh lies, and he that soweth discord among brethren."

This seemed to her to have so direct a bearing upon the situation in Tilling Green that it engaged her very particular attention. Whether these were the reflections of Solomon or not, how strong a searchlight they turned upon the darker recesses of the human mind, and what age-old wisdom they displayed. It was some time before she closed the book and addressed herself to her devotions.

When they were completed, she took off the dressing-gown and laid it across her folded clothes, after which she put out the light, drew back the curtains, and opened the farther of the two windows, reflecting as she did so how habits had changed in this direction. Her grandmother would never have dreamed of allowing the night air into a bedroom except during a period of summer heat. Not much more than a hundred years ago not only were the windows shut and the curtains drawn, but the beds were curtained too. Her common sense approved the change, though she considered that the young people of the present generation sometimes went too far in the opposite direction. Tonight the air was mild, and she pushed the casement wide. The night was a dark one. No moon was behind the cloud which veiled the sky. She could just see the path to the gate, but not the road, or the grass beyond it. As she stood watching, a car came out of the Manor gates on the far side of the Green. It was followed after a moment by another, and another. There had been a party there on the eve of the wedding, and the guests were going away. Miss Mettie Eccles was one of them. She and Connie Brooke, who was to be a bridesmaid, would be walking across the Green together. So pleasant for both of them. She was just about to turn away, when she heard, first footsteps, and then the click of a gate. Not the gate of Willow Cottage, nor of Miss Mettie's cottage on the left. The sound came from the other side. It was in fact the gate of Gale's Cottage that had clicked, and Gale's Cottage was the residence of Mr. Barton who had been described by Frank Abbott as the chief mystery of Tilling Green. He had called him a quiet, harmless old boy who kept cats and would not have a woman in the house, even to locking his door against them and doing his own cooking and cleaning.

Miss Silver leaned forward a little. She had not as yet set eyes on this next-door neighbour, though she had heard quite a lot about him from Miss Wayne. His seclusion, his cats, his nocturnal prowlings, did not commend themselves to the village. As Miss Renie said, "One tries to think kindly about everyone, but why go out at night?"

It was evident that Mr. Barton was returning from one of his rambles in the dark. She could just make out a tall figure standing by the wicket gate. It waited there for perhaps a minute and then moved on towards the house. The gate clicked to.

Gale's Cottage was the oldest of the cottages along the Green. Seen in the daylight, it was picturesque to the point of inconvenience. The roof sloped sharply, and since there were two storeys the rooms could hardly be more than six feet in height. The front windows were practically obscured by a growth of old neglected creepers. The entrance was at the side. By leaning farther out Miss Silver was able to observe Mr. Barton's approach to this entrance. Arrived, he produced a torch, which he held in his left hand. He focussed it upon the big old-fashioned keyhole, inserted a big old-fashioned key, and opened the door. As he did so he turned the torch downwards and stood to one side. A large tabby cat walked through the beam and disappeared into the darkness beyond. A second followed it, nose to tail, and after that a third, a fourth, a fifth, a sixth, a seventh. When the beam had lighted the last of the seven Mr. Barton himself crossed the threshold, shutting, and locking, the door behind him.

Miss Silver became aware that the night air was not as warm as it had seemed. She retired from the window and pulled up an eiderdown which she had previously discarded. Afterwards there was some impression of voices in the road outside—Miss Mettie's voice saying good-night, and a murmur of sound that answered it.

CHAPTER 11

The morning of Valentine's wedding day came up clear and bright. There was still some cloud in the west, but the rest of the sky was of the enchanting shade of blue which makes amends for days of mist and rain. The girl who brought up the early morning tea put the tray down upon the table beside the bed. The curtains were all drawn back, and the room was full of light. She said,

"You've got ever such a lovely day, Miss Valentine. I do hope it keeps up."

Valentine said, "Thank you, Florrie."

She sat up and turned to lift the cup. If there had been less light, it would have been easier to face it. She felt as if the day that lay before her was a steep hill which somehow she must climb, only she didn't know how she was going to do it. There was no firm, hard purpose in her, no resolve. She had come up out of deep belated sleep feeling light and relaxed. Somewhere far down there was a tremulous flutter of joy because Jason had come back, but how they were to cross all the things that lay between them, she had not even begun to think.

But she would have to think. Florrie went out of the room and shut the door. She was a nice girl, and she was looking forward to the wedding. She was going to be disappointed. A lot of people were going to be disappointed. Maggie had got a new hat. She couldn't marry Gilbert because Florrie would be disappointed if she didn't, or because of Maggie's hat, or the bridesmaids' dresses, or Mettie Eccles' new suede gloves. Just for a moment she could hear Mettie's voice quite distinctly— "I've had the others cleaned so often, and I'm sure they must be ten years old, so I'm getting a new pair in your honour." Mettie would certainly be very much annoyed.

She drank some of the tea, and found it warm and comforting. What was she going to do? She would have to tell Roger Repton that she couldn't marry Gilbert. He would want to know why, and she couldn't tell him. She couldn't go to him and say, "I can't marry Gilbert, because Jason has come back," any more than she could go to him and say, "I can't marry Gilbert, because he is Scilla's lover." It was a perfectly good reason, but she couldn't use it. She couldn't use it, because it would smash up his marriage. It wasn't a happy marriage, but to know that Scilla was unfaithful would be a terrible blow. He had been a fool to marry her, and it is a terrible thing to find out that you have been made a fool of. She couldn't hurt Roger like that.

And she had heard what she hadn't been meant to hear. She had stood and listened at a chink of the door in the dark. They might have been saying good-bye, and what they said hadn't been meant for her to hear. She thought that she could tell Gilbert what she had heard, but she knew she couldn't use it to break off their marriage, or to give Scilla away.

She finished the rest of the tea and turned to put down the cup. It was eight o'clock, and everywhere all over the house and in other houses people were either up or getting up and the preparations for her wedding were going on. There was a pile of letters on her tray with the tea things. There would be telegrams and telephone calls, and eleventh-hour presents to add to all the others which would have to be written about and sent back. She picked up the letters that were on the tray and began to go through them.

Janet Grant, in her characteristic sprawling hand, two words to the line and not more than four lines to the page.

"Darling—so devastated—Jessica prostrate—can't leave her—all my love—she sends hers."

Lexie Merridew's mother—Lexie was devastated too.

The next envelope was the kind you get in a village

shop or a very cheap shop anywhere, the kind they sell with the lower priced Christmas cards. Odd writing too, very large and clumsy. She had not to wonder about it—she knew. And then she was opening it and taking out a thin crumpled sheet with the same odd writing on it. It had no beginning, and when she turned the page there was no ending either. It said:

"You may not mind about his playing fast and loose with Doris Pell and driving her to take her life or about his carrying on with S R and if you don't know what I mean you are more of a fool than what I took you for but you had better find out about his marrying Marie Dubois under a false name when he was in Canada or you may find yourself in the cart along of the other pore gurls he as led astray."

There were no stops, and there was no signature.

Valentine dropped the letter back on to the tray and sat looking at it.

The time was half past eight.

On the stroke of the half hour Penelope Marsh jumped off her bicycle, wheeled it round to the garden shed, and opened the front door of the Croft with her latchkey. She was a tall girl with blue eyes, a brown skin, and very white teeth. She stood in the hall and yo-delled to Connie Brooke, her partner in the little kinder-garten school which was doing so well. When there was no answer, she called again, louder and more insistently. And then it came over her that there was something odd about none of the windows being open. The children arrived at nine, and they made a point of getting the rooms aired and then warmed up before they came.

She ran upstairs, still calling, knocked vigorously on Connie's door, and getting no reply, went in. Connie had taken off her dress, and she must have hung it up, because it wasn't anywhere to be seen, but she hadn't got any farther than that. She was lying on the bed in her slip with the eiderdown pulled round her, and at first Penny thought that she was asleep, but when she touched the hand that lay on the coverlet and tried to unclasp its hold she knew that Connie was dead, because the hand was quite stiff—quite cold—

Her mind knew that something dreadful and final had happened. It was like a thing which you read about in a book, a thing that happened to other people, not to anyone who was part of your own life like Connie was. She let go of that cold, heavy hand and backed away from the bed. It wasn't until she had reached the door that fear and desolation rushed in upon her. She found herself running down the stairs, out through the open door, and along the road to bang on Miss Eccles' front door and clamour that Connie was dead.

Miss Eccles was extremely efficient. It would be unfair to say that she enjoyed the situation, but she certainly enjoyed her own competence in dealing with it. She rang up Dr. Taylor, herself accompanied Penny back to the Croft, and there set her down to telling all parents who were on the telephone that Miss Brooke was ill and there would be no school to-day.

Dr. Taylor when he came had nothing to tell her that she did not already know. Connie Brooke was dead— had been dead for hours.

"We walked home together last night after the party at the Manor," she said. "She was all right then, except that she hadn't been sleeping too well. Maggie Repton had given her some sleeping-tablets."

Dr. Taylor was built on bulldog lines. He did not exactly bare his teeth, but he wrinkled up his nose and his voice was a growl.

"She had no business to do any such thing."

Mettie Eccles said,

"Well, you know what people are—they will do it. I told her she had better not take more than one. She was going to dissolve it in her bedtime cocoa. You'll remember she can't swallow anything like a pill."

He grunted. "Where's the bottle?"

They found it on the kitchen dresser, and it was empty.

"Know how much there was in it?"

"No, I don't. She just told me Maggie had given her some tablets, and I told her not to take more than one."

He said in a rough voice, because death always made him angry,

"Well, one wouldn't have killed her, nor two. I'll get on to Miss Maggie and find out how many there were in the bottle. You would have thought she would have had more sense than to hand over enough to do any harm. And where did she get them from? That's what I'd like to know. Not from me."

Maggie Repton took the call in her bedroom. She found the extension there a great comfort, because she did like to go early to bed, and it was so very trying to have to go down to the study in a dressing-gown if anyone called up and wanted to speak to her. She was only half dressed now. She threw her dressing-gown round her shoulders and pulled the eiderdown across her knees before lifting the receiver. It was much too early to ring up—nobody should ring before nine o'clock—it was almost certain to be for Valentine.

But it was for her. Dr. Taylor speaking.

"That you, Miss Maggie? . . . What's this I hear about your giving Connie Brooke sleeping-tablets?"

She began to feel flustered at once.

"Oh dear—I didn't think there would be any harm in it. She really looked wretched, and she said she hadn't been sleeping at all well."

"Well, you shouldn't have done it. How many were there in the bottle?"

"Oh dear—I'm sure I don't know. You see, there were a few left from the ones Dr. Porteous gave me when I was staying with my old cousin, Annie Pedlar. And then after Annie died there were some in another bottle—and I put the two together, but I never really counted them."

Dr. Taylor's voice came through very sharp and barking.

"You mixed the two!"

"Oh, but they were the same sort, or very nearly—at least I thought they were. Oh dear, I hope there isn't anything wrong!"

"You haven't got the other bottle, I suppose?"

"Oh, no. It would have been thrown away when we sorted out poor Annie's things. At least—no, I remember now, the nurse wouldn't let me mix them. I was going to, but she said it wouldn't be at all the thing to do, so I didn't."

He said with a sudden alarming quiet,

"Are you sure about that?"

"Oh, I think so. You confused me—but I think the nurse said not to mix them—Oh, I don't know—"

"Miss Maggie, can you form any idea of how many tablets there were in the bottle when you gave it to Connie Brooke?"

"Oh dear, I don't know—I really *don't*. But you can ask Connie. . . . Yes, why didn't I think of that before? Of course Connie will know. Why don't you ask her?"

He said, "Connie is dead," and rang off.

CHAPTER 12

Jason Leigh came down the
stairs at the Parsonage. He was whistling the odd haunting tune of a German folk song. He had heard it last in a very strange place indeed. He whistled it now, and the words went through his mind:

> *"On Sunday morning I go to the church,*
> *The false tongues stand and talk in the porch,*
> *Then one says this, and another says that,*
> *And so I weep, and my eyes are wet.*
>
> *Oh, thistles and thorns they prick full sore,*
> *But a false, false tongue hurts a heart far more,*
> *No fire on earth so burns and glows*
> *As a secret love that no man knows."*

There would certainly be a considerable stabbing of tongues over Valentine's broken marriage. Rough on Gilbert, but any man was a fool who married a girl who had nothing to give him. And if he didn't know that she had nothing to give him, he was so big a fool that he was bound to get hurt anyway.

He opened the dining-room door and came into a light shabby room full of the comfortable smell of bacon and coffee. But the bacon was cooling on the Reverend Thomas Martin's plate, the coffee in his cup skimming over, and both plate and cup had been pushed back. Tommy's chair was pushed back too. He was standing in front of the fireplace at which he had so often scorched his trousers. This morning he could not have told whether there was any heat in the grate or not. He had an open letter in his hand, and he looked across it at Jason with an expression of incredulous horror on his big good-humoured face. What he saw was what he would have given a great deal to see at any time in the past six months—a young man with rather odd dark looks and a quizzical lift of the brows—the nephew who was as dear to him as any son could have been.

Jason shut the door behind him. He said,

"What's the matter, Tommy—seen a basilisk or something?"

Tommy Martin held out the letter to him. It was written in a big awkward hand upon cheap white paper. Here and there the ink had run, as ink runs on blotting-paper. It began right at the top of the page without any form of address. With a slight intensification of his quizzical expression he read:

"I suppose you know what you are doing marrying Mr. Gilbert Earle to Miss Valentine Grey let alone his driving poor Doris Pell to take her life and leading another pore gurl astray as shall be nameless hadn't you better find out about the pore gurl he married in Canada Miss Marie Dubois before you go helping him to commit bigamy with Miss Grey."

Jason read it through to the end and came over to lay it down on the mantelpiece.

"Going to put it in the fire?"

"I can't. I shall have to think."

Jason's mouth twisted.

"Anything in it?"

"No, no, of course not—there can't be. We've had an epidemic of these things. That poor girl Doris Pell drowned herself because she got one. Just filth flung at random—nothing in it at all. But this suggestion of bigamy—that's awkward. One can't just ignore it."

"I imagine not."

Tommy Martin had a quick frown for that.

"Jason, you've known Gilbert Earle for a good long time, haven't you? Ever come across anything to make you suppose—" He came to a stop.

Jason laughed.

"That there was something in this Marie Dubois business? My dear Tommy!"

"Well, I don't like asking you, but I've got to."

"Oh, I wasn't at the wedding, you know."

"Was there a wedding?"

"Not to my knowledge."

"My dear boy, this is serious. I must ask you to take it seriously."

"All right then, here you are. I've known Gilbert on and off for quite a long time. I know him about as well as you know most of the people you are always running into because you go to the same houses and do the same sort of things. What you don't know about anyone like that would fill several large volumes—I've never felt any urge to wade through them. In case you're interested, your bacon is getting cold." He went to the table, uncovered a dish, and helped himself.

Tommy shook his head.

"The bacon can wait."

Jason looked shocked.

"Not on your life it can't! Mine is past its best. I should say yours was a total loss."

He was aware of an impatient movement and a more concentrated frown.

"My dear boy, you don't realize the position. I shall have to get in touch with Gilbert. And there's Roger—and Valentine—the wedding is at half past two—"

Jason helped himself to mustard.

"There isn't going to be any wedding," he said.

Tommy Martin stared.

"What do you mean?"

"There isn't going to be a wedding. The question of Gilbert being a bigamist doesn't arise, because he isn't going to get married. Valentine isn't going to marry him. There is no urgency about your seeing anyone. Relax and finish your breakfast."

Tommy Martin came across and sat down in the chair which he had pushed back after opening the anonymous letter. He sat down, but he did not pull it in to the table. He looked hard at Jason and said,

"What have you been up to?"

"What do you suppose?"

"You've seen Valentine?"

"If you can call it seeing her. There wasn't any light to speak of."

"Jason—"

"All right, I will dot the i's and cross the t's. When I got here last night and found you were up at the Manor, I had a nice chatty séance with Mrs. Needham. She told me all about everything. At first I thought of going up to the Manor and joining the festivities, but I wasn't dressed for the part, so I thought again. After which I wrote a line to Valentine telling her I would be at the gazebo until twelve—if she didn't come, I would be calling bright and early in the morning. I then walked up to the Manor, in at the front door, and up the stairs, where I stuck the note on Val's pincushion. I didn't meet anyone, and nobody saw me. Valentine came to the gazebo and we talked. She decided that she had better not marry Gilbert. And that, Tommy, is all. The proceedings were quite unbelievably decorous. I didn't even kiss her."

Tommy Martin's face had gone blank.

"She decided not to marry Gilbert?"

"She did."

"What did you say to persuade her?"

"Very little. I didn't have to. You can't pretend you thought she was happy about it."

The blank look broke up.

"No—no—it's been troubling me. But she wasn't happy at the Manor—she wanted to get away. Scilla and she are—" He paused for a word, and came out with, "Not very congenial."

"I should say an understatement."

Tommy Martin went on.

"There wasn't any word of you. I don't know how far the understanding between you went. There was no engagement—or was there?"

"No, there wasn't any engagement."

"And you might never have come back."

"It was more than likely that I shouldn't come back."

"Did Valentine know that?"

"She didn't know anything. As far as she was concerned, I just walked out on her."

"That was cruel."

Jason shook his head.

"Worse the other way. Besides, it is what everyone had to think. She might not have been able to resist the temptation to defend me. I couldn't afford to risk it. There were a good many chances against pulling it off as it was. I wouldn't have said anything, even last night, if you hadn't guessed."

Tommy Martin nodded.

"It wasn't just guesswork. James Blacker dropped me a hint. We were up at College together. That sort of friendship doesn't always last, but this one has. I ran into him the day after you went, and he told me where they were sending you. I may say now that when I walked in last night and you came out of the study to meet me, there was a moment when I wasn't quite sure—" his voice shook, and steadied again—"Well, I wasn't quite sure."

Jason put milk into his coffee.

"I wasn't quite sure myself. You know, there's the point of view of the ghost as well as of the man who sees one. When you come to think of it, there are things one would rather do than find oneself lingering superfluous on the stage without a part to play. I don't suppose the poor wretch enjoys seeing the odd friend or relations swoon at the sight of him."

Tommy hadn't swooned, but he had turned fairly green last night. The scene sprang into Jason's mind—the dimly lighted hall, Tommy coming in out of the dark, and himself in silhouette against the bright rectangle left by the open study door. There had been a moment when he had felt as if he were really a ghost come back to haunt the place that had been his home. The moment was between them—something shared which couldn't be put into words.

Neither of them would ever put it into words. Tommy Martin leaned forward, the letter still in his hand. He said abruptly,

"You went out again—after that?"

"Oh, yes."

"I didn't hear you."

Jason laughed.

"I shouldn't be much good at my job if I couldn't get in or out of a house without anyone hearing me."

Tommy Martin was looking at the letter, his shaggy brows drawn together, a lock of the hair that never would lie down falling over them. All at once his head jerked up.

"Jason, I don't think it—but I've got to ask you. This isn't your doing?"

"Mine? Oh, the letter? My dear Tommy!"

Tommy Martin said steadily,

"I just want you to say it isn't."

Jason's mouth twitched. He had disposed of the bacon on his plate, and now reached for some rather hard toast and the marmalade.

"But how completely illogical! Because, just supposing that after being brought up by you I had gone sufficiently down into the gutter to take up anonymous letter writing as a recreation, why should you imagine I would stick at a lie—or at any number of lies for the matter of that? Would you like to pass me the butter?"

Tommy Martin made a long arm for the butter, placed symmetrically by Mrs. Needham on the far side of the table. He gave it an impatient shove in Jason's direction and said in very nearly his ordinary voice,

"When one stops being illogical one becomes a machine."

Jason piled butter on the toast, and marmalade on the butter. He was laughing a little.

"All right, have it your own way! I may become a poison-pen addict yet—*'Il ne faut pas dire, fontaine, je ne boirai jamais de ton eau*—'but I haven't got there yet. You might have a little more confidence in yourself as an instructor of youth!"

The big hand which still held the letter relaxed.

"I said I didn't think it. I had to ask you. Roger—"

"Roger may have the same pretty thought. Well, if he does, just draw his attention to a few cold facts. I had a nice newsy gossip with Mrs. Needham before you turned up last night. She told me all about your poison-pen, and I gathered that a good few people had been having letters, and that it had been going on for quite a time. Well, I only got across the Channel yesterday, so I suppose I may be considered to have an alibi."

"Yes—yes—of course."

He had let go of the letter, picked up his knife and fork, and begun on the now congealed bacon, when the door was thrown open without ceremony. Mrs. Needham stood there, flushed and panting.

"Oh, sir! Oh dear me, isn't it dreadful! Who'd have thought of a thing like that happening! And Miss Valentine's wedding-day and all! Oh, sir!"

Jason's hand closed hard on the arm of his chair. Tommy Martin's back was to the door. He swung round to face it.

"What has happened, Mrs. Needham?"

"Miss Connie, sir—poor Miss Connie Brooke! Oh dear me! And no time at all since she was here and I couldn't help seeing how she'd been taking on!"

He got up out of his chair and towered there like a figure of judgment.

"Connie Brooke! Has anything happened to Connie Brooke?"

Jason's hand had relaxed. It wasn't Valentine. Nothing else mattered.

The tears were running down over Mrs. Needham's big flushed cheeks.

"Oh dear me, yes! Oh, sir—oh Mr. Martin—she's gone!"

"Gone!" This was his big pulpit voice that could fill the church.

She gulped and caught her breath.

"Oh, sir—the baker just brought the news! He come by, and there was Dr. Taylor's car, and the police from Ledlington! She's dead, sir—it's all right enough! Miss Penny found her when she come—and went running for Miss Eccles—and Miss Eccles rung up the doctor—and he rung up the police! But none of it wasn't any good!"

"You're sure about this?"

"Oh, yes—it's Gospel!"

The word struck ironically on Jason's ear. Gospel—good news! Connie Brooke suddenly dead! He had come from places where the wastage of life was so great that only the nearest and dearest regarded it, but this was a peaceful English village where life was secure. And he had known Connie all her life. A plain, shy creature, not very interesting to anyone, but part of the accustomed scene.

Tommy Martin said abruptly, "I must go." He pushed past Mrs. Needham into the hall. The front door opened and fell to behind him. Jason saw him go striding down to the gate and across the Green in his baggy, shabby suit. He had forgotten to take a hat.

CHAPTER 13

Miss Silver was greeted with the news when she came down to breakfast. She had already been aware of some unusual commotion. The Croft was visible from her bedroom window. When first one car and then another stopped before the gate, she supposed that parents must be delivering their children at the school. It was a little early of course, but that might be accounted for by other engagements—a father proceeding to his office in Ledlington for instance. But when the car remained stationary and there was still further evidence of activity, this supposition had to be abandoned, and at a quarter past nine when she came downstairs Miss Wayne informed her in a shocked voice that Connie Brooke had been found dead in her bed.

"It seems quite impossible to believe that it is true—it does indeed! You saw her at the rehearsal only yesterday afternoon. She was the substitute bridesmaid—the rather plain girl in the homemade red cardigan. So very becoming—but oh dear, I oughtn't to say that now, ought I? Poor Connie, I didn't think she looked at all well. In fact, you know, I thought she looked as if she had been crying, but of course I never dreamed there could be anything really *wrong*. Such a shock—and poor Penny Marsh finding her like that! She has her own key, and she let herself in, and there was poor Connie dead on her bed! She came running for Mettie Eccles, and they got the doctor, but it wasn't any use. Mettie says there wasn't any hope right from the start—she must have been dead for hours. Of course, my room being at the back, I didn't hear anything till Mettie came in just now and told me. But perhaps you—" She rubbed the pink tip of her nose and gazed hopefully at Miss Silver.

It appeared that at half past eight Miss Silver was in the bathroom and had heard nothing. Miss Wayne went on being shocked and telling her about what Miss Mettie had said, and what Dr. Taylor had said, and that, most shocking of all, the police had been sent for!

At the Manor Valentine was ringing up Gilbert Earle. From the call-box at the George he heard her voice, quiet and serious.

"Will you come up here as soon as you can?"

"I thought I wasn't supposed to see you until we met in church."

"I think you must come."

"Val—has anything happened?"

She said, "Yes." And then, "Just come straight up to my sitting-room. I want to see you alone."

She was telephoning from the study. When she had rung off she went directly upstairs to wait.

She had settled in her own mind exactly what she was

going to do, and she didn't want to see anyone else until it was done and couldn't be undone. She had had an emotional interview with Maggie Repton in which the news of Connie's death had been imparted and wept over.

"Such a terrible thing, and of course we must all feel it. But we can't let it make any difference—it wouldn't be *right*. My dear mother always used to say that nothing ought to be allowed to interfere with a wedding—not even the death of a near relative. Poor Connie is only a connection, and whatever Dr. Taylor may say, I cannot believe that I am in *any* way to blame. She looked terrible—you must have noticed it yourself. And she said she hadn't been sleeping, so I gave her my own sleeping-pills with the dose quite clearly marked on the bottle. At least I suppose it was—they generally are. And it is quite ridiculous for Dr. Taylor to expect me to remember just how many tablets there were, because I can't, and that is all there is about it."

The scene had broken down in tears, after which Maggie Repton had been persuaded to lie down for a little. Valentine emerged with a sense of complete unreality. None of the things that seemed to be happening were really happening. They were not the sort of things that did happen, but as long as they seemed to be going on you had to play your part and do the best you could. She stood looking out of the window in her sitting-room and waited for Gilbert Earle. She heard his step in the passage and turned to meet him. When he had shut the door he saw that she had put her hand up, as if to keep him away. He took a step towards her, and she said.

"No. I told you that something had happened. We have got to talk."

That halted him. But the news of Connie's death had reached the George—it had reached him just after Valentine rang off. Of course it was a frightful shock to her and everyone. He supposed there might be some idea that the wedding ought to be put off until after the funeral. He said,

"I know—I've just heard. What on earth was it? Mrs. Simpson at the George said something about an overdose of sleeping-draught. They don't think she took it on purpose, do they? And you won't let it make any difference, surely? I mean, it isn't as if she was a close friend or a near relation."

She had gone back a step or two. Her hands rested on the back of a tall chair. She said,

"I didn't ask you to come up here to talk about Connie."

He stared.

"But it's true, isn't it—she's dead?"

"Oh, yes, it's true. We can make it an excuse if you like. You see, I can't marry you, Gilbert."

"What on earth do you mean?"

"I mean I can't marry you."

The stare had become a very angry one.

"What do you mean, you can't marry me? You've left it a bit late in the day, haven't you?"

"Yes, it's late, but it isn't too late. There are things I could use for an excuse, but I'm not going to use them. I've thought about it, and I don't think it would be fair. I'm going to tell you the truth. I can't marry you, because Jason has come home."

"And what the devil has Jason got to do with your marrying me?"

She said quite simply,

"I've always loved him. We belong. I oughtn't ever to have said I would marry you. But he didn't say anything, and he went away."

He came a step nearer.

"Look here, Valentine, you can't treat me like this! Do you know what people will say? If you don't, I can tell you. It will be one of two things. Either you've found out something about me, or I have found out something about you. That's the sort of mud that sticks, you know. And it will be a damned sight worse for you than it is for me, because as far as I'm concerned they'll probably only credit me with a mistress, but it's a hundred to one they'll say it came out that you were going to have a baby, and that I turned you down. Pull yourself together and use some common sense!"

She shook her head.

"It's no use, Gilbert. It doesn't matter what anyone says or anyone does, I can't marry anyone but Jason. I ought to have known that all along. I've been so unhappy that I didn't seem to be able to think. We can just say that the wedding is put off. Everyone will think it is because of Connie."

Gilbert lost his temper with a crash.

"Don't be such a damned nitwit! What everyone will do is try and pin her suicide on to me. And if that doesn't make me a laughingstock—"

The colour came suddenly, vividly to her face.

"Gilbert!"

"Connie Brooke—that fatuous white rabbit! I see myself!"

He gave a furious laugh.

She hadn't meant to show him the letter, she hadn't meant to shelter behind it in any way. If she loved him, she wouldn't have believed it. If she had loved him, she wouldn't have shown it to him. And if he had left Connie alone, she wouldn't have shown it to him. But Connie hadn't ever given him a thought, and Connie was dead. She was going to show it to him now.

She went over to her writing-table, took out the letter

from between the leaves of the account-book where she had laid it for safety, and came back with it in her hand, her mind so concentrated on what she was doing and why she was doing it that it had no knowledge of whether Gilbert had gone on talking or not. When she held it out to him he said angrily, "What's that?" and she put it into his hand.

She said, "You had better read it," and backed away to stand by the tall chair again and rest her hands upon it.

Gilbert stared at the cheap paper, the big clumsy writing. He read:

"You may not mind his playing fast and loose with Doris Pell and driving her to take her life or about his carrying on with S R and if you don't know what I mean you are more of a fool than what I took you for but you had better find out about his marrying Marie Dubois under a false name when he was in Canada or you may find yourself in the cart along of the other pore gurls he as led astray."

He read to the end, looked across at her with blazing eyes, and demanded,

"What the devil is this?"

Valentine's colour stood high.

"I got it this morning. I wasn't going to show it to you—I wouldn't have if you hadn't said those things about Connie."

"I never looked the same side of the road as Connie! Who would?"

There was a bright flame of anger in her. She cried back at him,

"She's dead! How can you talk like that about her when she's dead!"

It was like a head-on clash between them. Where had it come from suddenly, this hot antagonism? She thought, "Oh, God—I might have married him!" And he, "She won't marry me now. There was something about Scilla in that damned letter. Better go on talking about Connie."

His eyes went to the paper in his hand, and like a flash Valentine knew why. "You may not mind his carrying on with S R—" He was talking about Connie because he didn't want to talk about that. He said in a moderated tone,

"Oh, well, I lost my temper. I didn't mean to hurt your feelings, and I'm sorry if I did. I hardly knew the girl, but of course you did, and it's been a shock and all that. I'm sorry if I said anything I shouldn't. As for this—" he beat on the paper with his hand—"it's just pure poison-pen! I suppose you're not going to ask me whether I was really planning to commit bigamy?"

She said, "No—it doesn't arise. I'm not asking you about Marie Dubois—I'm not asking you about Scilla."

"Scilla—"

Her colour had begun to fade again, the flame in her was dying down. She said,

"I don't need to ask about Scilla. I came in through the drawing-room last night. The door into her sitting-room was ajar, and I heard you. I suppose I shouldn't have listened, but I did."

He made a creditable effort.

"I don't know what you heard. I've known her a long time. There's never been anything serious. If you heard anything at all you would have gathered that whatever there had been, it was over."

She said,

"It doesn't matter. No, I suppose I oughtn't to say that, because of course it matters to Roger. But it doesn't matter to me—it didn't matter last night. You see, I knew then I couldn't marry you. I knew it as soon as Jason came back. I oughtn't ever to have said I would. We don't belong. Jason and I do. Now will you please go?"

Gilbert Earle went.

CHAPTER 14

It was late on the following day that Miss Silver was called to the telephone. Since the instrument was in the dining-room and supper was in progress, she hoped that her tact and discretion would not be put to too great a test. Mrs. Rodney had handed her the receiver without saying who the caller was, but no sooner had a deep, pleasant voice pronounced her name than she was aware that it was Rietta March, the Chief Constable's wife.

"Dear Miss Silver, how are you? I do hope this is not an inconvenient moment. You are not in the middle of a meal or anything?"

Miss Silver coughed.

"We are at supper, but I feel sure that my kind hostess will not mind a temporary interruption."

Rietta, having been thus informed that the Tilling end of the conversation would be public property, and having in any case been instructed not to say anything that could not be proclaimed aloud upon the village green, continued.

"I should have rung up before, but Randal hasn't had a moment. Now when are we going to see you? You can't be in Ledshire without at least coming over to tea. Could you manage tomorrow?"

"Well, I don't know, my dear—"

Rietta went on.

"Oh, please do come! George has grown tremendously, and you haven't even seen little Meg. Look here, Randal says he will be over in your direction tomorrow—some tiresome business or other—and he could pick you up at half past three if that will suit you. Do please say that it will. He sends his love, and we both want to see you so much."

Miss Silver returned to her cocoa and scrambled egg. The tip of Miss Wayne's small pink nose twitched in a manner which strongly suggested a white mouse in the throes of curiosity. In her scholastic days Miss Silver had more than once had to contend with the passionate partiality which little boys seem to entertain for these creatures. She had never been able to share it. She found herself wishing that Miss Wayne did not so often remind her of them. She hastened to explain Rietta's call.

"The Marches are old friends. Mrs. March has very kindly invited me to tea tomorrow. Her husband was once a pupil of mine. No one would ever think so to look at him now, but as a little boy he was considered too delicate to go to school, so he shared his sisters' lessons."

Miss Wayne quivered with interest.

"Do you mean the Chief Constable? Such a fine looking man! No one would ever think that he had been delicate. Now let me see—I am afraid you will have to start rather early, but if you take the three o'clock bus and change at the Merry Harvesters. . . . No, we had better look it up—I am not quite sure about the connection. I hope we have a really up-to-date timetable. My dear sister was so methodical about these things."

Miss Silver explained that Mr. March would call for her—he had business in this direction.

Miss Renie dabbed her nose.

"Oh dear—do you suppose that it would be something to do with poor Connie? It seems so terrible that people should think it could be anything except a dreadful, dreadful accident! I won't say it wasn't foolish of Maggie Repton to let poor Connie have those sleeping-tablets, because I suppose it was. Esther was always so very particular about things like that. Prescriptions should never be passed on, she used to say, because of course what agrees with one person may not agree with another. Let them go to the doctor themselves and not go borrowing, she used to say. So Maggie Repton ought not to have done it, but I'm afraid poor Connie must have been careless too. But I can't see why the police should be interested. Mettie says poor Maggie Repton is quite prostrated. They keep asking her how many tablets there were in the bottle, and of course she has no idea. As if one counted things like that!" She gave a little tittering laugh and then dabbed her nose again. "Oh dear—I didn't mean—of course one ought not to make a joke of it."

Miss Silver went on talking about the March family.

"I have always kept up with them. The girls are very happily married."

She discoursed upon the theme at some length—Isobel's children—Margaret's services during the war—the valued friendship of the elder Mrs. March.

There was a moment after supper when she and Joyce Rodney were alone. Plates and dishes had been cleared, and Joyce was washing up whilst Miss Silver, always anxious to be helpful, dried for her. In the dining-room Miss Wayne was engaged in setting out the breakfast things. The door through to that part of the house being shut, Joyce said quick and low,

"I am taking David to a friend of mine in Ledlington tomorrow. I don't want him to hear anything—about Connie. Penny means to go on with the school, but it will have to be at Lower Tilling. Her mother has a big-gish house there, but it would be a good deal farther for David to go—I should have to take him on my bicycle. Anyhow I thought if I could get him away until after the inquest and the funeral—"

Miss Silver registered approval.

"A very sensible idea. Your friend has children?"

"Two—and such a nice Nannie. David loves going there, and I shall be much happier about him."

Miss Silver polished a tablespoon and laid it down on a baize-covered tray.

"People are sadly incautious about what they say in front of children," she observed.

"They are frightful! Hilda Price was here this morn-ing—you know, she comes to Aunt Renie on Wednes-days and Fridays—and I'm sure as far as getting on with her work was concerned she might just as well have stayed at home, because all she could do was talk about Connie. I told her when she came that I didn't want David to hear anything, and she agreed with every word, and then about five minutes later there she was, talking to Aunt Renie at the top of her voice, going over some long story about Connie having gone up to the Parsonage in tears on Tuesday evening."

Miss Silver finished the last tablespoon and began on the forks.

"Indeed?"

Joyce gave an emphatic nod.

"And there was David only a yard away drinking it all in. Aunt Renie should have known better, even if Hilda didn't. Of course, I hustled him off to play in the garden at once, and I stayed around to see that he didn't come back."

Miss Silver said in a thoughtful voice,

"And pray how did Hilda Price come to know what had happened at the Parsonage?"

"Well, she has a sister-in-law who is a cousin of Mrs. Gurney who keeps the village shop, and she had it from Mrs. Emmott who is a friend of the parson's house-keeper, Mrs. Needham."

Miss Silver was not unaccustomed to villages. She found this a perfectly satisfactory explanation.

"Pray continue, Mrs. Rodney."

"I do wish you would call me Joyce."

"I really do not think it would be wise. I should like to know what is being said about Connie Brooke's visit to the Parsonage."

Joyce put the last plate up in the rack and emptied the washing-bowl.

"Mrs. Needham told Mrs. Emmott, and she told Mrs. Gurney, that Connie had been crying. She said her eyes were all red and swollen. She rang up, you know, and Mr. Martin was out. Mrs. Needham said she thought Connie was crying and she was dreadfully upset because he wasn't there. Then whilst she was speaking he came in, so Connie said she would come along. Mrs. Needham was very much put out because of it being his supper time. She hates people like poison when they come and bother him at meal times, so she probably lurked in the hall and clattered with the tray. Anyhow she was there when Connie went away, because she heard Mr. Martin say that she had better think it well over, and if she really did know who was writing those poisonous letters it would be her duty to go to the police. Mrs. Needham said Connie cried dreadfully and said things like 'Oh, poor Doris!' and she didn't know what to do but once she had said it she couldn't take it back, could she? And Mr. Martin said no, she couldn't, and got out his own handkerchief and gave it to her, which seems to have annoyed Mrs. Needham quite a lot. And he told Connie to go home and think it over. If that was all over the village by Wednesday, and I expect it was, because I know we had it here, the person who wrote the letters would have heard about it too."

Miss Silver said, "Yes."

"I thought at the rehearsal that Connie looked as if she had been crying her eyes out. If she really knew who had written those letters—but how could she—"

"Some accident may have placed her in possession of a clue. Pray finish what you were going to say."

Joyce looked at her in a distressed manner.

"Well, it looks as if it was someone she knew quite well. She wouldn't have been so distressed if it wasn't. And that ties in with her going to see Tommy Martin and coming away in floods of tears without telling him anything. You see, when Mrs. Needham heard her say, 'Once I've said it I can't take it back, can I?' and Tommy said no she couldn't, and to think it well over, well it does sound as if perhaps she just couldn't face up to it and Miss Maggie's tablets might have been the answer. Do you think it was like that?"

Miss Silver looked at her with gravity.

"There is another possibility, Mrs. Rodney. The person who wrote those letters would have been ruined by exposure. He, or she, would have had a very strong motive for silencing Connie Brooke."

CHAPTER 15

Randal March drew up at Willow Cottage at a little after half past three on the following afternoon, whereupon Miss Silver came out of the front door in her black cloth coat and the new hat which she had intended to wear for the wedding. After an unbroken succession of black felts trimmed with ribbon and little bunches of flowers it really was, as Ethel Burkett had declared, "Quite a change," being more of a toque, and the material black velvet. Three pompons nestled against the crown, grey, black, and lavender. As they drove away, Randal said with an affectionate smile,

"Surely that is a new hat. I like those what-you-may-call-'ems at the side."

Miss Silver experienced a glow of modest pleasure. She supplied the name.

"They are pompons."

"Most becoming."

From this promising opening they proceeded to solicitous enquiries from Miss Silver and a budget of family news on the part of Randal March. Isobel's second girl was demanding to go on the stage. Margaret and her husband were going to run a chicken farm in Devonshire—"And how anyone can deliberately set out to get mixed up with hens is beyond me."

Miss Silver confessed that she would not care about it herself, but added that Margaret always knew exactly what she wanted to do, and that once her mind was made up it was no use trying to stop her.*

"Obstinate as a mule," said Randal March.

It was obvious that no serious business would be discussed while they were still upon the road. Arrived at the house, they were met by Rietta March. The beauty which had once been rather austere was now softened by happiness. Miss Silver recalled the lines which she had heard applied to her when they had first been

*Miss Silver Comes to Stay.

thrown together—"A daughter of the gods, divinely tall—" Her favourite Lord Tennyson had completed them with "and most divinely fair," but Rietta Cray was a dark goddess, and in those days a tragic one, since the shadow of murder had rested upon her and hers—a shadow which Miss Silver had been instrumental in lifting.* She looked younger now than she had then, and there was a carnation bloom in her cheeks. She kissed Miss Silver warmly and enquired, "When would you like to talk—now or after tea?"

Randal March said,

"Now, I think. And I want to take her into the drawing-room. This has got to be just a social visit, and you never know how things will get round."

"Very well, I'll go up to the children. You can call when you are ready for me to come down."

Miss Silver watched her go away from them up the stairs graceful and gracious in a dress of dark red wool, one of the chrysanthemum shades. Then Randal was taking her into a pleasant room with flowered chintzes and big jars of dahlias, golden rod, and Michaelmas daisy. Seating herself and looking about her with pleasure, she reflected upon the happy atmosphere which filled the house. Although she had disciplined herself very severely in the matter of having favourites amongst her pupils, there was no contesting the fact that Randal March had always had a very special place in her affections. He had been a spoilt, delicate little boy when she arrived to superintend the schoolroom which he shared with two elder sisters. Previous governesses had pronounced him unmanageable, and he was too delicate to be sent to school. After two years of a rule which had combined authority, interest, and beneficence the deli-

*Miss Silver Comes to Stay

cacy had been outgrown, and a deep and enduring respect had been implanted in his mind. When, many years afterwards, he encountered Miss Silver in her capacity as a private enquiry agent, the respect was enhanced and the lively affection of the little boy developed into the enduring friendship and affection of the man. It was the horrible affair of the Poisoned Caterpillars which brought them together, and he had been forward to maintain that she had saved his life. Since those days he had become, first Superintendent at Ledlington, and then Chief Constable of the county, and their paths had continued to cross. He leaned back now in one of the comfortable chintz-covered chairs and said,

"And how are you getting along at Tilling Green?"

Miss Silver took a moment before she said soberly,

"I do not know that I can answer that. I need not tell you that there is a great deal of talk about the death of Connie Brooke. I do not know how much of it will have reached you."

"Let us assume that I haven't heard any of it. I may have done so, or I may not, but I would like to have your angle."

She repeated what Joyce Rodney had told her. Randal March looked thoughtful.

"So you think she knew something about the anonymous letters, went to the Vicar to tell him what she knew, and came away without doing it on the grounds that once she had said it she couldn't take it back. What do you make of that?"

"That the person whom she suspected, or against whom she really had some evidence, was someone she knew and someone who could not be lightly accused."

He nodded.

"Had you met the girl at all? How did she strike you?"

"I saw her at the rehearsal of Valentine Grey's wedding. Miss Wayne asked me to accompany her. That, as you may know, was on Wednesday afternoon. In the evening the poor girl attended a party at the Manor from which she walked home across the Green with Miss Eccles who lives at Holly Cottage next door to Miss Wayne."

"Yes, I have seen her statement. She says they separated there, and that Connie Brooke went on alone."

"Yes, I believe I heard them say good-night to one another."

"Oh, you did? That might be quite an important point, you know."

"I would not like to swear to it, Randal. I was dropping off to sleep. It was just an impression."

"I see. Well, you saw the girl at this wedding rehearsal on Wednesday. That would be after her visit to the Vicar?"

"The following afternoon."

"How did she strike you?"

"She had been brought in as a substitute for a Miss Merridew who had developed German measles. Shyness, nervousness, or excitement would not have been surprising, but there was no evidence of any of them. The first thing I noticed was that she had been crying. Not within the last few hours, but at some time previous to that—probably during the night. The eyelids were still reddened, and there was some swelling. There had been an unskilful attempt to cover up these traces with powder. The rehearsal was rather a fiasco, the bridegroom having been delayed by an accident to the car in which the best man was driving him down. Those present at the rehearsal were all more or less affected by this delay. There was a general uneasiness, a disposition to fidget, to whisper. Connie Brooke just stood there. I had the impression that she hardly knew what was going on."

"You think she had something on her mind?"

"Yes, I think so."

"And that practically everyone in the village was aware of the fact?"

"I suppose most people would know that she had been to see Mr. Martin about the anonymous letters and had come away without telling him what she knew."

He leaned forward to put a log of wood on the fire. A little shower of sparks flew up.

"That sort of secret could be a dangerous one to keep. You know, she had taken, or been given, a tremendously strong dose of that sleeping stuff. I've had the report on the post-mortem. It wasn't a case of an extra tablet and a weak heart or anything like that. She had had about twice as much as would have been necessary to kill her. Now a very large dose like that points to suicide. You can't swallow a whole lot of tablets without knowing what you are doing."

Miss Silver gave the slight cough with which she had been accustomed to call a class to order.

"You should, I think, be informed that Connie Brooke had a nervous inability to swallow anything in the form of a pill or tablet. Miss Eccles, Miss Wayne, and Mrs. Rodney having all told me this, I should think it unlikely that anyone in Tilling Green was ignorant on the point. Anything in the form of a tablet must therefore have been crushed and dissolved, probably in her bedtime cocoa."

"She was in the habit of taking cocoa when she went to bed?"

"Certainly. She found that it helped her to sleep. It

seems she told Miss Eccles whilst they were walking home across the Green on Wednesday night that she had left this cocoa all ready mixed in a saucepan so that it wouldn't take her any time to heat it up. They talked about the tablets Miss Repton had given her, and she said she would dissolve them and put them into the cocoa. Miss Mettie said why couldn't she just swallow them. She says they went on talking about it all across the Green, and she is very insistent that she told Connie on no account to take more than one tablet."

"Yes, she put that in her statement. I wonder if she is speaking the truth."

Miss Silver did not reply. When he realized that her silence was deliberate he spoke again.

"It is quite an easy thing to say. And it puts Miss Mettie Eccles in a very favourable light. Is she the sort of person who sees to it that the light is favourable?"

Miss Silver's small, neat features were expressionless. She said in a noncommittal voice,

"I suppose, Randal, that most of us would place a certain value upon the impression made by our conduct in an emergency."

"You mean we all like to stand well with each other."

"And with the police, Randal."

He frowned.

"How does Miss Eccles strike you?"

She met his look with one of bright intelligence.

"She is a busy person. She has a hand in everything that goes on in the village. Her connection with the Reptons gives her a certain standing."

"A finger in every pie, and quite a lot to say as to know the pie is baked!"

"She is efficient. What she does is well done. She talks a great deal. She has decided opinions. Her house is very well kept, the garden neat and formal."

He laughed.

"Well, I've met her, so I know what she looks like. Most women would have started off with that, but you left it out—I wonder why."

She gave him her peculiarly charming smile.

"There is no mystery about it, my dear Randal. She told me that she had met you."

"I see. Well, well—Now look here, either this girl melted down a large number of tablets in her cocoa, or someone else put the drug into the cocoa and either left it there hoping she would take it, or came in with her and persuaded her to do so. I find considerable difficulty in believing in either of these theories. As to the first, I don't believe there were anything like so many tablets in that bottle Miss Repton gave her. I've seen Maggie Repton myself. I thought I should probably get more out of her than Crisp."

"And did you?"

"Yes, I think I did. She's the well-meaning, nervous kind—afraid to commit herself, afraid to be definite about anything. The kind who holds up a statement for half an hour while she tries to think whether something quite irrelevant took place at half a minute to seven or half a minute past. I spent quite a lot of time getting her sufficiently soothed down to say anything at all, and even then she qualified everything until neither of us knew where we were. But I did emerge with an impression—in fact you can say almost with a conviction—that there weren't very many tablets in that bottle."

"Indeed, Randal?"

He nodded.

"It sounds a bit vague, but then so is Maggie Repton."

Miss Silver was looking at him.

"Would it be possible that she desired to give you that impression?"

"My dear Miss Silver, you simply can't have Maggie Repton as a suspect."

"You say that with a good deal of confidence."

He laughed.

"Come now, what motive could she possibly have?"

She replied soberly.

"The person who wrote the letters would have a motive. If, in fact, Connie Brooke was deliberately removed, there could be only one possible motive for removing her, the fact that she knew, or guessed, the identity of the person who wrote the anonymous letters. The person, and that person alone, would have the necessary motive."

"You are right about that of course. But Maggie Repton is an impossibility. She is the mildest, vaguest, and most blameless of women—the kind of stay-at-home daughter and sister who is rapidly becoming extinct. She nursed her parents, she kept house for her brother until he married—in fact I believe she still does so. The domestic arts are not much in Scilla Repton's line."

Miss Silver gave her slight deliberate cough.

"But do you not see that it is amongst just such people that the anonymous letter-writer is to be found? Too little occupied with their own affairs, having in fact no affairs with which to occupy themselves, too timid and ineffectual to express their own opinions—do you not see that it is to just such a person that the writing of an anonymous letter might appeal? It affords an opportunity for the release of concealed resentments, suppressed desires, the envy, the grudge which has been secretly cherished. There may, or may not, have been some specific sense of injury, but I believe that in most cases it is a feeling of inferiority or frustration which provides the background of these painful cases. As in so many other circumstances, it is only the first step which is hard to take. Once that has been taken, the vice grows rapidly. In a village the effect of each letter can be observed. A sense of power and importance comes to the writer, the letters become more numerous and more poisonous, the appetite grows with what it feeds upon. And then there comes the threat of discovery. A timid person does not suddenly become brave, but he or she may become desperate. Timidity may itself be the incentive to a crime. If Connie Brooke was in a position to ruin such a person, would not that provide a motive for her murder?"

The word had been skirted round, now it had been said. Miss Silver was reminded of poor Connie's words, "Once I've told it, I can't take it back." They had been discussing the possibility of murder, but it had not been named until now.

Randal March threw out a hand.

"Of course everything you say is perfectly true, but—if you knew Miss Maggie—"

She said mildly,

"I do not wish you to think that I am accusing her. I am only anxious that in this matter there should be no one so privileged by place, position, or character, as to be withdrawn from the most careful scrutiny. In the case of Miss Repton, she has the background which I have suggested as a probable one, and she is known to have pressed a bottle of sleeping tablets on Connie Brooke. We do not know how many there were in the bottle, nor do we know whether anything was said as to the number it would be prudent to take. If it could be proved that there were only a few tablets, Miss Repton would be exonerated, since it would not have been possible for her to have left the Manor at any time during the evening. There is, in fact, plenty of evidence to show that she did not do so. It would not, therefore, have been possible for her to have tampered with the cocoa which Connie had left in readiness for her return."

He said,

"Quite. And that brings us to the second of my two theories. As I have said, I don't believe there were so many in that bottle. If there were, the girl could have committed suicide, but if there were not, then someone murdered her by putting a fatal dose of that stuff into her cocoa. Only just consider how appalling it must have tasted. How could the murderer have counted on her swallowing it? The natural reaction would have been to pour the cocoa away and make fresh."

Miss Silver recalled a piece of gossip not really heeded at the time.

"Connie Brooke had an illness in her teens which practically destroyed her sense of taste and smell. I have known of such a case before. She would not, therefore, notice the taste of the drug, and this fact would be known to the person who murdered her. Even if she had been aware of an unpleasant taste, you must remember that she had intended to use what Miss Maggie had given her."

He made an impatient movement.

"I've no doubt it would be known to everyone within a five-mile radius. No one can complain that there is a lack of possibilities. Anyone in the county could have done it, provided he could have got into the house. What have you got to say about that?"

"People are extremely careless about their keys. If anyone was planning to get into the house whilst Connie was out, a key might have been abstracted or a window unlatched."

"A *window?*"

"I thought of that at once, Randal. If this girl was

murdered, it was by someone whom she knew, someone who could have had a quite natural reason for coming to the house. You must remember that it was being used as a school. The older children would be there till four o'clock. In the bustle of their departure it would not be difficult to lock the back door and go away with the key or leave it hidden under a mat. It would be even simpler to contrive that a window should be left unlatched. Or, simplest of all, the person who desired to effect an entrance might have possessed a key which would open one of the doors of the Croft."

"Do you know of anyone who had the opportunities you speak of?"

"Mrs. Rodney and I walked along to the Croft to fetch her little boy at four o'clock on Wednesday—"

"Are we to suspect Joyce Rodney?"

"I think not, though she certainly entered the house, as did also Miss Eccles who had undertaken to fetch a little girl whose parents live just outside Tilling Green. They are young people of the name of Black, and they had invited Miss Eccles to tea."

He frowned.

"And Miss Eccles walked home with Connie Brooke after the party."

"She walked with her as far as Holly Cottage, which is next door to Miss Wayne's."

"And you think, but you are not sure, that they said good-night there. Even if they did, there wasn't anything to prevent Miss Eccles changing her mind, was there? There wasn't anything to prevent her saying, 'Well, I'll walk the rest of the way with you.' She could have done just that, and then have gone in with her and found an opportunity of slipping those extra tablets into the cocoa. She would have had to have them all ready ground up, but of course the whole thing must have been very carefully planned. Here's another possibility. I wonder whether Miss Eccles went to the party with Connie as well as returning from it. If she picked her up at the Croft, there might have been an opportunity for tampering with the cocoa then."

"I think not, Randal. They did go together, but it was Connie who came to Holly Cottage to pick Miss Eccles up. I was in my room and saw them start. There is, of course, one very strong reason for exonerating Miss Eccles. It must have occurred to you that if it were she who was under suspicion, Connie would not have willingly undertaken to cross the Green with her both on her way to the party at the Manor and on the way back."

"She might not have been able to help it."

"That is true. It could all have been arranged before her suspicions came to a head. Once the arrangement had been made it would have been very difficult to alter it. And she would not know that part of her interview with Mr. Martin had been overheard and repeated all round the village."

"In fact Miss Eccles remains a suspect."

Miss Silver became slightly aloof.

"I have not said that I suspect her. I go no farther than to say that she had the opportunity."

He nodded.

"As you say." After a slight pause he continued. "There is something that I think you ought to know. The post office has been on the look-out for those poison-pen letters. Well, there were three of them posted in Ledlington on Wednesday. They were collected from a box in the High Street, and they were delivered in Tilling Green next morning. As you know, the envelopes are cheap white stuff, and the writing awkward."

"Are you going to tell me to whom they were addressed?"

"Yes, I think so. Colonel Repton had one, the Vicar another, and a third was for Miss Valentine Grey."

"Well, Randal?"

"I understand that the wedding has been put off."

She inclined her head. He said,

"On account of Connie Brooke's death? Or because of something in those letters? Or because Jason Leigh has come home?"

Miss Silver gazed at him. After what seemed like a deliberate silence she said,

"Mr. Gilbert Earle has returned to London."

"Yes—we knew that. It may, or may not, be significant."

"It has been remarked that he has neither written nor telephoned. The postman is naturally acquainted with his writing, and the two girls who work in the telephone exchange are familiar with his voice."

"There are, in fact, no secrets in a village."

"Very few, Randal."

"Then perhaps you can tell me who went into Ledlington on Wednesday morning."

Miss Silver considered.

"I went in myself on the ten o'clock bus. The wedding was next day, the rehearsal that afternoon, and Miss Wayne had decided to purchase a light pair of gloves. I accompanied her and—now let me see—Miss Eccles was also going in, and I think for the same purpose. We met in Ashley's, where she was buying a blue evening scarf. Such a good shop. I always enjoy going there. We had quite a pleasant time. Miss Wayne met a number of friends." She appeared to hesitate for a moment. "She also pointed out to me someone who was not a friend."

"Are you being mysterious?"

She did not respond to his half laughing intonation, but said gravely,

"No, I am only trying to be accurate. The person pointed out to me was Mr. Barton, the occupant of Gale's Cottage. He is Miss Wayne's neighbour on the side nearer the village, and he attracts a good deal of local attention because he does his own housework and cooking and keeps his house locked up. He also keeps seven cats who accompany him on his nocturnal rambles. I believe he very seldom goes out in the day."

"And he was in Ledlington on Wednesday morning? I presume without the cats."

"Yes. Miss Wayne remarked on it as a most unusual occurrence."

"And how did he strike you?"

"He is tall and thin, and his clothes are old and shabby. He has a listening look. I wondered if he was perhaps a little deaf."

"I believe not."

She said, "It is a look which elderly people sometimes have."

"You had not seen him before?"

"Not by daylight. But perhaps I had better tell you that I did see him on Wednesday night."

"At what time?"

"It was just after half past ten. I had put out my light and was opening the window, when I heard, first footsteps, and then the click of a gate. I leaned out a little and saw that it was the gate of Gale's Cottage. Mr. Barton was standing by it. After a little he shut the gate again and went up to the door of the house, which is at the side. He switched on a torch and opened the door, allowing the beam to fall upon the threshold. Seven large cats entered the house, after which he went in himself and locked the door behind him."

"I don't wonder the village talks. It sounds like the Arabian Nights. Did you notice from which direction he came?"

"From the direction of the Croft. Two or three cars had just come out of the Manor Gate, and most of my attention was taken up with that side of the Green, but I heard the footsteps and the click of the gate."

He frowned.

"Are you aware that quite a number of people at Tilling Green are firmly persuaded that Mr. Barton is the author of those anonymous letters?"

She said in her most restrained manner,

"They would naturally suspect a stranger and one whose way of life does not conform to the village pattern."

"Has no one suggested him to you as a suspect?"

"My dear Randal, no one except Mrs. Rodney has mentioned the anonymous letters to me at all."

"Well, I suppose that is natural. You are a stranger too, and this is a village affair. But they do suspect Barton, and if you saw him coming home at half past ten he could have been along at the Croft taking steps to silence Connie Brooke, though one would hardly expect a would-be murderer to pursue his nefarious purpose attended by a retinue of cats."

Miss Silver said,

"Since it was his habit to go out with them at night, to leave them at home would attract more attention than to take them with him—always supposing that he was about some unlawful business."

He laughed.

"Of which there is no proof! Let us return to your expedition with Miss Wayne to Ledlington on Wednesday morning. Were you together the whole time?"

"Oh, no. I found that Ashley's had some extremely

pretty wool. I bought enough to make a jumper and cardigan for my niece Ethel Burkett for Christmas—a really charming shade of red. And then I had the great pleasure of meeting dear Mrs. Jerningham."

Old memories rose between them. There had been a time when Lisle Jerningham had stood on the very edge of death and these two had watched her. Randal March said,

"She's a lovely creature and Rafe is a good chap. They are very happy now. But to get back to these Tilling people. As far as I can make out from the bus drivers there were quite a lot of them in Ledlington on Wednesday morning. Odd thing human nature. With all the other days of the week to choose from, they make a bee line for Wednesday because it is early closing, so the shops and the buses are packed. The herd instinct, I suppose. A string of Tilling people as long as your arm were in Ledlington that morning. The Reverend Thomas Martin was there. Roger Repton was there, and his decorative wife, and his sister Maggie. Valentine Grey was there, and a girl who was going to be one of her bridesmaids, Daphne Hollis. And Miss Mettie Eccles and at least a dozen others. I don't hail from Tilling myself, but I was in Ledlington on Wednesday morning and so was Rietta, and I saw quite a number of Tilling faces. And every single one of those people could have posted those three letters."

Miss Silver was silent for a moment, then she said,

"What do the people who received the letters say?"

"Tommy Martin says yes, he got a letter. No, he couldn't tell me what was in it. Not exactly secrets of the confessional, but getting on that way. It wouldn't be any help if he told me, and anyhow he wasn't going to. Valentine Grey flushed up and turned pale. Then she said she had had a nasty letter and she had put it in the fire, and she didn't want to talk about it. Things like it being her duty to help the police just rolled off. I don't know whether you—"

She shook her head.

"I have not even met her. There would have to be some natural opportunity."

"Something might be contrived. So far it's no more than one might have expected—a parson in his office, a girl and her secrets. But when you come to the third letter, there's something odd. The postman says he delivered it, but Roger Repton says it never reached him."

CHAPTER 16

After a pleasant interlude during which tea was partaken of and the March children were cordially admired Miss Silver returned to Willow Cottage. So far from being reticent about her visit, she expatiated upon it at considerable length.

"Such a charming house. Such charming people. Mrs. March in such delightful looks. She even quoted Lord Tennyson."

Miss Wayne was all interest.

"I haven't met her myself, but surely wasn't there some story?"

Miss Silver smiled.

"There could be no possible story about Mrs. March which did not redound to her credit."

Miss Renie became extremely confused.

"Oh, no—of course not—I didn't mean—I had no idea of suggesting—that is the worst of living in a village, people do talk so. And as an old friend of my mother's used to say, there don't seem to be enough

kind words to go round. I really shouldn't have alluded
to what I am sure was just ill-natured gossip. My dear
sister used always to say, 'Whatever you do, don't repeat things, Renie,' but somehow they just seem to slip
out. And it's really only because one does take an interest in one's neighbours. For instance, if my dear Esther
were here now, even she would find it very difficult not
to talk about poor Connie. Nothing *unkind* of course,
but one can't help wondering, can one?"

Miss Silver was winding the red wool which she
had bought at Ashley's. It always kept so much better
in balls, and Miss Renie having offered to hold the
skeins for her, the two ladies were brought into very
close proximity. Nothing could have exceeded the
sympathetic warmth of Miss Silver's attention as she
said,

"Oh, no. One cannot withdraw from the life of the
community. Injury to one member of it cannot fail to
be the concern of all. As St. Paul puts it, 'Whether one
member suffer, all the members suffer with it.' "

Miss Wayne dropped one end of the skein she was
holding in order to apply a somewhat crumpled handkerchief to her nose.

"How well you put it. Oh dear, I'm afraid I have tan-
gled the skein! How stupid of me!"

Miss Silver adjusted the wool with the dexterity of
long practice.

"Now if you will just keep it quite taut. I do not really
think that you should reproach yourself for being concerned about Connie Brooke. It is a very sad incident,
and must be felt by all her friends."

Miss Renie sniffed.

"I did think she looked as if she had been crying at
the rehearsal, but one couldn't have *dreamed*—"

Miss Silver said "Yes?" in a manner that made a question of it. The skein dropped again, Miss Renie burst into tears.

"I keep thinking of how she looked. We could all see that she had been crying. They say she must have had something on her mind. If only someone had gone home with her and found out what it was. But no one did, and now it is too late."

She had withdrawn both hands from the wool and was pressing the handkerchief to her face in a feeble and ineffectual manner.

"It is all these terrible letters." She peered round the corner of the handkerchief. "But perhaps you haven't heard about them—or have you?"

Miss Silver replied with composure.

"An anonymous letter was mentioned in an account of the inquest upon Doris Pell. These things can cause great distress."

Miss Wayne gave a small stifled sob.

"They are terrible! I wondered whether you knew, but I did not like to say anything—only sometimes one feels as if it would be a relief. Joyce is always so afraid of David overhearing something. Which is all nonsense, because how can a child of five know anything about anonymous letters? Why, he wouldn't even know what the word meant."

Miss Silver said gravely, "It is surprising what quite young children will pick up, and remember."

Miss Wayne emerged from the handkerchief with a slight toss of the head.

"Joyce has not been very sympathetic. I used to discuss *everything* with my dear sister. She would have been quite horrified about these letters. You know, some years ago they had the same sort of trouble at

Little Poynton which is only about ten miles from here. Two people committed suicide, and Scotland Yard was called in. That stopped it, but they never really found out who wrote the letters. Some people thought it was the postmistress, but my sister and I could never believe it. She was such a regular church-goer, and always so obliging if you went into the shop. They had a very good grocery counter as well as the post office. An old aunt of ours lived almost next door, so Esther and I were in the way of hearing a good deal about the trouble, and Aunt Marian always said she couldn't believe anything against such an obliging woman as Mrs. Salt. It is her sister Mrs. Gurney who has the post office here—and I suppose no one would suspect *her* of having anything to do with the letters people have been getting in Tilling Green."

Miss Silver's hands were busy with the red skein. She said,

"Would there be any grounds for such a suspicion?"

Miss Wayne became very much flustered.

"Oh, no—oh dear, no—of course not! Oh dear, what did I say to make you think of such a thing? Of course Mrs. Gurney can't help knowing a lot about what goes on in the village, because everyone goes in and out, and when they meet their friends they talk to them. My dear sister used to say what a lot of time was wasted in this way. 'If you are going to shop,' she said, 'then do your shopping and come away. Lingering and gossiping go together, and a great deal of mischief is done by it.' Of course it isn't always easy to get away, but I do my best—I suppose no one listens to what is being said less than I do. Why until Hilda Price absolutely insisted on pouring it all out to me I had no idea that poor Connie Brooke was supposed to know who had been writing these dreadful letters. Everyone else in the village seems to have known, but I really hadn't the slightest idea."

Miss Silver said in a concerned voice,

"What made them think that Connie knew about the letters?"

The story of the telephone call to the Parsonage and Connie's subsequent visit was reluctantly disclosed, if at first with such remarks as, "I don't like repeating things," and "One can really hardly believe it." Miss Renie's version did not differ substantially from that communicated by Joyce Rodney. Connie had been crying when she rang up the Parsonage, and she wept as she went away. She knew something about the letters and she had come to tell Mr. Martin what she knew, but had gone away without doing so. Her words as reported by Mrs. Needham were, "Once I've said it, I can't take it back." To which Mr. Martin replied, "No, you couldn't take it back, so you had better think it well over. But if you know who has been writing these anonymous letters, you may have a duty."

"And now," said Renie Wayne with a sob, "whatever it was she knew, it is too late to find out, because she's dead! And it all goes to show that if there is anything that ought to be done, it's better to do it at once. Esther always did say that. She said there was a proverb about it in Latin, but I'm afraid I don't remember what it was."

Miss Silver's Latin extending to some of the commoner proverbs, she was able to supply the words in question—"*Bis dat qui cito dat*—he gives twice who gives quickly."

CHAPTER 17

The inquest on Connie Brooke took place at eleven o'clock on Saturday morning. Only formal evidence was taken, after which the police applied for an adjournment. Miss Wayne having announced her intention of attending, Miss Silver offered to accompany her, and was profusely thanked.

"Oh, if you would! I should find it such a support! These things are so painful, and until last year I went nowhere without my dear sister."

In other circumstances Miss Silver might have pointed out that the painful experience could easily be avoided by the simple expedient of staying at home. As, however, her professional interest was engaged, she made no attempt to dissuade Miss Renie, who duly appeared in the full mourning outfit which she had worn at Miss Esther's funeral. She provided herself with an extra handkerchief, confiding to Miss Silver that an inquest always made her cry—"And it seems no time at all since I was at poor Doris Pell's."

The inquest was at the George, its largest room having been placed at the Coroner's disposal. It was packed. After the medical evidence had testified to the very large number of tablets which the dead girl must have swallowed, Miss Maggie Repton was called to the chair which had been set at the far side of the Coroner's table. She took the oath in a series of gasps and sat pulling at the corners of her handkerchief. It is to be assumed that the Coroner himself was able to hear her replies to the questions which he put, but it was only when he repeated them that they reached anyone else.

Asked if she had given Connie Brooke a bottle of sleeping tablets, she was understood to indicate that she had.

"What made you do that, Miss Repton?"

Her murmured reply appeared as, "She hadn't been sleeping."

"Did you tell her how many tablets to take?"

There was a slight movement of the head, followed by another murmur.

"Oh, you think the dose was on the bottle. Are you not sure about that?"

Here the Police Inspector intervened to state that the dose was on the label, but the lettering was rubbed and faint. The bottle was produced and scrutinized. The Coroner said,

"Yes. It is not at all clear. Now, Miss Repton, how many tablets did this bottle contain?"

It emerged that Miss Maggie had no idea. After a series of such questions as "If you can't say exactly, can you make a guess? Was it half full—a quarter full—very nearly empty?" it had still been impossible to draw her into expressing any opinion. She gasped, she whispered, she pressed the by now extremely crumpled handkerchief to her eyes, but no faintest gleam of light was cast upon the number of tablets in the bottle which she had given to Connie Brooke.

Miss Eccles succeeded her, taking the oath clearly and giving her evidence with businesslike precision. She had walked across the Green with Connie Brooke as far as Holly Cottage and said good-night to her there. They had talked about the sleeping-tablets, and she had cautioned Connie strongly against taking more than one. Pressed upon this point, she repeated it with emphasis.

"She wasn't accustomed to anything of the sort, and I told her she ought not to take more than one."

"Did she make any comment?"

"No, she didn't. We got off on to her not being able to swallow anything like a pill. She said she would crush the tablet up and put it in the cocoa which she had left ready on the stove. I told her it would taste horrible—and then I remembered and said, 'Oh, but you don't taste things, do you?' "

"Yes, that was in Dr. Taylor's evidence—she had lost her sense of taste after an illness. Now, Miss Eccles, when you were referring to the dose she was going to dissolve you used the words '*a tablet.*' Is that what Miss Brooke said?"

Mettie Eccles said,

"I'm not sure. I was thinking about her taking *a* tablet. I had just told her she ought not to take more, but I'm not sure whether she said 'a tablet' or 'tablets.' I'm sorry, but I can't be certain about it."

Under the Coroner's questioning she gave a very clear and composed account of Penny Marsh running over to fetch her next morning, and of how they had found Connie Brooke lying dead upon her bed. She was questioned as to the saucepan that had held the cocoa.

"Did you wash it up and put it away?"

"Oh, no. She must have done that herself."

"It is not for us to assume what Miss Brooke did."

Mettie Eccles did not exactly toss her head. There was just some slight indication that she might have done so if she had not been restrained by respect for the court. What she did do was to say very firmly indeed,

"Connie would never have left a saucepan dirty."

There was very little more after that. The police asked for an adjournment. The Coroner left his seat, the spectators streamed away by ones and twos, the room at the George returned to its normal uses.

CHAPTER 18

*Valentine Grey was walk-*ing in the woods behind the Manor. She had come there to meet Jason. When he came he put his arms around her and they stayed like that for quite a long time, just holding one another. Presently he said,

"When are we going to get married?"

"I don't know. You haven't ever asked me."

"I don't need to ask you. I couldn't before I went away, because it didn't seem so very likely that I should come back. And now there's no need. You know."

"I might like to be asked."

"On bended knee in the proper romantic style!" He went down on the carpet of pine needles and kissed both her hands. "Will you do me the very great honour of marrying me?"

She looked down at him, her eyes shining, her lips not quite steady. This was not the Valentine who had stood at the chancel step to rehearse her marriage to Gilbert Earle. Her hands shook in his, her colour came and went. She said,

"I don't know—" Her voice shook too.

"You do. You know perfectly well. And mind you, it's your only chance, because I certainly shouldn't let you marry anyone else."

Her lips quivered into a smile.

"How would you stop me?"

He got up without letting go of her.

"I should forbid the banns. You know it's a thing I've always wanted to do."

"Does anyone ever?"

"Oh, I believe it's been done. You stand up and get it off your chest good and loud, and the parson stops and says he will see you in the vestry afterwards. And no one listens to another word of the service, least of all you, because of course you are thinking up what you are going to say in the vestry."

"And what would you be going to say? It would have to be a just cause or impediment, you know."

He said,

"There's an old posy ring of my mother's that I want to give you. It has been in the family since about the same time of the Armada. The writing inside is so small that you have to use a magnifying glass to read it, and it has had to be renewed a great many times. It says:

'If you love me as I love you,
Nothing but death shall part us two.'

"Don't you think that's a just cause and impediment to your marrying anyone else?"

"I suppose—it might be—"

It was some time later that she said, "Will you have—to go—again—"

"Not to the same places. They got wise to me this time, so I shouldn't be very much use. Would you like to settle down and farm?"

"I'd love it."

"Then when will you marry me?"

"Jason, I don't know. You see, as far as anyone can tell I'm still engaged to Gilbert. People just think the wedding was put off on account of Connie Brooke."

He gave a half angry laugh.

"That is all you know! I get the low-down from Mrs. Needham. Half the village is talking about poor Mr. Earle, and the other half thinks he must have blotted his copy-book pretty badly or you wouldn't have done it. But they are all quite sure that he has been given the push, and that the wedding is definitely off. The postman has noticed that he doesn't write, and the girls in the telephone exchange are quite positive he hasn't rung up, so the matter is considered to be settled. You had better get on with informing the family and putting a notice in the papers."

"Oh, I've told Roger and Maggie, and I suppose Roger has told Scilla. She hasn't said anything."

"And what did Roger and Maggie say?"

She lifted his hand and laid it against her cheek.

"Oh, Maggie cried and said marriage was very uncertain, and she had often felt thankful that she had escaped it."

"Poor old Maggie."

"Darling, she was rather pathetic. She said how unhappy my father and mother had been, and she talked about Roger and Scilla."

"And what did Roger talk about?"

"He hardly said anything at all. I told him I shouldn't be marrying Gilbert, and he didn't even ask why. He stood with his back to me and looked out of the window, and all he said was, 'Well, I suppose you know your own business.' So I said yes, I did, and that was just about all."

Jason did not speak. After a moment she went on.

"I had one of those horrible letters on Thursday morning. I can't help wondering whether Roger had one too."

"Tommy did."

"Tommy!"

"Yes, I saw it."

"Jason—"

"Look here, this is just between you and me."

"Of course. What did it say?"

"Accused Gilbert of intending to commit bigamy, and asked Tommy if he was prepared to aid and abet. Put him in quite a spot. On the one hand you don't take any notice of anonymous letters, and on the other you can't take a chance about letting a girl in for a bigamous marriage. Tommy ought to be blessing us for getting him out of the mess."

She was leaning against him. Gilbert was gone, and everything felt very safe and comfortable. She said,

"Did Tommy's letter say Gilbert had married a girl called Marie Dubois in Canada?"

"It did. Without saying where or when. Anonymity strictly preserved throughout. Let me see—he was in Canada, wasn't he?"

"A long time ago. He couldn't have been more than about twenty. I wonder if he really did marry Marie."

"May have done. If he was had for a mug when he was all that young and she was dead, he might not have thought it necessary to mention her. Or there might have been a divorce. I should hardly think he would risk being run in for bigamy. We'll ask him about it some day. Just casually, you know—at a cocktail party, or a railway station, or any of the other places where you are liable to have a head-on collision with the people you don't want to meet."

"Darling, what a fool you are!"

What a heavenly feeling to be able to laugh at something that had been a nightmare. They laughed together. Jason said,

"What do you bet I don't do it? Some day when we are safely married. I would, you know, for tuppence. Something on the lines of 'Oh, by the way, what happened to that girl you married in Canada, Marie Dubois?' "

"You *wouldn't!*"

"You wait and see!"

CHAPTER 19

*Scilla Repton lifted the tele-*phone receiver in the study and asked for a London number. Of course the girl in the telephone exchange would listen if she thought there was anything to listen to, but what did it matter? If you lived in a village you didn't have any private affairs to speak of anyway. If you heard too often from anyone, Mrs. Gurney at the post office got to know the writing and could make a pretty shrewd guess at the writer. Scilla had heard her say quite openly across the counter things like, "Oh, no, Mrs. Lawson, there's nothing from your Ernie to-day—just a card from your sister in Birmingham."

She waited for the click of the receiver and thought what she was going to say. It took her some time to get hold of Gilbert Earle, and when she did get him he couldn't have sounded stuffier. He heard her laugh.

"Really, Gilbert—what a voice! Anyone would think we had quarrelled!"

He said in very good French, "A little discretion, if you please."

She sounded amused.

"I can't be bothered. Besides there's nothing to bother about. Roger tells me the wedding is off, and a good job too. Anyone could see with half an eye that it was going to be a case of marry in haste and repent at leisure, so you're well out of it, if you ask me."

"I didn't ask you."

She allowed her voice to soften.

"It'll all come out in the wash, darling. Look here, I've got to come up to town, and I thought we might lunch together. What about it?"

"I hardly think this is the moment."

"What a foul thing to say! It's Val who has turned you down, not me. I thought I might provide a little hand-holding—you sound as if you needed it. Nothing like being seen about with somebody else as soon as possible. I mean, darling, how much more agreeable to have people coming up and asking you who was the smashing blonde you were lunching with, instead of drifting along to condole at some horrid solitary snack bar. You know, what you want at the moment is a tonic, and so do I. I'll say I'm going to the dentist. That always goes down well, and as a matter of fact I'm about due for a date with him. And Mamie would lend us her flat and not ask any questions. So Monday at the old place at one o'clock. The best of everything!" She rang off in a hurry because she thought she heard a movement behind her.

But she had not rung off in time. The sound which she had heard was not the sound of the opening but of the closing door. Roger Repton was already in the room. The latch clicked, he leaned back against the panels, and said in an odd dead voice,

"Who were you talking to?"

She said the first name that came into her head, the one she had used to Gilbert Earle.

"Mamie Foster. I've got to go and see the dentist, and I thought I'd go back to her flat afterwards and have a bit of a rest before coming down again. He may want to give me gas."

He stood there with his hand on the door behind him.

"That is a lie."

"Roger!"

His voice had not altered. She knew his temper to be a violent one. There was something unnatural about this leaden tone. He said,

"You were not talking to Mamie Foster, you were talking about her. You were going to meet Gilbert Earle, and you were talking to him. You said, 'I'll say I'm going to the dentist—that always goes down well. And Mamie would lend us her flat and not ask any questions.' And you would meet him at the old place at one o'clock on Monday. You see it's no use telling any more lies, because I know. If you have been in the habit of meeting him at Mamie Foster's flat, it should be possible to get evidence of the fact, in which case I shall divorce you. Someone was kind enough to send me an anonymous letter informing me that you have been having an affair with Gilbert. I think Valentine probably had a letter too. I haven't asked her, and she hasn't said so, but I imagine that you have had your share in breaking up her marriage. You can go to Gilbert Earle, or you can go to your accommodating friend Mamie Foster, or you can go to hell. But I should like you to get out of my house." He stood away from the door and opened it. "You had better go and pack."

She was between fear and anger. Something desperate in her was urging her to burn her boats. Why not kick over the traces, upset the apple cart, and get back to the old life? She was better looking than she had ever been, and her figure was just as good. She could get back into the show business, and Gilbert would come to heel all right. She was fed to the teeth with the country and with Roger. But she was frightened of this desperate urge. She could remember the times when she had been out of a job—when she was cold, tired, hungry, and nobody cared a damn whether she lived or died. If Roger divorced her she would lose the money he had settled on her. There were the horrid words in the settlement which the lawyer had been careful to explain to her—*dum casta,* whilst chaste. If she went through the divorce court she wouldn't get a penny. But if she stayed here—if she could stick it out—and Roger died. . . . She wouldn't be so badly off at all. . . . He was getting on. . . .

All these thoughts were in her mind like birds beating against a window. It was the fear that broke through. She heard herself saying in a loud scornful voice,

"An anonymous letter? One of those filthy things that have been going round? How dare you!"

He made no response to her heat as he said,

"A filthy letter about a filthy thing."

"Lies—lies—*lies!*"

He shook his head.

"I don't think so. The letter was quite circumstantial. You were with Gilbert Earle and you were spied on, and I think I know by whom. I think I know who wrote the letter."

She put up her hand to her throat. The pulse of anger beat there—the pulse of fear.

"Who was it?"

"You would like to know, wouldn't you? Perhaps it was you yourself. It would have been one way of breaking off Valentine's marriage, wouldn't it? It would have been one way of getting out of your own! What do you and your friends care about divorce—it doesn't mean anything to you! But you had better be sure that Gilbert will marry you before you walk out."

She said in a voice that was edged with anger,

"I thought you were *turning* me out! Suppose I

haven't got anywhere to go to! Suppose I just say I'm going to stay!''

He had a sense of having gone too far, of having embarked upon a course which would involve them all in a devastating scandal. If he went any farther, there could be no turning back. How far had she really gone herself—how far had she meant to go? Gilbert wouldn't marry her if he could help it. He had an empty title coming to him. He couldn't afford a scandal, and he couldn't afford to marry a woman who wouldn't have a penny. These were not consecutive thoughts. They were there in the cooling temper of his mind.

They had both forgotten the open door. Roger remembered it now. He pushed it to as he said,

"I have no desire to put myself in the wrong by turning you out. You can make your plans, and you can take your time. In any case you'll have to stay over Tuesday. There must be no scandal before that poor girl's funeral."

It was very disappointing for Florrie Stokes when the study door was closed. She had come through into the hall on her lawful business of seeing to the fires and drawing the curtains before dinner. She couldn't help hearing the angry voices in the study, because it was the first room she came to, only of course when she heard the way Colonel Repton was talking she knew better than to go in. She didn't mean to listen—well, not really—but the way the Colonel was talking, not loud but ever so distinct and bitter—well, she just couldn't help it. And the very first thing she heard was something about getting evidence of Mrs. Repton meeting Mr. Gilbert at her friend Mamie Foster's flat and going for a divorce. And he went on, "You can go to Gilbert Earle, or you can go to your accommodating friend Mamie Foster, or you can go to hell. But I should like you to get out of my house." And when he got as far as that the door began to open, and it was all she could do to get back out of sight. Even then if Mrs. Repton had come out, she would have been caught. But Mrs. Repton didn't come out. She said very clear and angry—something about an anonymous letter and, "How dare you!"

After that Florrie just couldn't tear herself away. With the door open, she could stand right back against the baize door which went through to the kitchen premises. If one of them put a foot into the hall she would be just coming through to her work and nothing to say how long she had been there. She could hear everything they said, and it was as good as being at the pictures. Of course everyone knew Mrs. Repton was flighty, just the same as they knew she'd been carrying on with Mr. Gilbert on the sly. And serve her right if the Colonel had found her out. She'd got a husband of her own, hadn't she, and it was a downright shame doing anything to upset Miss Valentine's marriage. Only of course now that Mr. Jason was back Miss Valentine would never want anyone but him—they all knew that.

When Scilla came out of the study with an angry spot on either cheek Florrie had just let the baize door swing to behind her.

CHAPTER 20

It was Florrie's afternoon out. Her mother worked at the George because Mr. Stokes enjoyed bad health. There were three daughters and a son, and they all lived at home and contributed to Dad's upkeep. They were a very affectionate family, and if it was fifteen years since Mr. Stokes had earned anything, he was at any rate a very good cook and always had something tasty ready for tea when the family came home. He had a very light hand with pastry, and as Florrie said, though not in Mrs. Glazier's hearing, he could cook bacon and sausages and fry fish to beat the band. It was well known that alluring offers had been made to him from several quarters, but Mr. Stokes was not to be lured. He had mysterious turns which no doctor had ever been able to diagnose. He had not, in fact, a great deal of faith in doctors, an attitude fully reciprocated, Dr. Taylor going so far as to allude to him as an old humbug. This was doubtless the case, in spite of which the whole family was a very cheerful and united one.

When Florrie came in he was reading the paper and sipping herbal tea, a quite horrid beverage the recipe for which had been handed down in his family for a hundred years and was a closely guarded secret. Nothing would have induced any of his children to touch it. Florrie wrinkled her nose at the smell, kissed the top of his head, and plunged into gossip.

"There's been ever such a row up at the Manor."

Mr. Stokes allowed his paper to slide onto the floor. It contained nothing as exciting as what might have been termed The Repton Serial. What with the talk there had been about Mrs. Repton—her clothes, her make-up, the rumours about her having been a model, to say nothing of what he stigmatized as her carryings on, and then Miss Valentine's wedding being broken off—and anyone could guess why that was—and Connie Brooke dying off sudden as she had, and the police looking into it—well, there hadn't been a dull moment. He enquired with avidity,

"Why—what's up now? Been any more of that poison pen?"

Florrie shook her head.

"Not that I know of."

"Miss Valentine had a letter Thursday?"

"I told you she did."

"And the Colonel too? And Sam Boxer says there was one went to the Parsonage—all of them the spit and image of each other. And the police been at him about them. I told him straight, what he did ought to have done was to face up to 'em and say, 'I'm a postman, that's what I am—I'm not a detective. I got enough work to do delivering of my letters. It isn't no part of my business to be studying of 'em.' That's what he did ought to have said and saved himself a lot er trouble. It's got nothing to do with him, and so I told him. Or anyone else that I can see. Spilt milk won't go back in the jug, nor broken-off weddings won't come on again, not for the police nor yet for no one, so what's the row about now?"

Florrie was bursting with it, but it wasn't any good for her to start anything till Dad had had his say. You might just have been seeing a murder, but if there was something Dad wanted to talk about, you had to let him get in first.

But as soon as the coast was clear it all came tumbling out.

"Colonel and Mrs. Repton have had ever such a row. I could hear them in the study. Their voices was ever so loud—at least not the Colonel's but there was something about it—it seemed to come right through the door. I was coming through to draw the curtains, and I could hear him say she could go to Mr. Earle, or she could go to her friend Mamie Foster—that's the one she's always writing to—or she could go to hell."

Mr. Stokes sat with a cup of herbal tea in his hand. He had been going to take a sip, but the movement had been checked. His eyes fairly sparkled and his small monkeylike features displayed the liveliest interest as he said,

"He never!"

Florrie nodded.

"Cross my heart he did! And told her to get out of his house, and the sooner the better—at least that's what it sounded like—and threw open the door and told her to go and pack."

"Well, I *never!*"

Florrie nodded again, even more emphatically.

"And I got caught as near as a toucher. I don't know how I got out of the way in time, I don't reelly. I wouldn't have, only they didn't come out—not then. And the door stayed open, so I could hear all the rest of it—and my goodness if it wasn't a Row! There was something about a letter he'd had—and that would be the one that came Thursday morning—and he said it was a filthy letter about a filthy thing."

"He didn't."

"He did, *straight!* And she screaming out that it was all a lie! And then he said he knew quite well who it was as had written all those letters, and she said who was it, and he said wouldn't she like to know. And then—Dad, what do you think he said then? He said maybe she'd written the letters herself! It didn't sound sense to me, but that's what he said. He said it would be one way of breaking off Miss Valentine's marriage and getting out of her own, only she'd better make sure Mr. Gilbert would marry her before she walked out!"

Mr. Stokes took a sip of the sickly looking greenish fluid in the cup he was holding and swallowed it with relish. He said,

"Who'd er thought it! Has she gone?"

Florrie shook her head.

"No—nor doesn't mean to, if you ask me. Said how

was he going to make her go if she didn't want to? And I'd say that brought him up with a bit of a turn, but I didn't rightly hear any more, because that's where he shut the door, and I didn't like to go near it again."

"Then how do you know she isn't going off?"

Florrie giggled.

"I've got eyes and ears, haven't I? The Colonel, he banged out—took the car. He just told Miss Maggie he wouldn't be home to lunch and off he went. Mrs. Repton, she come down as if nothing had happened, and she hadn't been packing neither, for I looked in her room. And at lunch, when Miss Maggie was talking about poor Miss Connie's funeral and saying of course they would all go, and had they anything like mourning that they could wear, Miss Valentine said she hadn't anything but grey, but she could wear a black hat with it. And Mrs. Repton—you know how bright she dresses— she said all she'd got was a smart navy suit which wouldn't be at all right, but she supposed it would have to do. So the funeral not being till Tuesday, it doesn't look as if she was thinking of getting off in a hurry, does it?"

"She wouldn't want to make talk," said Mr. Stokes. "There'd be a lot of talk if she went away before the funeral. Not but what there'll be a lot of talk anyway."

It would not be the fault of the Stokes family if there were not. When Florrie's elder sister Betty came in the whole story had to be gone over again. And when Ivy was added to the family party, and the son Bob, and presently Florrie's boy friend and Betty's boy friend dropped in, it was all repeated. And with each repetition there was a tendency to place more and more emphasis on the fact that Colonel Repton had said he knew who had written the anonymous letters.

Later on that evening Florrie and her boy went over

in the bus to Ledlington to the pictures. Waiting in the bus queue were Hilda Price and Jessie Peck. After such preliminaries as, "You know how I am about not talking," and, "You won't let it go any further, will you?" Florrie passed from hinting to narrative, the story lasting most of the way over in the bus, with the result that the boy friend, who was not really very much interested in anything except himself and his motorbike with Florrie a bad third, began to show signs of temper. How many people Hilda and Jessie told is not on record, but they were competent news-mongers.

Betty Stokes, who had been going steady with Mrs. Gurney's son Reg for the past two years and was expecting to be engaged at Christmas, went round with him to his mother's, where they spent the evening. In the intervals of playing rummy she related the latest installment of the Manor serial. It was received with a good deal of interest.

Ivy, who was only sixteen, ran over to a girl friend who was also one of a large family. Her version of the row at the Manor was certainly the least accurate of the three, but not on that account the least interesting. She had a lively imagination and a good deal of dramatic sense. Her performance in a play got up in aid of the local Women's Institute had been noticed in the Ledshire *Observer*. Her rendering of the Repton quarrel was an exciting one.

"Florrie, she was right next the door and she couldn't help hearing him tell her he knew all about the way she'd been carrying on, and she could go to hell. Those were his very words, and they didn't half give Florrie a turn. She came over ever so queer, because she thought whatever should she do if the Colonel got reelly violent. She couldn't just stand there outside the door and let Mrs. Repton be half killed—now could she? And the

Colonel might have turned on her if she'd come between them. Just like something out of a film it was. Florrie said her heart beat ever so. And the Colonel says, 'Leave my house!' he says. And she says, 'How are you going to make me, I'd like to know.' And they get on to those poison-pen letters, and he carries on something dreadful and he says he knows who wrote them. . . ." And so forth and so on, the girl friend's family coming in with appropriate responses and a good time being had by all.

It was not until late that night and just before she dropped asleep that the girl friend's mother was suddenly visited by the thought of Connie Brooke. It was a vague ghost thought without clarity or definition, but it went with her into her sleep and it was still there when she woke in the morning. If she could have put it into words they would have been something like this, "Connie Brooke knew who wrote those letters, and she is dead."

CHAPTER 21

There are days which come up so bright and fair that they hardly seem to belong to the workaday world. When Miss Silver rose next morning to golden sunshine and an unclouded sky she reflected that it was doubly pleasant and appropriate that such halcyon weather should adorn a Sunday. She recalled George Herbert's words:

> *"Sweet day, so cool, so calm, so bright,*
> *The bridal of the earth and sky—"*

The end of the verse, with its reference to the dew which would weep the fall and death of the lovely day, she considered to be morbid, and did not therefore allow her thought to dwell upon it. She found the service in the old church most pleasant and restful, the lessons read plainly and well, a simple sermon, hearty untrained singing, and Mettie Eccles at the organ.

As they walked home afterwards, Miss Rennie said in a plaintive voice,

"Mettie has always played. She has so much energy, but my dear sister used to say that her touch was hard. Esther had a very cultivated musical taste."

Miss Silver remarked that she had liked Mr. Martin's sermon. Miss Rennie's very slight sniff might have escaped a less acute observer.

"He has been here a long time, and people are fond of him, but he does not keep up his dignity," she said. Then, with an abrupt transition, "I suppose you noticed that there was no one in the Manor pew?"

The following day was dull and rainy. It was Miss Maggie's afternoon for the Work Party which, begun during the war, had proved so pleasant a social gathering that it had established itself as a permanency. There were, unfortunately, always the displaced and the distressed to work for, and no lack of piteous appeals for their relief. The party met at a different house each week, and its members vied with each other in the provision of simple refreshments. There had been some considerable speculation as to whether Miss Maggie would take her turn this time or allow it to pass to someone else. Opinion was divided on the subject, some ladies considering that the Reptons had really had enough on their hands, and that it would really be more delicate if they remained in retirement until after Connie's funeral, whilst others held the view that the Work Party was not so much a Party as a Good Work and as such nothing should be allowed to interfere with it. Mettie Eccles made herself the mouthpiece of this second view, and not without authority, since she allowed it to be known that Miss Maggie had consulted her.

"She asked for my advice, and I had no hesitation in saying that if she felt up to it, the Work Party should go on. After all, none of us know when some distant connection may pass away! If a charitable activity like the Work Party is to be chopped and changed whenever anything like that happens, we shall none of us ever know where we are. I told Maggie very decidedly indeed that she ought not to let it make any difference, always provided she felt up to seeing us all, and she said at once that it would be the greatest help. And I said to her, 'It isn't as if poor Connie was anything but the *most* distant connection. It was your grandfather's sister Florence who married Connie's great-grandfather on the mother's side as his third wife. And she never had any children of her own, which was just as well, because there were fifteen already, but I believe she made the most admirable stepmother.' "

After which there was no more to be said.

In spite of the damp afternoon there was quite an unusual attendance. The Manor had been the centre of interest all the week, and now on the top of everything else there was a perfect buzz of talk about the Reptons having had a really terrible quarrel.

"It came from one of the maids. . . . It came from Florrie Stokes. . . . All the Stokes family are such terrible talkers, and Mr. Stokes is the worst of the lot. . . . They say Scilla Repton was carrying on with Gilbert Earle, and that's why the wedding was broken off. . . . My dear, how dreadful! . . . They say Colonel Repton is going to divorce her. . . . He was crazy to marry her in the first place—he was old enough to know better. . . .

Oh, my dear, no man is ever too old to make a fool of himself over a woman. . . ."

And first, last, and all the time,

"He said he knew who had written the anonymous letters. . . . Florrie heard him with her own ears. . . . The door was open and he shouted it out quite loud. . . . He said he knew who had written the letters, and perhaps it was Scilla herself. . . ."

Nobody in Tilling Green was going to miss an opportunity of mingling with the characters in so exciting a drama. Not that they really expected Roger to mingle with them. The utmost that anyone expected to see of him would be a brief encounter in the hall on arrival or when going away. Scilla Repton was also not to be counted upon. She would occasionally make a brief appearance in corduroy slacks, crimson or emerald, worn with a vividly contrasting jumper, drawl out a few bored sentences, and then vanish from the scene. When the Work Party was actually in the Manor she did as a rule come in at tea-time. If she absented herself to-day, Florrie's story would be confirmed. And anyhow Miss Maggie would be there, and Valentine, and it should be perfectly possible to tell from their looks and manner whether anything was going on.

When Maggie Repton was worried she couldn't keep her fingers still. She had be fidgeting with this and that and the other. As she received them this afternoon, it was quite obvious to these people who knew her so well that she had something on her mind. Her long sallow face twitched, and when she was not actually shaking hands, her bony fingers were plucking at the cut steel chain about her neck or feeling for the handkerchief which she as constantly mislaid.

She had thought that she could manage to get through the afternoon, but now she didn't feel as if she could. Roger had said that she ought to do it, and Mettie had said that she ought to do it, so here she was in the drawing-room in the dress which she always wore on these occasions. Not her best, because that would look pretentious, and though it was only purple and that counted as half mourning, she wouldn't quite like to wear it until after the funeral. Her usual dress was fortunately quite suitable—two years old, and of a very dark grey with a little black fancy stitching on the yoke and cuffs.

She had consulted Roger again, a few minutes ago, just to reassure herself about the party. He had said very emphatically,

"Oh, yes, yes—go on and have the Work Party! What difference does it make? Except that if you don't have it, you will start everyone talking all over again." He went as far as the door, put his hand on it, and spoke without turning round. "There'll be plenty to talk about, but let us get this funeral over first."

Miss Maggie gave a little gasp.

"What—what do you mean?"

He threw her a brief glance over his shoulder.

"Divorce—Scilla is clearing out. You may as well know it now as later."

"Clearing out—"

"And not coming back. She has been having an affair with Gilbert Earle—if that's the worst of it. I've come to the end. She must go." He jerked at the handle of the door and went out, shutting it sharply behind him.

Maggie Repton felt her way to a chair and sat down. It was quite a long time before she went through to the drawing-room. When she did so, people were already beginning to arrive. They glanced uneasily at her and at one another. Maggie Repton was always sallow, but this afternoon her skin had a curious greyish tinge. It might have been partly due to the light, the rain having turned into the kind of mist which drains the colour out of everything, but it wasn't the light that gave her that wandering look and set her fingers shaking.

Valentine, on the contrary, did not look in the least like a deserted bride. She was not in colours—she wore a cream jumper and a grey tweed skirt, a compromise which was very generally approved. But there was a kind of bloom and glow about her which had been rather noticeably absent during the days preceding what should have been her wedding. After no more than a single glance there was a warm and unanimous feeling that whoever was plunged in gloom and distress, it was not dear Valentine.

Miss Silver had by now met quite a number of the ladies present. She found herself impressed by the efficiency with which Miss Eccles appeared to be presiding in what was, after all, someone else's house. Certainly no one who did not know would have taken Miss Maggie for the hostess. It is true that she was not wearing a hat, but after the first few minutes this failed to distinguish her, since Mettie Eccles and quite a number of the other ladies had preferred to remove their headgear before sitting down to do needlework. For this purpose they adjourned to the hall, either by ones and twos or in small groups. There was a mirror there, and a chest upon which coats, hats and scarves could be piled.

They came back into the room and disposed themselves on the comfortable old-fashioned chairs and sofas. Thimbles were put on, scissors laid ready, half-made garments produced, knitting-needles and wool extracted from capacious bags. Miss Silver found herself on a sofa next to large and important looking lady in black and white tweeds. She wore pearl studs in her ears, and she had very fine dark eyes. She was also the only woman in the room who was not provided with some sort of work. At first occupied in exchanging nods and greetings with some of the other women, she turned presently to her immediate companion and remarked,

"How very well you knot. Let me see, you are Renie Wayne's p.g. aren't you? Miss Silver isn't it? I'm Nora Mallett—Lady Mallett. I'm a relation of the Reptons, and I'm here under completely false pretences, because I really came over to see Maggie. This poor girl Connie dying so suddenly and Val's wedding being put off, I thought I had better just make sure that Maggie hadn't packed up altogether. If I had had any idea that there would be this Work Party business going on I shouldn't have come. As it is, I'm just waiting for a chance to get Maggie to myself for five minutes, so I don't want to get involved with anyone it will be difficult to get away from."

Oddly enough, this bluntness did not give offence. There was so much warmth in voice and manner, so strong an expression of kindness, as to make her seem merely frank. Miss Silver found herself forming a favourable impression. She said with a smile,

"My own work, I am afraid, is of quite a private character. I am making a twin set for my niece's little girl. The jumper is finished. This is the cardigan."

Lady Mallet admired the stitch, asked a number of questions about little Josephine, about her brothers, her parents. Always ready to talk of her dear Ethel, Miss Silver responded, and it was not until some time had passed that they reverted to their more immediate surroundings, Miss Silver reproaching herself for having been led into taking up too much of Lady Mallet's attention.

Nora Mallet gave her rolling laugh.

"Oh, I'm always interested in people, you know, and

there isn't really any particular hurry." She carefully dropped her voice as she continued. "I just don't want to get buttonholed by Mettie Eccles. We're some sort of cousins, you know, and she always tries to lay down the law to me. As for getting Maggie to myself, I don't suppose there's a hope." She turned to look across the room to where Miss Repton drooped over a pattern which she and at least three other people were endeavouring to accommodate to what was obviously too short a length of material. With a laugh and a shrug she turned back again. "They might as well give it up—and so might I! I wonder how long before Mettie—Oh, she's going over to them. And now, my dear Miss Silver, you will see that the pattern will be made to behave itself and come out right. If Mettie wants things to go a certain way, well, they go that way. The only time she didn't bring it off was the one that mattered the most to her, poor thing."

Nora Mallet's tongue was notoriously indiscreet, but she would probably not have proceeded any farther if it had not been for that something about the quality of Miss Silver's listening which had caused her to receive so many confidences. And after all, there really wasn't any secret about the fact that Mettie Eccles had always been devoted to Roger. The words slid off her tongue.

"Odd, isn't it, but you stop being clever when you care too much, and that's a fact. She would have made Roger just the sort of wife he ought to have had, and I don't suppose it ever occurred to him. Men are so horribly stupid! There she was under his nose—he saw her every day of his life—and so he really never saw her at all! Have you met his wife?"

"I have seen her."

Lady Mallet shrugged the ample shoulders under the black and white tweed.

"Oh well, then, there isn't much need to say any

more, is there?" Like so many people who make this type of remark, she then proceeded to say quite a number of things. "Thirty years younger than he is, and a great deal too ornamental! What was it one of those old poets said about someone being too bright and good for something or other? I don't know that I should use the word good, but she is certainly too *bright* for Tilling Green."

With a slight preliminary cough Miss Silver supplied the information that the poet was Wordsworth, and that what he really said was:

> *"Not too bright or good*
> *For human nature's daily food."*

Nora Mallet laughed good humouredly.

"Daily food! My dear, what a cannibal! You know, I'm being horribly indiscreet, but sometimes it's a tremendous relief just to let go and say what you feel, and if you do it to a stranger it matters so much less than giving yourself and everyone else away to an intimate friend who is quite certain to pass it on."

Miss Silver's needles were moving briskly. She looked at the blue frill which was lengthening there and said,

"It is sometimes much easier to talk to a stranger."

Lady Mallett nodded.

"The looker on who sees most of the game! Now tell me—what is everyone saying about the wedding? Do they think it's just put off, or what?"

"Mr. Earle's absence has occasioned some comment."

Lady Mallett laughed.

"Well, it would, wouldn't it! Gilbert goes off, the other young man stays put, and Val has got stars in her eyes. I don't mind saying that I like Jason the better of the two, though I'm sure I don't know why. He can be shockingly rude, and he has been making Val unhappy, but if she wants him she'd better have him, so long as he doesn't go off into the blue again and leave her to break her heart."

Since she had only seen Jason Leigh in the distance, Miss Silver could do no more than reply that it was extremely difficult to lay down any rules for happiness in marriage, but that kindness, unselfishness and mutual consideration must always be important factors.

"Most people would say that sounded very old-fashioned!"

Miss Silver smiled.

"The institution of marriage has been going on for a very long time."

"And people still go making a mess of it! Well, some of us are lucky. When I married Tim you've no idea the things everybody said!" She laughed with gusto. "I said quite a few myself!—'He had come up from nowhere,' and the answer to that was—'You can't keep a good man down.'—'Nobody had ever heard of his people.' 'Perhaps not,' I told them, 'but they are going to hear about *him*.' 'He's nothing to look at.' 'Well, well,' I said, 'I never did care about having everything in the shop window.' You know, I think that's why I don't like Gilbert Earle—there's such a lot in his shop window that it sets me wondering whether there's anything in the shop. In my husband's case there was such a lot put away behind that I'm not through with finding out about it yet. The only thing that hasn't panned out is the family we were going to have. It just never came along, which I suppose is the reason why Mettie and I have got to have our fingers in other people's pies. If I'd had half a dozen children to worry about, I shouldn't have had nearly so much time to run round interfering with my neighbours' affairs."

For a moment there was a brightness which might have been moisture in the fine dark eyes. Then she laughed and said,

"Oh well, I've got plenty on my plate for one woman. What were we talking about before I got off on to me? Scilla, wasn't it? I'll tell you one thing, I don't wonder she's bored to death down here. I'm not, and you wouldn't be, but what about a girl who has never lived where there weren't lamps in the streets, buses, neon lights, oodles of shops, and a cinema round every corner? Why, even when the war was on those poor women who were evacuated to this kind of place—it only took them about two minutes to get over being blown up in their beds and to start hankering after going back again. And of course one can see their point. As long as they weren't actually being bombed, the town gave them everything they wanted—company, crowds, the fried fish shop, and lots and lots going on. And what had the country got to give them in exchange—dark frightening lanes, the general shop, no one to speak to, and nothing to do. You see what I mean? And Scilla hasn't even got the possibility of bombs to put her off that life she used to live. I don't pretend I like her, but I'm sorry for her all the same!"

CHAPTER 22

*They went into the dining-*room for tea. As they crossed the hall, Scilla Repton came out of her sitting-room. The word which Lady Mallet had employed to describe her immediately sprang to Miss Silver's mind—bright. In contrast with the black, grey, and drab of all the other female garments present Mrs. Repton's appearance might even have been stigmatized as garish. She wore a skirt of an imitation tartan in which the predominant colours were scarlet, yellow and green. Her shoes were red, and her pale shining hair hung down over a jumper of emerald wool. Perhaps it was all these colours which gave her a curiously hard look. It occurred to Miss Silver that without her make-up she might have been pale. She spoke to one or two people, and as she entered the dining-room she came face-to-face with Maggie Repton. Miss Silver, a little behind her, had a most vivid impression of Miss Maggie's recoil. She not only stopped, but she stepped back and put up a shaking hand as if to ward off any contact. For a moment her face was contorted. It was as if she had suddenly seen something that shocked her. Afterwards, when Miss Repton had given her evidence, Miss Silver knew what it was that she had seen— Roger's unfaithful wife who was leaving him, the woman who had broken off Valentine's marriage. She had shrunk away from the sight and felt the room go round with her.

The hand that steadied her was Miss Silver's. She found herself guided to a chair, and was glad to sink down upon it. A voice that was as kind as it was firm advised her to bend forward.

"If you will drop the handkerchief you are holding and stoop to pick it up, no one will notice anything. Just stay here, and I will bring you a cup of tea."

During the general movement in the direction of the long table at which tea was being served the incident had passed unnoticed. When Miss Silver returned with a cup in either hand Miss Maggie had recovered sufficiently to thank her.

"How very kind of you. I really don't know what came over me. You are staying with Renie Wayne, are you not? I think I saw you with her on Wednesday at that unfortunate rehearsal."

"Yes, indeed."

"Then you will understand that we have had a great deal to trouble us this week. I haven't been able to sleep. I am afraid I am not as strong as I should like to be."

Nothing could have exceeded Miss Silver's sympathetic attention.

"Why do you not just slip away and lie down for a little? Your niece could look after the Work Party, and I am sure that everyone would understand."

Miss Maggie had got no farther than, "You are very kind—" when Mettie Eccles emerged from the crowd about the tea-table and came towards them. She held a large cup in one hand and a plate with sandwiches and cake upon it in the other. She paused to say briefly,

"I'll take these in to Roger. Florrie tells me he is in the study. It's too much to expect him to join such a mob of women for tea."

"My dear Mettie!"

Mettie Eccles gave a short laugh.

"Well, we are a mob, aren't we? Men prefer women one at a time, my dear."

She went on her way, and presently came back again, her face cold and shut down. Miss Maggie made a small vexed sound.

"There—I knew he wouldn't like it—her taking him in his tea, you know. I'm sure she meant it so very kindly, but I think he would rather she had let it alone. I am afraid she may have noticed that he wasn't pleased, and it has hurt her feelings. She is a cousin, you know, though rather a distant one, and we have known her always. Dear me, how good you are to me! I am really feeling quite revived. Do you think I could just sit here quietly with you for a little longer? I am finding it so restful. Or do you think it would be remarked?"

Miss Silver smiled benignly.

"What could anyone say or think, except that you were most kindly entertaining a stranger?"

Later on when the tea interval was nearly over Miss Eccles passed them again. She said in a determined voice, "I am going to see whether Roger will have another cup," and went on and out of the door.

The room had been emptying. Ladies who were going to handle light-coloured needlework made their way to the downstairs cloakroom to wash their hands. Scilla Repton had disappeared. There were not more than half a dozen people left in the dining-room. About as many more were crossing the hall, amongst them Miss Maggie and Miss Silver, when the study door was wrenched open. Mettie Eccles stood on the threshold. She held onto the jamb and her face was ghastly. Her lips moved, but for once she had no words. Then, as Miss Silver went quickly towards her, the words came—

"He's dead—Roger is dead!"

CHAPTER 23

The sound trembled and died. It is to be doubted whether anyone who was more than a few feet away could have heard it. But it had reached Mettie Eccles herself. The hand that had clutched at the jamb went up to her throat. She turned back into the room. Miss Silver, following her, saw that Roger Repton had fallen forward across his desk. His hands were clenched and his face was hidden. The cup of tea which Miss Eccles had brought him had been overturned. the plate with its sandwiches and slice of sodden cake was awash. To the right of the table there was a miniature decanter. It was empty, with the stopper beside it. A broken tumbler lay in a scatter of glass. There was a cut on Colonel Repton's clenched right hand, but no blood flowed from it. With one side of her orderly mind Miss Silver took note of all these things. With another and wholly womanly part she felt a deep compassion for Mettie Eccles, who knelt by the dead man, saying his name over and over in a tone of agonized protest.

"No—no—no, Roger! Oh, Roger, *no!*"

A fire burned on the hearth, the room was full of tobacco smoke. On that warm, still air there floated a smell of almonds. It was not the first time that Miss Sterling had encountered it in a criminal case. She had knelt over the body of a woman poisoned by cyanide, and been aware of it. When she laid her steady fingers upon Roger Repton's wrist she did not expect to find a living pulse. There was none.

As she stood there, a few people had begun to cluster round the door and to look in. Scilla Repton pushed through them. Walking up to the table, she said abruptly,

"What is going on? Is Roger ill?"

Miss Silver lifted her hand from the dead wrist and turned to meet her.

"Mrs. Repton—I'm afraid—"

Mettie Eccles got to her feet.

"You needn't be," she said. "And you needn't trouble to break it to her, because she knows."

Scilla's delicate make-up appeared suddenly ghastly

as the natural colour beneath it drained away, leaving her face like a mask with vermilion lips. She said, "What do you mean?" and Mettie Eccles told her.

"You know very well that Roger is dead, because you killed him."

Lady Mallet had loomed up beside them. She put a hand on Mettie's arm and said in a horrified voice,

"You can't say things like that—oh, my dear Mettie, you can't—"

The hand was shaken off. Those very bright blue eyes blazed at her. Mettie said loudly,

"I shall tell the truth, and no one is going to stop me! She never cared for him, and now she has killed him! Do you suppose I am going to hold my tongue? She is an adulteress, and he found her out! He was sending her away, and he was going to divorce her! So she has killed him!"

Miss Silver said in her quiet voice,

"Lady Mallett, the police must be notified. No one else should come in. I think the door should be locked. Perhaps you will kindly see to it. Mrs. Repton—"

Scilla Repton turned on her.

"Who do you think you are—giving orders in my house! Who does Mettie Eccles think she is—talking like that! Everyone knows she's been off the deep end about Roger for years and he woudln't look at her! A damned interfering old maid with a finger in everybody's pie! I'll have the law on her—that's what I'll do! You heard what she said, and I'll make her pay through the nose for saying it!"

As her voice rose loud and shrill, Miss Silver reflected how quickly fear and anger can strip off the veneer of breeding. The languid, graceful woman with her tones modelled to the current fashion was gone. Instead, there was a London girl who knew what it was to fight for her own hand and was perfectly capable of doing so. Her colour had come back with a rush.

Mettie Eccles stood as if she had been turned to stone. The anger had gone out of her. Her limbs were heavy and her eyes dazzled. All she wanted now was to sit in the dark and weep. But she came of a fighting stock—she would not go back on what she had said. She repeated it with a dry tongue.

"You killed him—"

It was at this moment, and just as Lady Mallet was about to close the door, that Maggie Repton had come down the hall. There had been a whisper of talk, and it had reached her. If Roger was ill, she must go to him. It didn't matter if she felt ill herself, she must go to Roger. She saw Nora Mallet, but she was not to be stayed.

"Maggie—"

"If Roger is ill, I must go to him."

She walked past her, and saw what was to be seen—Roger lying sprawled across his desk, and the three people who were standing there and were not doing anything to help him—

Miss Silver who was so kind—but she was a stranger.

Scilla who was his wife, his unfaithful wife.

And Mettie who loved him.

Why were none of them doing anything to help Roger? She heard Mettie Eccles say, "You killed him—" and she saw Scilla Repton step forward and strike her across the face.

CHAPTER 24

Maggie Repton lay on her bed with the eiderdown drawn up to her chin. Like everything else in the room it was old and rather shabby. Miss Repton remembered her mother buying it at the Army and Navy Stores in Victoria Street. The cover was only cotton, but the down was of the very best quality, and it had cost £2.10.0., which in those days had seemed quite a large price for an eiderdown. It was still very warm, and light, and comforting. She became aware of a hot water-bottle at her feet. That was comforting too. And there was something else—kindness and the sense of a reassuring presence. It was getting dark outside. A small shaded lamp stood on the washstand. It was beyond her range of vision, so that it did not dazzle her, but the light was pleasant in the room. She turned her head on the pillow and identified the presence which she found consoling. Miss Silver sat beside her knitting.

For a little while the warmth, the soft light, the sense of comfort and security, were between Maggie Repton and the things that had happened at the Work Party. Then they came back—Roger lying dead across his own writing-table—the smashed glass and empty decanter—poor Mettie calling his name, accusing Scilla, and Scilla striking her. She put out a long, thin hand and said with a gasp, "Oh, no, it isn't true!"

Miss Silver laid down her knitting and took the hand.

"Yes, my dear, it is true. You must be brave."

Two slow, weak tears rolled down Miss Maggie's cheeks. Her thoughts moved slowly too. Roger was

dead. She must be a very bad, unloving sister, because it
didn't mean very much when she said it. She didn't seem
to be able to feel anything. She said that aloud.

"I don't seem to be able to feel anything."

"That is because it has been a shock." Miss Silver's
hand was warm and steady. Maggie Repton clung to it.

"I was speaking to him just before the people arrived.
He said it was the end. You don't think he meant—you
don't think—"

Miss Silver looked at her gravely.

"You will have to tell the police just what was said."

"I ought not to have left him," said Miss Maggie.
"But I never thought—indeed I never thought—"

"What did you think he meant, my dear?"

"He was talking about Scilla. They had had a terrible
quarrel. He said she had been having an affair with Gilbert Earle. Such a dreadful, wicked thing—because Gilbert was going to marry Valentine, you know, and it has
all been broken off. Roger talked about a divorce, a
thing I never thought I should have in our family, but
he said he couldn't go on. It is all so *dreadful*. It doesn't
seem as if it could possibly have happened."

It had become a relief to talk, to pour it all out. After
a little Miss Silver drew her hand away and began to
knit again. When she rose from her chair, Miss Maggie
said with a sob,

"You're not going?"

"Not if you wish me to stay."

"Oh, if you could—" The weak voice faltered and
broke. "Valentine is a dear child, but she is young,
and—and Scilla—" she jerked herself up in the bed—
"she is an unfaithful wife—Roger was sending her
away. There ought to be someone here with Valentine,
and Mettie—it wouldn't do for Mettie to come. Scilla
hit her, didn't she? What a dreadful thing! Poor Mettie

couldn't come here after that! Scilla hit her, and then I don't seem to remember what happened."

"You fainted, my dear."

"Oh dear—I oughtn't to have done that—it must have given so much trouble." Then, on a faint and trembling note, "Did they—did anyone—send for the police? You said—I thought you said—"

"Yes, my dear, they are here. I am sure you will find them all that is kind and considerate."

The door was opened a little way. Valentine Grey first looked round it, and then came in. Seeing that Miss Maggie was awake, she bent down to kiss her. Miss Silver, withdrawing to the window, was aware of a murmur of words.

After a little Valentine came to her. Her starry look was gone, and she was white and distressed, but quite sensible and controlled. She said very low,

"She is better?"

"She will do very well now."

"The Chief Constable is here. He said to ask you whether she is fit to see him. He said he wouldn't press it if you thought not."

Miss Silver turned back to the bed.

"Let us ask her. It may be better for her to get it off her mind."

Miss Maggie had drawn herself up against the pillows. She discovered to her surprise that she was in her nightgown, with the pretty blue bed-jacket which Valentine had given her for her birthday.

"Did you say Mr. March was here? Does he want to see me? I don't know—I don't feel that I can get up and come down—"

Valentine bent over her.

"No, darling, of course not. He would come up here."

She murmured, "How good of him. I am sure he is very kind to come like this. A man is such a help. And if you think he wouldn't mind—Only, my dear, am I quite tidy?"

The customary pins had been removed from the wispy hair which they so often failed to control. It lay now neat and flat on either side of the narrow brow. With a lace scarf thrown over it, nothing could have been more decorous. Miss Silver was most reassuring on this point.

"And you will stay?" said Miss Maggie, beginning to flutter. "I do know Mr. March—he is always so nice. But you won't leave me, will you? Renie Wayne was telling me you know him quite well. She told me you went over to tea there on Friday. Mrs. March is so very goodlooking, is she not—and they have two lovely children." Her eyes filled with tears. "You know, when things go wrong, as they have with us, it is a help to think about the people who are really happy."

Randal March came into the room and took the chair which had been set for him. Nothing could have been kinder than voice and manner as he told her how sorry he was to disturb her, and how much he regretted the reason.

"But if you do not mind answering a few questions. Time may be of importance, and Miss Silver will see that I don't tire you. We are old friends, you know."

Miss Maggie showed a definite interest.

"Oh, yes, Renie Wayne told me. Miss Silver has been so kind—so very kind."

He said warmly, "She is the kindest person I know." And then, "Now, Miss Repton, will you tell me when was the last time you saw your brother—I mean the last time before you came into the study and found him there with Miss Eccles and Miss Silver and Mrs. Repton."

Miss Maggie gazed at him.

"Nora Mallet was there too. She is a cousin, you know, and so is Mettie Eccles."

"Yes. Now when did you last see Colonel Repton before that—and where?"

She said in a distressed voice,

"It was in the study, just before all the people came. We had the Work Party here—I suppose they told you. And Roger was dreadfully angry. Oh, not about the Party—it wasn't that at all. It was—Oh, do I have to say?"

Miss Silver had drawn up a chair at the other side of the bed. She said gently but firmly,

"I am afraid so, my dear. Mr. March will have heard already that there was trouble between your brother and his wife."

"Yes, Miss Maggie, you had better tell me. Was that what he was angry about?"

"Oh, *yes*. He said he had come to the end."

Randal March looked at Miss Silver, who very slightly shook her head. She said,

"I think Mr. March will want to know just how that was said. He had told you that his wife was going away for good, had he not, and the word divorce had been mentioned?"

Miss Maggie caught her breath.

"Oh, yes, it had. He thought she had been—had been—unfaithful."

"With Gilbert Earle?"

"Yes—yes—"

"He really said she was leaving him, and he spoke of a divorce?"

"Oh, yes—poor Roger."

- "Then how did he say that bit about having come to the end? Will you see if you can give me his exact words?"

"Oh, I don't know—it seems so dreadful to repeat them."

March looked across at Miss Silver.

"I think she should understand what is involved. You will explain it better than I can."

She took her cue mildly, but with authority.

"Dear Miss Repton, I know it is distressing for you, but a good deal depends on just how these things were said. If the words 'I have come to the end' are taken by themselves, they would seem to point to suicide."

Miss Maggie's "Oh, no—" was only half articulate.

Miss Silver went on.

"If you do not think he meant that, you must try to remember what else was said at that time. A man who intends to commit suicide would not be thinking of divorce. You are sure that he did mention divorce?"

A little faint colour had come into Miss Repton's face. She said in quite a strong voice,

"Oh, yes, I am quite sure he did, because it shocked me dreadfully. We have never had such a thing in our family. And Roger would never have taken his own life—he had a great deal too much principle."

March said,

"Then just how did he say those words about having come to the end?"

Maggie Repton put up her hand to her throat.

"He said Scilla was going away and not coming back. He said, 'She's been having an affair with Gilbert Earle—if that's the worst of it.' And then he said, 'I've come to the end. She must go.' And then he went out of the room and banged the door."

Randal March looked across at Miss Silver and nodded.

"There you have it. Three words, and they make all the difference. He had come to the end of his patience with his wife. Then 'She must go' makes that perfectly clear—if that is how it went. You're quite sure about it, Miss Maggie?"

Oh, yes, she was quite sure. Now that it was said it had relieved her very much. She repeated it all again quite slowly, and when he had written it down she signed her name.

CHAPTER 25

Miss Silver went downstairs with the Chief Constable. As soon as they had come out upon the landing he said,

"I want to see that girl Florrie. Crisp has taken a statement from her. I want to go over it with her, and I should very much like you to be there. In the case of a young girl I think it is always advisable that another woman should be present. Do you think she would be likely to object?"

Miss Silver made a slight movement of the head.

"I have found her all that is pleasant and helpful. Perhaps you would like me to let her know that you wish to see her. My presence would then be brought about in quite a natural manner."

He went into the study, and after telling Valentine that Maggie Repton was alone, and that she considered that some light nourishment would now be beneficial, Miss Silver acquainted her with the Chief Constable's desire to interview Florrie Stokes. The bell was rung.

Florrie appeared to answer it, and far from showing any objection to Miss Silver's presence, evinced a disposition to cling to her. She had been crying and was obviously in a frightened and emotional state, which made March congratulate himself on Miss Silver's presence. The Inspector, who had encountered her before, responded to her greetings in the briefest and most formal manner.

Colonel Repton's body had been removed. The room had been aired, but the heavy smell of smoke remained. The broken glass, the decanter, the cup and saucer and plate conveyed to the dead man had been taken away. There was a damp patch on the already much worn and stained green leather of the writing-table. When it dried there would be nothing to show that it had given mute evidence of a violent death. Where Roger Repton had sprawled the Chief Constable now sat with Florrie's statement in his hand, whilst Crisp on his left kept pencil and notebook ready.

Florrie sat on the couch beside Miss Silver. She was upset, but she was excited too. It was an awful thing to have happened, but it would be something to talk about for the rest of her life. The Chief Constable was ever so goodlooking, and so was Mrs. March. Miss Silver was ever so kind. She was glad she hadn't got to talk to that Inspector Crisp again. Jumped down your throat something awful, for all the world like one of Joe Blagdon's terrier dogs when it was after a rat. She didn't like rats, but she didn't like to see anything killed.

March took her through her statement, which began with her coming into the hall on the Saturday and hearing Colonel and Mrs. Repton quarrelling on the other side of the study door. The quarrel was about Mr. Gilbert Earle. She had told the story so often that it was like something she had got by heart, and she could repeat it and scarcely vary it by a word. The Colonel had said that Mrs. Repton had been carrying on with Mr. Gilbert—he had had one of those letters about her. They had been meeting at her friend Mrs. Foster's flat, and he would be able to get evidence about it and divorce her.

March said, "You heard him mention the word divorce?"

"Oh, yes, I did."

"You are quite sure about that?"

"Oh, yes, sir."

He went on.

"Now, about these anonymous letters—you say Colonel Repton spoke of them?"

"Yes, sir."

"He said he had had one?"

"Yes, sir—and so he did, for I took it up to him myself."

Inspector Crisp lifted his head with a jerk. March said,

"You took it up to him?"

"Oh, yes, sir. There was one for him and one for Miss Valentine."

"And how did you know what kind of letters they were?"

Florrie was more at her ease every moment. If there was a subject that had been thoroughly discussed in Tilling Green, it was the subject of the anonymous letters—the cheap white paper on which they were written, the flimsy envelopes which matched it, the large awkward writing. Sam Boxer, who was the postman, had given far too particular a description of these points for her to be in any doubt about them, and she had actually seen the one which Mrs. Pratt had had, because she had been there when Mrs. P. came in and showed it to Mum and Dad—a horrid spiteful letter about her Joe having been had up in court over breaking a shop window. And he wasn't a bad boy really, only a bit wild. But the letter said everyone hoped he would go to prison and he was bound to come to a bad end anyhow. And Mrs. Pratt had taken on something dreadful.

Florrie explained all this with artless confidence.

March turned to Crisp.

"Did the police know about this letter?"

Crisp really did resemble the terrier of Florrie's fancy. At the moment he was the terrier whose rat has been killed by another dog. He was at his most abrupt as he said,

"No, sir."

March had a moment of exasperation. How could you help people if they wouldn't help themselves? They would talk endlessly to each other, but when it came to reporting anything to the police a tomblike silence engulfed them. Sam Boxer having already stated that the Colonel, Miss Valentine, and the Vicar had each received a letter answering to the description of the poison-pen letters, he himself having delivered them with the first post on Thursday morning, March decided that Florrie's evidence could be considered to establish the fact that the letter addressed to Roger had certainly reached him, though he had not seen fit to admit that it had. Since it appeared to have dealt with the subject of his wife's unfaithfulness, this was not surprising.

Florrie maintained that the Colonel had not only talked about the letter, but that he and Mrs. Repton had quarrelled very bitterly about it, and that in the course of this quarrel the Colonel had said that he knew who had written the letters. And had gone on to say that perhaps it was Mrs. Repton herself.

"You are sure he said that?"

She repeated the words in her statement.

"Mrs. Repton said it was all lies, and the Colonel said

it was a filthy letter about a filthy thing, and he knew who wrote it. And Mrs. Repton said, who was it then? And the Colonel said wouldn't she like to know, and perhaps she done it herself, because that would be one way of breaking off Miss Valentine's marriage, wouldn't it, and one way of getting out of her own. And what did she and her friends care about divorce, he said. Only she had better make sure that Mr. Gilbert would marry her before she walked out."

She might almost have had the statement in front of her as she tripped through the quarrel which had taken place in this very room. Both March and Miss Silver received a clear impression of how it had gone—suspicion turned suddenly to certainty and blazing up into an anger which defied control, followed by what the Chief Constable, but not perhaps Miss Maud Silver, would have described as a slanging-match. And then a certain cooling down, so that what had begun with a demand that Scilla Repton should get out and leave his house then and there seemed to have concluded with a realization of the scandal which such a course must provoke, and a desire to keep on the right side of public opinion.

As March said later on when they were alone, "He just blazed off at her, and then, I fancy, he realized what he would be letting himself in for if he turned her out neck and crop. I gather that he was supposed to be out, but he had forgotten a letter he wanted to post. He came back for it, found her having a pretty compromising conversation with Earle. Not unnaturally, he went in off the deep end, and then had to get back to a more dignified position. But from what Miss Maggie says, after two days to think it over he was still all set to divorce her, and was only waiting for Connie Brooke's funeral to be over to insist on her leaving the house."

Miss Silver agreed.

"Do you suppose that he was serious when he suggested that Mrs. Repton might herself have written the letter which accused her?"

"It is difficult to believe that he was. He was furious with her, and I should say at a guess that he wouldn't be too particular about what weapon he was using. They are talking about the letter he had received, or rather shouting at each other about it, and he snatches at something that he thinks will frighten her."

"You think, then, that he did not really know who had written the letter?"

He lifted a hand and let it fall again.

"He said that he knew. Florrie is quite definite about that, and she strikes me as a truthful witness."

"Truthful and accurate."

He nodded.

"So he said that he knew. The event rather bears that out, doesn't it? Connie Brooke said she knew who had written the letters, and she is dead. Roger Repton said the same thing, and he has gone the same way. It rather looks as if somebody had believed what they said."

But all this was afterwards. At the time, there was Florrie, rather pleased with herself, and thinking what a story she would have to tell them at home. She would have to tell it at the inquest too—a daunting but at the same time an uplifting thought.

Miss Silver's voice broke in upon it. She was addressing the Chief Constable.

"I wonder whether you will object to my asking Florrie a question."

Inspector Crisp had his quick frown for that. He had been on a case with Miss Silver before, and he considered that she took liberties, and had been allowed to take them. He did not doubt that she would be allowed

to take this one. And sure enough there was the Chief
Constable giving way to her.

"Oh, certainly, Miss Silver. What is it?"

She said with formal politeness,

"Thank you very much, Mr. March. When we were
having tea in the dining-room I was sitting near the door
with Miss Repton, who had been feeling faint, when
Miss Eccles came by with the cup and plate which were
afterwards found on the desk in the study. She said that
Florrie had told her Colonel Repton was there, and she
was taking him a cup of tea. I thought I would like to
ask Florrie how she knew that Colonel Repton was in
the study—whether she had actually seen him there, and
when, and whether he was alone at the time."

March said, "Well, Florrie?"

Her colour came up.

"There wasn't anything wrong about my telling Miss
Eccles?"

He gave her his pleasant smile.

"Oh, no, nothing like that. You are being a great
help, you know."

Thus encouraged, she relaxed again.

"Well, he'd been there ever since lunch. Miss Maggie,
she was there with him just before the Work Party ladies
came. She come out when I went through to answer the
door. What with them coming in by twos and threes, I
was backwards and forwards to the door for the best
part of half an hour. One time I went past the study
there was Colonel Repton talking, and another man."

"Another man!"

Florrie nodded.

"I hadn't let him in, and I was ever so puzzled until I
thought, 'Well, it'll only be Mr. Barton, and he must
have gone round the house and knocked on the window
for the Colonel to let him in.' The study door was on the

jar the way Miss Maggie would have left it. She always gives the handle a little turn so that it springs open again. So I went up close, and sure enough it was him."

"Did you say Mr. Barton?"

"Oh, yes—with the rent, sir. And I thought he couldn't have known about the Work Party, or wild horses wouldn't have dragged him, the way he is about ladies."

"Mr. Barton was in the habit of coming up here and paying his rent?"

"Oh, yes, sir—once a month he'd come. And some funny sort of rent too. He'd come round mostly after dark, and sometimes he'd ring the bell, and sometimes he'd just go round to the study window."

"You said something about the rent being a funny one. What did you mean by that?"

Florrie let off a faint giggle.

"Well, sir, it was what the Colonel was saying when I come up to the door. He said, 'Come to pay your peppercorn rent, James?' and something about always being pleased to see him. And then he said, 'Break through your rule for once and have a drink.' And Mr. Barton said, 'If you don't know by now that it's a waste of time to ask me, you won't ever. It's wicked stuff,' he said, 'and you'd be better without it yourself.' "

March's eyebrows rose.

"Oh, they were on those sort of terms, were they?"

Florrie looked demure.

"Yes, sir—it was all very friendly when Mr. Barton came."

"And was it all very friendly this afternoon?"

"So far as I know, sir. I just heard what I said."

"You're sure about it being Mr. Barton?"

"Oh, yes, sir."

"How can you be sure?"

"Because of what the Colonel said, and Mr. Barton's voice. He's got ever such a deep voice, and sort of gaspy. My Dad says he was gassed in the war—the first war, that was, not the one my Dad was in."

"Then as far as you know, Mr. Barton was the last person who saw Colonel Repton before Miss Eccles took him his tea?"

"Oh, no, sir."

"Well, who else was there?"

Florrie had run on easily enough, but now she wasn't easy any more. She wouldn't have let anyone say she was frightened—there wasn't anything to be frightened about. It was just that the Colonel being dead and the police in the house, it didn't seem right to say what she had heard, but of course she would have to say it. She opened her mouth and shut it again. March said,

"Come—who was it?"

She was astonished to hear how small her own voice sounded.

"It was only Mrs. Repton."

"I see. And you were passing the study door?"

"Yes, sir."

"Perhaps you heard what was being said."

"Well, sir—"

It all came back to her with a rush and she couldn't go on—the door flying open like it had, and Mrs. Repton turning on the threshold. It had shaken her at the time, and it shook her now, the way Mrs. Repton had looked and the thing she said. Florrie had been brought up to go to church and Sunday school. She thanked God very fervently that Mrs. Repton hadn't seen her.

Miss Silver laid a hand upon the arm that had begun to shake.

"There is nothing to be afraid of, Florrie."

Florrie blinked.

"Oh, miss, you didn't see her."

March said, "You saw Mrs. Repton?"

She gulped and nodded.

"Just tell us what happened."

The words came tumbling out. It did her good to get rid of them.

"I was coming through to the dining-room. They were talking ever so loud—I could hear their voices, and they sounded ever so angry. And then the door opened sudden and Mrs. Repton come out. I didn't want her to see me, so I stood against the wall, and she turned right round and looked back into the room. Oh, sir, it was the dreadfullest look you ever saw—and she said to the poor Colonel—oh, sir she said, 'You'd be a lot more good to me dead than alive,' she said, and she come away and banged the door."

CHAPTER 26

Florrie had gone away, shaken but resilient. When the door had shut behind her Randal March said,

"That being that, we had better see Mrs. Repton. In the circumstances, I didn't think it would be tactful to send a message by Florrie. Perhaps, Crisp, you wouldn't mind—"

When the Inspector had gone out March said,

"Well, what do you make of it?"

Miss Silver gave the faint cough with which she was wont to emphasize a point.

"It is, I think, too soon to draw any conclusion. We know that there was anger between them, and people do not always mean what they say."

He was silent. After a moment she said,

"I do not think Mrs. Repton will wish me to remain, in which case—"

"You will have to go? Yes, I am afraid so. But I would much rather you stayed."

Scilla Repton came into the room with Crisp behind her. She was still wearing the tartan skirt and emerald jumper, but she had taken time to put on fresh make-up, and her hair shone under the ceiling light. It had been in her mind to put on a black dress and play the disconsolate widow, but something in her rebelled. And what was the good of it anyway when there wasn't anyone in the house that didn't know that she and Roger were all washed up? He had talked to his sister—he had told her so—and no doubt she would make the most of it to the police, so why not be honest and have done with it? There would be another of those awful inquests, and she supposed she would have to stay for the funeral, but once all that was over Tilling Green wouldn't see her again in a hurry. So what did it matter what any of these people thought or said about her? She didn't give a damn.

Observing Miss Silver, she raised her carefully shaped eyebrows and said without anything in her voice to soften the words,

"What is she doing here?"

March said,

"Miss Repton and Florrie Stokes preferred to have another woman present, and Miss Silver was kind enough—"

She interrupted him with a short hard laugh.

"A chaperone! My dear man, how prehistoric! I should have thought Maggie was past wanting one anyhow, but of course you never can tell, can you!"

"If you object to Miss Silver's presence—"

She drew a chair to the other side of the writing-table, sat down, and proceeded to light a cigarette.

"Oh, no, I don't object. Why should I? If Maggie wants a chaperone, I'm sure I do."

She flicked out the match and dropped it among the pens and pencils which Roger Repton would not use again. She drew on the cigarette and the tip brightened. She had quite deliberately turned her back upon Miss Silver, who now as deliberately changed her own position, moving from one corner of the leather-covered couch to the other, an adjustment which gave her a very good view of Mrs. Repton as she sat, her legs crossed, the mesh of the stockings so fine that it hardly seemed to be there at all, the red shoes a little too ornate, a good deal too high in the heel.

If Miss Silver's own garments were quite incredibly out of date, it was because she liked them that way and had discovered that an old-fashioned and governessy appearance was a decided asset in the profession which she had adopted. To be considered negligible may be the means of acquiring the kind of information which only becomes available when people are off their guard. She was fully aware that she was being treated as negligible now. She thought that Scilla Repton was putting on an act, and she wondered why she had chosen just this pose of callous indifference. She would not have expected good taste, but what was behind these bright colours, this careful indifference? A sudden death in a household must shock even its most indifferent member, and this was Roger Repton's wife.

Randal March was speaking.

"I believe you had had a very serious quarrel with your husband on Saturday, Mrs. Repton."

She withdrew her cigarette and blew out a little cloud of smoke.

"Who says so?"

He did not answer this.

"In the course of this quarrel the question of the anonymous letters came up."

"What anonymous letters?"

"Oh, I think you have heard of them. One of them was in evidence at the inquest on Doris Pell. Colonel Repton had interrupted a telephone conversation between you and Mr. Gilbert Earle. During what followed he spoke of having received one of these letters, accusing you of carrying on an affair with Mr. Earle. A very serious quarrel developed, in the course of which divorce was mentioned and he said that you must leave this house immediately. The actual words were that you must get out. Later this was to some extent modified. He had begun to think about the scandal, and said that it would be better if you stayed here till after Miss Brooke's funeral."

She said with an accentuation of her usual drawl,

"You were listening at the door?"

"Somebody was," said March drily. "Voices raised in a violent quarrel do attract attention, and for part of the time at any rate I understand that the door was open."

She lifted a shoulder in the slightest of shrugs.

"Oh, well, people do have quarrels, you know. Roger and I had lots, but we always made them up again."

"Do you wish to imply that this was not the first time he had accused you of infidelity?"

"I don't mean to imply anything of the sort, and you know it!"

"Then do you mean to imply that this particular quarrel was no more serious than others that had taken place, and that it was likely to have been made up?"

She said easily,

"He wouldn't have turned me out, you know."

"Mrs. Repton, Miss Maggie Repton has stated that she had a conversation with her brother this afternoon just before three o'clock in which he told her that he had come to the end, and that you must go. Now I think you saw him after that."

"Who says so?"

"You were seen coming out of the study."

She drew at the cigarette and let the smoke go up between them.

"All right—so what?"

"The person who saw you states that both you and Colonel Repton were talking very loudly. She received the impression that you were quarrelling. Then the door opened and you were coming out, but you turned back again and spoke. And she heard what you said."

A little ash dropped on the front of the emerald jumper. Scilla Repton brushed it off with a careless flick.

"Really, Mr. March?"

"She states that she heard you say, 'You'd be a lot more good to me dead than alive,' and after that you came away."

"Quite a good curtain," said Scilla Repton.

March said gravely,

"And within an hour he was dead."

"It didn't mean anything. It was the sort of thing one says."

"Not, I think, with a reconciliation in sight."

She leaned over to stub out the cigarette where she had left the match in Roger Repton's pen-tray.

The action set off a curious spark of anger in him. She had quarrelled with the husband who had found her out, she had wished him dead to his face, she had heard another woman accuse her over his dead body, and here, on the very spot where these things had happened, she could lean over and stub out her cigarette! It was a small thing, but it got him. He said sharply,

"You wished him dead, and he was dead within the hour. You have been accused of having brought that death about."

She actually laughed.

"You've been listening to Mettie Eccles. My dear man, don't be silly! She was head over ears in love with Roger—always has been, I can't think why. And she has always been just about as jealous of me as anyone could be, so naturally if there was anything wrong it would be my fault. I should think even a policeman could see that."

He said abruptly,

"There was cyanide in the gardener's shed, wasn't there?"

"Cya—what?"

"Cyanide. I suppose you've heard of it?"

"No. What is it?"

"I haven't had the surgeon's report yet, but it could have been the poison which caused Colonel Repton's death."

She stared at him.

"And what would it be doing in the gardener's shed?"

"It is used to destroy wasps' nests."

She gave quite a natural shudder.

"I can't sit in the room with a wasp! That's the worst of the country—all these insects! But if this cya stuff was used for them, how did it get into the house—unless—Oh, do you mean that Roger took it on purpose?"

Randal March said very gravely indeed,

"No, Mrs. Repton, I didn't mean that."

CHAPTER 27

About half an hour later
March stopped his car on the other side of the Green,
lifted the latch of a gate, and made his way with the help
of a torch to the sideways-looking door of Gale's Cottage. His knocking upon it brought a somewhat delayed
and reluctant answer. There was no bell and no
knocker. He was obliged to switch off his torch and use
that, and he was beginning to wonder whether Mr.
James Barton could be out, when there was the sound of
a slow footstep and the door was opened a bare two
inches, and on the chain at that, since an unmistakable
rattle came through the gap. A deep breathy voice said,
"Who's there?"

"My name is March. I am the Chief Constable of the
county, and I would like to have a word with you."

The voice from within said, "Why?"

"Because you were one of the last people to see Colonel Repton."

There was a gasp, the rattle of the chain which held
the door, and the sound of the door creaking back upon
its hinges. There was no light in the narrow passage, but
a door on the right stood half open and enough light
came from it to throw up the figure of a tall man standing back about a yard from the threshold.

"What's this about Colonel Repton?"

"I believe you were one of the last people to see him."

Barton repeated the words almost in a whisper.

"To see him?"

March said, "Mr. Barton, if Colonel Repton was a

friend of yours, I'm afraid you must be prepared for a shock, because he is dead."

James Barton said, "Oh, my God!" And then, "But he can't be—I was talking to him—Oh, come in!"

The room with the half open door was the kitchen, and it was warm and comfortable, with an oil lamp on the dresser, a bright fire, and thick red curtains at the window. There was a table covered with a crimson cloth, an old leather-covered armchair, and a strip of carpet in front of the fireplace upon which lay seven large tabby cats.

In the light Mr. Barton was seen to be a thin and rather stooping person with a good deal of grizzled hair and a straggling beard, but even the beard and the bushy eyebrows did not hide the terrible scar which ran across his face. Before March had taken in these particulars he was saying,

"Colonel Repton—what has happened? I was up there—he wasn't ill."

"Yes, that is why I have come to see you. He wasn't ill, and he is dead. I believe that he was murdered."

"Murdered—"

There were a couple of plain wooden chairs in the room. Barton sank down on one of them and leaned forward over the table, folding his arms and dropping his head upon them. His breathing quickened into sobs. After a minute or two he straightened himself.

"He was a very good friend to me. It's knocked me over. Will you tell me what happened?"

"He was poisoned—we believe, with cyanide."

"That's the stuff they use for wasps?"

"Yes."

"Who would do such a thing?"

March had taken the other chair. He said,

"I hope you can help us to find out."

Barton raised a hand and let it fall again.

"Isn't that what the police always say when they're talking about the chap they've got it in for?"

"If you mean have we any special reason to suspect you at present, the answer is no. But since you were one of the last people to see Colonel Repton alive—By the way, just when did you leave him?"

"It would be four o'clock, or a little later. I don't carry a watch."

"Do you mind telling me why you went to see him, and what passed between you?"

"I went to pay my rent."

"I see. And just what do you pay for this cottage?"

Barton was leaning on an elbow, staring down at the red tablecloth. He jerked his head up at that and said roughly,

"What's that got to do with the police?"

"Is there any reason why you should mind answering the question?"

"Oh, no—no—I just wondered why you should ask it, that's all. If you must know, it was what is called a peppercorn rent."

"You mean you didn't pay him anything at all?"

"No, I don't. I mean I paid him a peppercorn—one a month—and we'd sit talking for a bit. He was about the only one I ever did talk to, and I suppose you'll try and make out I did him in."

"Will you tell me what you talked about this afternoon?"

Barton went back to staring down upon the red tablecloth.

"Most times I'd go up after dark, but I didn't today."

"Why was that?"

"I don't know. I'd a fancy to go when I did, that's all. I'd been thinking of things, and I'd got to the point where they didn't bear thinking about, so it came to me I'd go up and see the Colonel."

March's memory produced a date. He wouldn't have sworn to it in court, but short of that he was as certain of it as makes no difference. This was the thirteenth of October, and on the thirteenth of October some thirty years ago . . . He said,

"Well you went up to see Colonel Repton. What did you talk about?"

"Him." Barton stared at the cloth. "I went round to the study window and knocked on it because they'd got company—a lot of women visiting Miss Repton for a sewing-party. Miss Wayne from next door, she was there, and the one that's staying with her. I'd forgotten about it, but I wasn't going to let it put me off. I knew he wouldn't be having any truck with it anyway. So I went round by the far end of the Green and got in over the wall and round to the study window. I'd done it before."

"And when you got there Colonel Repton asked you if you'd come to pay your peppercorn rent and offered you a drink."

He got a startled sideways look.

"If you know all the answers you can find them for yourself."

March was made to feel that he had been clumsy. He hastened to make amends.

"Mr. Barton, please do not be offended. It would be a natural way for Colonel Repton to receive you, wouldn't it? And I am really anxious to know about the drink, because, you see, the cyanide—we are practically sure that it was cyanide—was in a small decanter of whisky on his writing-table, and I would like to know whether you saw the decanter there."

He was staring at March now.

"Oh, yes, I saw it. And he offered me a drink out of it all right, but that was just a joke between us—he knew I wouldn't take it. It's devil's stuff, and I don't use it. He knew that well enough. It's always the same when I go up—he says, 'Have a drink,' and I say, 'No,' the same as he knows I'm going to."

"Well, that being over, you say you talked about him."

"Yes—about him and about women—he knows what I think of them. He talked about his wife."

"What did he say about her?"

"Said she'd done the dirty on him and he was going to divorce her. I never spoke to her in my life—I don't have any truck with women—but I could have told him she was that sort right from the word go. I could have told him, but it wouldn't have been any good. That's the sort of thing you have to find out for yourself. Cats and dogs, they go after their nature, and you know what that nature is—it's the way they're made. And women are just the same, but they're not honest about it the way an animal is. They lie, and creep, and go round corners, pretending to be holy angels—angels of light, and not the drabs and sluts they are."

March broke in.

"Are you perfectly sure that Colonel Repton spoke of divorcing his wife?"

"Of course I'm sure. Why should I make it up? He said he was all through with her and she'd be clearing out just so soon as Connie Brooke's funeral was over. He said he'd been telling his sister, and once the funeral was over everyone would know."

"That was a very confidential way for him to talk."

The hand that was resting on Barton's knee moved and clenched. He said in his deep hoarse voice,

"Sometimes it eases a man to talk. I've had troubles myself."

March waited for a moment before he spoke again. Then he said,

"Well, he talked to you in this confidential way. Did he say anything—anything at all to suggest that he had the thought of suicide in his mind?"

He got a quick angry look.

"No, he didn't!"

"Because that would be a possible alternative to murder. A man who had, or thought he had, discovered that his wife was unfaithful might have taken his own life."

Mr. Barton brought his fist down upon the table.

"Not if it was Colonel Repton, he wouldn't! And I'll take my Bible oath he wasn't thinking of any such thing. He talked about getting rid of her—said it oughtn't to take so long to get a case through the courts now. Well, if he was planning about that, he wasn't thinking of killing himself, was he?"

"Not then."

"When did it happen?"

"He was seen alive at half past four, and found dead at his desk just after five o'clock."

"That means the stuff was there in the decanter when I was with him. He'd never have offered me a drink the way he did if he knew there was poison in it."

"He might have if he was sure you wouldn't take it."

The fist came down on the table again.

"Not on your life! It's not what any man would do—not to a friend! Cyanide? That's the stuff that kills you dead in a minute. There's something in a man that would turn at offering it to a friend."

"He knew you wouldn't take it—you said so yourself."

Barton shook his head.

"He'd not have done it. Just thinking of it would have turned him. And he wasn't thinking about suicide—I'll swear he wasn't."

CHAPTER 28

Miss Silver walked across the Green to fetch the few things that she would need for the night. Miss Wayne displayed some incredulity.

"You are going to stay at the Manor?"

"Miss Repton would like me to do so. It has been a great shock to her."

Miss Renie's handkerchief dabbed sketchily at eyes and nose.

"Oh, yes *indeed*—and to us all. But surely a stranger—one would have thought Lady Mallet, or at any rate a *friend*—"

"Lady Mallet was herself a good deal distressed. Sometimes it is easier to be with a stranger whose personal feelings are not involved."

Miss Renie sniffed and dabbed.

"I should have thought that Mettie Eccles would have stayed."

Miss Silver gave a slight reproving cough.

"I am afraid the shock has been worse for her than for anyone, since it was she who made the dreadful discovery."

"I offered to wait and go home with her," said Miss Rennie. "The police wished to question her, and she was obliged to stay. I was feeling the shock a good deal myself, but I was perfectly willing to remain there with her. And all she said was, 'For God's sake let me alone!' Really quite profane! After that, of course, I couldn't say any more, could I?"

Whilst Miss Silver was putting a few things into a case Joyce Rodney came in. She shut the door and sat down upon the bed.

"Oh, Miss Silver, I'm so thankful I took David away."

Miss Silver looked up from folding a warm blue dressing-gown.

"I think you did wisely, and I am sure he is very happy with your friend in Ledlington."

"Oh, yes, he is. I'm so thankful I was there today, and not at the Manor. It must have been dreadful." She hesitated, and then went on. "Penny Marsh came to see me this morning. She wanted to know whether I would take Connie's place and help her to run the school."

"Yes, Mrs. Rodney?"

Joyce Rodney made an impatient movement.

"I do wish you would call me Joyce! Everyone does."

Miss Silver's reply was kind but firm.

"I have told you that I do not consider it advisable."

"Yes, I know. All the same I wish you would. When Penny spoke to me about the school I felt as if it might be a very good plan. Of course I couldn't go on doing so much for Aunt Renie, but I would be able to pay for my board, and she could have extra help—only with these dreadful things happening—" She broke off, looked very directly at Miss Silver, and said, "About Colonel Repton—you were there when it happened. Was it suicide? Aunt Renie says it was—but was it?"

Miss Silver laid the dressing-gown in the suitcase.

"Neither Miss Wayne nor myself is in a position to say."

"Well, you know, everyone says that he and Scilla had had a frightful quarrel, and that she was only waiting until after Connie's funeral to clear out. They say he was going to divorce her."

Miss Silver said mildly, "That scarcely appears to be compatible with suicide."

"No, it doesn't, does it? Frankly, I shouldn't have thought anyone would kill himself because Scilla was walking out on him. Of course she's pretty, but she doesn't do a single thing that a man like Colonel Repton expects his wife to do—why, she doesn't even keep house. And she's got an odious temper."

Miss Silver put a sponge, a nailbrush, a toothbrush, and a tube of toothpaste into a blue waterproof case which had been a last year's Christmas gift from her niece by marriage, Dorothy Silver, who was the wife of Ethel Burkett's brother. She said,

"Men do not take the same view of these things that we do. Mrs. Repton has the type of looks which is apt to render them indifferent to practical considerations."

Joyce laughed.

"How right you are! And I was being thoroughly catty. I daresay she is all right against her own background, and she must have been hideously bored down here, but I do hate to see anyone take on a job and then not lift a finger to make a success of it. Look here, I'll walk back across the Green with you and carry that case."

It was when they were alone under the night sky with the empty Green stretching round them that Joyce Rodney said out of the middle of what had been quite a long silence,

"Miss Silver—about Colonel Repton—you never did say whether you thought it was suicide. Do you know, I don't somehow feel as if it was. Florrie has been telling everyone that he said he was going to divorce his wife.

Well, as you say, if he was going to do that he wouldn't commit suicide, would he?"

To this bald but commonsense statement of a problem upon which she did not desire to enlarge, Miss Silver thought it best to observe in a noncommittal manner that suicide was sometimes due to a sudden impulse, and that there was not at present enough evidence to show how Colonel Repton had met with his death.

It was about this time that Valentine was saying to Jason Leigh, "He didn't himself. Oh, Jason, he didn't—he *wouldn't!*" She stood in the circle of his arms and felt safe. But outside of that charmed circle there was a world of which the foundations had been shaken. She had never known her father, and she could only remember her mother as someone very vague and shadowy who lay on a sofa, and then one day wasn't there any more and Aunt Maggie said she had gone to heaven. But Roger had always been there, part of the established order of things. He was not at all exciting, but always a kind person round whom the house revolved. It had never occurred to her to think whether she loved him or not. Now that he was dead, it was like being in a house with one of the walls sheared off and letting in all the winds of calamity. She pressed against Jason and heard them blow, but they couldn't touch her as long as he held her close. He said,

"I shouldn't have thought he would either."

"He didn't. I am quite sure he didn't. He talked to me about suicide once, and he said it was running away. He said he didn't believe it got you out of anything either. It was shirking, and if you shirked you only made things harder for yourself and everyone else."

"You had better tell that to the Chief Constable."

"I have. He didn't say anything. Jason, what is so frightful about it is that if he didn't do it himself, there is only one person I can think of who would have done it."

"Scilla? You'd better not go about saying that, darling."

"As if I would! As if I wanted to! I've been trying not to say it to myself, but it keeps on coming back. There was a story I read once about a room in a house. Someone had been murdered there, and the door wouldn't stay shut. It's like that—about Scilla—in my mind. I try to shut it away, but the door won't stay shut." Her voice had gone away to just a breath against his cheek. They were so close that he couldn't be sure whether he heard the words or just knew that she was saying them. He kept his own voice down, but it sounded too loud.

"Why should she?"

"He was going to divorce her. He told Maggie. That is why she looked so ghastly at the Work Party this afternoon—he had just been telling her. There was an affair—with Gilbert—and he had found it out."

"Is that why you broke it off?" The words came hard and hot before he could stop them.

"No—no, it wasn't. You've got to be quite sure about that, because it's true. I didn't know—I hadn't any idea until that Wednesday night. When I left you and came back to the house they were in her sitting-room. I was coming in through the drawing-room window, and the door between the rooms wasn't quite shut. I heard—something—and I oughtn't to have listened—but I did. He was telling her it was over. He said he was—fond of me."

"That was very kind of him."

"It was quite *horrid*," said Valentine with sudden vigour. "I came away after that. In the morning I got one of those poison-pen letters. It said Gilbert had been carrying on with Scilla. But you are never to think that that was when I made up my mind to break it off, because it wasn't. It was quite, quite made up when I was with you in the gazebo. You told me I couldn't marry Gilbert, and I knew I couldn't. I knew it the way you know something that you don't have to think about. It was just there."

They kissed.

CHAPTER 29

Miss Repton was better in the morning. She was in deep grief, but the sense of shock was lifting. She found herself able to read her Bible, and expressed a wish to see Mr. Martin, with whom she presently had a very comforting talk. It appeared he did not adhere to the school of thought which believed that those who passed away remained asleep in their coffins until the Day of Judgment, a belief which had been entertained by her parents and handed down to her by them. It had never occurred to her to question it before, but she found the Vicar's more modern view very comforting indeed. She was also extremely grateful for the continued presence of Miss Silver, both on her own account and for the sake of Valentine. As she put it with rather touching simplicity,

"I do not wish to have unkind thoughts about anyone, and I have been praying to be delivered from any harsh judgments, but I am afraid that everyone will know by now that dear Roger was going to divorce his wife, and one can't help wondering—no one can help wondering whether—whether—And it does seem more suitable that there should be someone else with dear Valentine."

Late in the morning the Chief Constable came over.

He asked to see Miss Silver, and she came down to him in the study, where she found him looking out of the window. He turned as she came in, informed her briefly that the *post mortem* had established the fact that death was due to cyanide poisoning, and went on.

"Crisp saw the gardener last night, and he says it was used to destroy wasps' nests near the house in July. Everybody knew it had been used. He had pointed the nests out to Roger Repton and told him something ought to be done about them or they would be over-run with wasps hatching out in August, and then what was going to happen to the fruit? Scilla Repton came along while he was talking and wanted to know all about it, and said she was scared of wasps. Was he sure there was something that would kill them, and what was it? In fact considerable interest was displayed, and when he was destroying the nests she came out and watched him. He said he had to tell her not to touch the stuff, because it was the worst kind of poison. Casting back to my interview with her yesterday, it seems to me that she rather overdid her ignorance of cyanide and all its works."

Miss Silver had seated herself in the corner of the leather-covered couch which she had occupied at that interview. Then Scilla Repton in her tartan skirt and emerald jersey had been sitting by the writing-table. An excellent memory recalled the naive manner in which Scilla had stumbled over the very word. It had been "Cya what?—Cya stuff." As she opened her flowered knitting-bag and took out little Josephine's now almost completed cardigan she said gravely,

"I do not feel that too much attention should be paid to that. She is not a young woman of any education. She practically never opens a book, and her knowledge of current events is obtained from the more sensational headlines in the papers, a brief glance at the papers, and the news-reel at the cinema. I think it more than possible that an unfamiliar word like cyanide would leave her mind as casually as it had entered it. It was, in any case, the possibility of a plague of wasps which she found interesting and alarming. The cyanide would only come into it as a means of averting that threat."

March had taken the opposite sofa corner. He said grimly,

"Unless it occurred to her that it could be used to remove an inconvenient husband as well as a wasps' nest." Then, with half a laugh, "She is everything you don't like, but you'll put the case for her with scrupulous fairness, won't you?"

She smiled.

"Naturally, my dear Randal."

"Well, now that you have discharged your conscience, suppose you tell me what you really think."

She knitted for a while in silence.

"I suppose," she said, "that you can see what is on the surface as well as I can. Her looks have been cultivated to the utmost, her mind has not been cultivated at all. I do not know what her parentage may have been, but I think she has had to fend for herself from an early age. Miss Maggie tells me that no relations have ever been mentioned, no old friends have ever been asked to stay. She has been a show girl and a mannequin, a precarious and intermittent form of employment and a very bad preparation for life in the country as the wife of an impoverished landowner nearly double her age. She may well have felt that she had made a disastrous mistake, especially if she was attracted by Mr. Gilbert Earle. I do not think that she had any affection for her husband, or for his family. Miss Maggie tells me that Colonel Repton made a settlement on her at the time of the marriage. It amounted to about two hundred a year.

She may have felt two hundred a year and her freedom preferable to a continuance of her life at the Manor, where she had no ties either of affection or interest. All this is arguable, but in all of us there are certain factors which set a barrier between what we would prefer and what we are prepared to do in order to obtain that preference. A young woman might wish to be free and independent, and yet be quite incapable of murder as a means to that end."

He nodded.

"As to the settlement, I've been seeing Repton's solicitors this morning. They are an old Ledlington firm, Morson, Padwick, and Morson. I had an extremely interesting talk with Mr. James Morson, the head of the firm. Scilla Repton would have forfeited her settlement if she had been divorced for adultery. Asked whether she were aware of this fact, Mr. Morson looked down his nose and said he had personally made it his business to explain it to her at the time the settlement was made, pointing out the words *dum casta* and telling her what they meant. He had been a good deal scandalized by the fact that she had immediately burst out laughing and said in a drawling voice, 'Oh, then, if I get bored with Roger and run away with somebody else I don't get a bean. What a shame!' So you see she was perfectly well aware that she would be left penniless if he divorced her. And he had not only told her that he was going to divorce her, but he had informed his sister and his solicitor. I gather that she had been meeting Earle in the flat of a complaisant friend, of which evidence would probably have been forthcoming. Now so far everything rather adds up against her, but yesterday morning Roger Repton went in to Ledlington and altered his will."

Miss Silver knitted placidly.

"Indeed, Randal?"

He could not believe her to have missed the implication, but he proceeded to put it into words.

"He altered his will and cut her right out of it. He insisted on doing it then and there in what Mr. Morson had obviously considered a very precipitate manner. Now—point one—it might be argued that this is evidence of an intention to commit suicide. And—point two—when he saw his wife in the study some time within an hour of his death and Florrie heard them quarrelling, did he, or did he not, tell her that he had altered his will? Because if he did, and she knew he had cut her out of it, her interest in his death would be considerably reduced, whereas if she only thought he was going to alter it, it would be very much enhanced."

Miss Silver coughed.

"There is, of course, no evidence upon either point. But suppose him to have informed her of the change in his will. She would certainly have been extremely angry. It must by then have been after four o'clock. The cyanide was, in all probability, already in the stoppered decanter. If it was added to the contents by Mrs. Repton, this may have been done much earlier in the afternoon, or during that very interview at some moment when Colonel Repton's attention had been diverted. His death had in either case already been resolved upon, and the means were to hand. Would an angry young woman who had planned her husband's death be in any state to weigh the alternative advantages of pursuing this plan or changing it? If he lived to divorce her, she would lose her settlement. If he died now, she might, or might not, be able to keep the settlement. That, I suppose, would depend upon the line taken by the family and the amount of evidence as to her infidelity. I think it would probably appear to her that she would keep it, because if he were dead he couldn't divorce her. As to the will, had he any considerable amount to leave?"

March said,

"Very little. As there is now no male heir, the estate, including the farms from which practically all his income was derived, passes under the entail to Valentine Grey. Indeed, if it hadn't been for her very generous contributions, the place would have had to be sold long ago. Scilla Repton probably knew all this."

Miss Silver pulled upon the ball of blue wool. She said,

"It is common knowledge, Randal. I had not been here twenty-four hours before Miss Wayne had told me very much what you have told me now."

"Then you think she did it?"

"I think we may say that there was a good deal of motive. She was threatened with divorce and with the loss of her settlement. She was also threatened with the loss of her lover. I do not know to what extent her feelings were involved, but Mr. Earle is an attractive young man who is said to have a career before him, and he is the heir to a title. Even nowadays he could not afford to marry a woman about whom there had been a serious scandal. As Roger Repton's widow she would be in a much more eligible position."

"Yes, that is true."

"So much for the motive. As to the opportunity, it would of course have been easier for her than for anyone else to add cyanide to the contents of the decanter. It could have been done in the morning when Colonel Repton was out, or at any time during the afternoon when he was absent from the study for a few minutes. This is also true about anyone else in the house, but nobody else appears to have any motive. Apart from the household, two other people would have had the opportunity required."

He raised his eyebrows.

"Two?"

"Mr. Barton and Miss Eccles."

He shook his head.

"Well, doesn't the same thing apply? What motive could either of them have had?"

Miss Silver's needles clicked.

"The one which we have not touched upon, the one which I believe to have been the real motive for the deaths of both Colonel Repton and Connie Brooke. Each was believed to have identified the author of the poison-pen letters. In the case of Colonel Repton there may have been contributory motives. If it was his wife who poisoned him, there certainly were. He told her he knew who had written the letters, and he said, 'Perhaps you wrote them yourself. It would be one way out of Valentine's marriage and of your own.' This was at the height of a violent quarrel, and may not have been very seriously meant. He did not repeat it to Miss Maggie when he told her that his wife had been unfaithful to him. In the meanwhile Florrie's story of the quarrel had gone all round the village, and it was being repeated everywhere that Colonel Repton knew who had written the letters. His death followed, just as Connie Brooke's death followed upon the rumour that she possessed the same knowledge. I find it difficult to dissociate the two cases. Therefore, unless Mrs. Repton was the writer of the letters, I am disinclined to believe that it was she who poisoned her husband."

"According to Florrie he accused her of having written them."

"Not quite in that way, I think, Randal. What she put in her statement was that Colonel Repton had received one of the anonymous letters, and that it had accused Mrs. Repton of having been unfaithful to him. She then continued, 'Mrs. Repton said it was all lies, and the Colonel said it was a filthy letter about a filthy thing, and he knew who wrote it. And Mrs. Repton said who was it then? And the Colonel said wouldn't she like to know, and perhaps she had done it herself, because that would be one way of breaking off Miss Valentine's marriage and getting out of her own.' You see, it was more of a taunt than a direct accusation, and he did not repeat it to his sister."

"I don't know that that proves anything. His personal reaction to her infidelity could very well have been uppermost in his mind, with the anonymous letters a good deal in the background. And if it wasn't Scilla Repton who poisoned him, who was it?"

She said soberly, "We were talking of Mr. Barton and Miss Eccles, both of whom are to some extent linked with the deaths of Connie Brooke and Colonel Repton. I do not say that either of them is guilty, but in each case there was opportunity."

"Barton?" His tone was one of surprise. "Well, he certainly saw Repton within a very short time of his death, but he was, according to Florrie, received on the friendliest terms, and there is no evidence of a quarrel or of any other motive. He had every reason to feel grateful to Repton, who had been a very good friend to him. I believe he was devoted to him. I saw him after I left here last night, and I am sure that the news of Repton's death was a severe shock. And what possible connection could he have with Connie Brooke?"

"None, unless he was the writer of the anonymous letters. A very strong one if he was. And there is this slight connection. On the Wednesday night—that is, the night on which Connie Brooke met her death—I had put out the light and I was opening my bedroom window. The party at the Manor was breaking up. I saw two or three cars go away, and I saw Mr. Barton come home from one of his nocturnal rambles. He had his cats with him, and he came from the far end of the Green—that is, from the direction of Connie Brooke's house. It proved no more than that he was in that neighborhood at a time when, provided he had access to the house, he could have drugged her cocoa."

Randal smiled.

"It is scarely evidence."

She continued to knit.

"I do not advance it as such. I have mentioned it because I do not wish to keep anything back. I think, however, that with regard to Mr. Barton you have by no means told me all you know about him."

He nodded.

"No, I haven't. And I am in two minds whether to tell you now. If I were not a good deal more sure of your discretion than I am of my own, I would hold my tongue. As it is, I am going to tell you. Barton isn't the chap's real name. There isn't any need to tell you what it is, but you will probably remember the case. I think we'll just go on calling him Barton. He got a commission from the ranks of the battalion in which Repton was. A year or two later they were on foreign service in the Far East, a gruelling sort of job. Barton got a nasty face wound which left him badly scarred. Then he had sunstroke and was invalided home. He found his wife living with another man, and he killed them both—pitched the man out of the window and strangled the woman. There is no doubt that he was not sane at the time. They sent him to the Criminal Asylum at Broadmoor, and after some years he was released. Repton let him have this cottage at a peppercorn rent and has befriended him in

every way. He could have no reason to destroy his bene-
factor."

Miss Silver regarded him in a manner which recalled
his schoolroom days. It suggested a conviction that he
could do better than this if he tried. She said firmly,

"Where there is a history of insanity it is possible that
there may be a recurrence. The writing of what are commonly called poison-pen letters points to a mind not
truly in balance. In the case of a man who has had so
serious a breakdown as you described, and who has for
years been living the life of a complete recluse, is there
not at least the possibility that, deprived of all normal
companionship, he might seek this abnormal means of
contact with his neighbours? It is generally attributed to
some form of frustration, and few lives can have been
more painfully frustrated than that of this unfortunate
man."

March's mind went back with discomfort to the date
which had presented itself during his interview with
James Barton. He said in a lowered voice,

"When I asked him why he had gone to see Repton in
the afternoon instead of waiting as he usually did till
after dark, he said, 'I'd been thinking of things, and they
had got to a point where they didn't bear thinking
about, so it came to me that I'd go up and see him.' And
when he said that, it came up in my mind that it was
somewhere about the middle of October that he had
come home and found his wife with the other man. And
I think it was on the thirteenth—in fact I'm pretty sure
about that. I read up the case in the file of the *Times*
when I came here, because I had it passed on to me that
the chap was living here under the name of Barton. The
date stuck, because I remember thinking it had been an
unlucky thirteenth for him."

There was silence between them for a little before he spoke again.

"I suppose you are right, and that he might have done it. If he had been sitting there brooding over the old tragedy, and then came up here to find himself taxed with the writing of those anonymous letters, I suppose he might have gone off the deep end. Only if it was like that—where did he get the cyanide? It's not the sort of stuff you have knocking about in your pockets. No, if Barton was going to do anyone in, I should expect something more on the lines of the previous affair—a blow, or an attempt to strangle. There is a noticeable tendency amongst the insane to stick to a pattern of murder."

Miss Silver inclined her head.

"That is very true, Randal. There is also another point in Mr. Barton's favour. As you say, if it was he who poisoned Colonel Repton, he must have gone there provided with the means of doing so. Florrie's story must have reached him, and he must therefore have been aware that Colonel Repton had said he knew who had written the letters. But how did the story reach him? He went nowhere, and he saw no one. He did not go to the George, and his door was locked against everyone. It is difficult to see how he can have heard what was common gossip to everyone else in Tilling Green, and unless he knew that he was suspected he would not have gone to the Manor provided with the means of poisoning Colonel Repton. I do not wish you to think that I suspect Mr. Barton of the crime. I only feel that he cannot as a suspect be lightly dismissed from it."

"Which brings us to Mettie Eccles. And what have you got to say about her? Everyone says she was devoted to Repton."

"Yes, that is undoubtedly true. She was in an agony of distress after she had found his body, and she immediately accused Mrs. Repton of having killed him. In neither case was she acting a part. But consider for a moment. Jealousy and jealous resentment are amongst the most frequent causes of violent crime. Miss Eccles had always cared deeply for this distant cousin. She undoubtedly hoped to marry him. And then he comes back suddenly with the least suitable wife in the world. There is a complete disparity of age, of breeding, of tastes. The marriage took place two years ago. About a year later the poison-pen letters began. As we have agreed, this sort of thing almost invariably springs from some painful frustration. But in this case Miss Eccles continued to be the centre of all the village activities. She played the organ, she visited the sick, she was active in the Village Institute. She would not seem to have had much time for the morbid brooding which must have preceded the production of those letters. But as to opportunity, it is she who, in both cases, had enough of it and to spare. She could have gone all the way home with Connie Brooke and drugged her cocoa which was waiting for her on the stove. As I told you, I have just a faint impression that I heard them saying good-night, but even if I could swear to it, there would have been nothing to prevent Miss Eccles from appearing to change her mind. It would have been quite easy to catch poor Connie up and say that she would like to see her all the way home. It would be a perfectly natural gesture from an older woman to a girl who had been looking desperately tired and ill. In the case of Roger Repton, we would have to suppose that she had heard Florrie's story and believed that she might be accused. Consider for a moment what a disaster that accusation would have been. If it had been brought and proved, or if it had only been believed, she would have been utterly and irretrievably ruined. There would have been nothing left for her at all. Is it impossible to believe that she would provide herself with a means of escape? The cyanide could in the last resort have been intended for herself. But she is of a bold and managing temperament. She has the courage to seek an interview with Colonel Repton. The Work Party offers her an opportunity. She knows that he is in the study. She says Florrie told her he was there, which means that she had asked where he was. She goes in, ostensibly to take him his tea. She stops beside Miss Repton and myself to announce that she is doing so. Now suppose that Colonel Repton took advantage of their being alone together to accuse her of having written the letters. He could have done so, and he could have been prepared to go to extremities by making the matter public. She had known him all her life, and she would know whether this was likely to be his course of action, in which case she might have been desperate enough to silence him. She could, no doubt, have found an opportunity of adding the cyanide to the contents of the decanter."

He was regarding her with a kind of quizzical respect.

"Do tell me how you would distract the attention of a man whom you were going to poison."

Miss Silver turned her knitting and measured the sleeve against her hand.

"I think I should say I saw a strange dog in the garden. The cyanide would, of course, be dissolved and contained in some small bottle which would go easily into a handbag or a pocket."

"I see you have it all worked out. How fortunate for society that you do not devote your abilities to crime!"

The gravity of her look reproved him. He hastened to say,

"I suppose it could have happened like that. How long was Mettie Eccles away from the tearoom?"

"It was quite a long time."

"You noticed her return?"

"Yes."

"Was there any change in her appearance?"

"Yes, Randal, there was. She was, she had been, agitated. There were signs of tears. Her face was freshly powdered. It is, of course, quite possible that Colonel Repton had been informing her that he intended to divorce his wife. He had already told his sister and Mr. Barton of his intention. If Miss Eccles was not the person he had in mind as the author of the anonymous letters, he might very easily have taken the opportunity of confiding in so old a friend."

He shook his head.

"You are building houses with a pack of cards. Very ingenious houses, I'll give you that, but you no sooner set one up than you proceed to knock it down again. As a plain man, I don't mind telling you I'd give all your ingenious suppositions for a ha'p'orth of real evidence. And it is only in the case of Scilla Repton that there is really any evidence at all. Plainly, she had a motive. Even if she knew that Repton had altered his will—and she may not have known that he had already done so— his death would save her settlement, her reputation, and any chance she might have of marrying Gilbert Earle. She had knowledge of the presence of cyanide in the gardener's shed, and she had easy access to it. She had an angry interview with him within an hour of his death, and could have introduced the cyanide into the decanter either then or at some previous time. The interview closed with the damning words overheard by Florrie as Mrs. Repton left the study—'You'd be a lot more good to me dead than alive.' This constitutes a strong case."

"Undoubtedly. But it does not link up with the anonymous letters, or with the death of Connie Brooke."

He let that go.

"To return for a moment to Mettie Eccles. Your last remark about her was to the effect that if she were not the author of the letters and Repton had therefore no accusation to bring against her, the agitation which you noticed might have been due to his having told her that he intended to divorce his wife. Don't you think this possibility derives a good deal of support from the fact that she immediately and directly accused Scilla Repton of having killed him? Such an accusation might very well have sprung from a belief that, driven by her infidelity, Colonel Repton had taken his own life. It certainly seems to me to be the most natural explanation."

"What does Miss Eccles herself say about her interview with Colonel Repton?"

"Nothing that amounts to anything. She just says she took him in his tea, and that he was sitting at his table and appeared to be as usual. She says that she didn't stay, and that she went up to Miss Maggie's room to tidy herself before going back to the others. I can press her, of course, as to whether Repton said anything about his wife. But look here—do you seriously suspect her?"

Miss Silver was silent for a moment. Then she said, "Suspicions are not evidence, as you have pointed out. But I believe that somewhere there is the evidence which would convict the person who is responsible for at least a double murder. It occurs to me that this evidence may lie farther back in the case than has been supposed. I feel quite sure that the question of the anonymous letters is fundamental. I would like, therefore, to go back to the letters received by Doris Pell, the girl who was found drowned in the Manor Lake. She lived with an aunt, who was formerly maid to Mrs. Grey, and they did dressmaking. I suppose the aunt was interviewed by the police?"

"Oh, yes, Crisp saw her. There had been more than one letter, but she was only able to produce the last one. It was the usual disgusting type of thing, full of what seem to have been completely unfounded suggestions of immorality."

"And what did Miss Pell have to say to Inspector Crisp?"

"Oh, nothing at all. The poor woman just went on crying and saying what a good girl Doris was, and how no one had ever had a word to say against her or against anyone in their family. They were Chapel people and very religious, and Doris just couldn't bear the shame of it."

Miss Silver was casting off. As the last stitch fell from the needles, she looked across them at the Chief Constable and said,

"Would you have any objection to my going to see Miss Pell, Randal?"

CHAPTER 30

Miss Pell lived three houses beyond the post office. Now that she was alone there, the house was too big for her and she was thinking of taking a lodger. Only of course she would have to be very particular about the sort of person she would take. A man was not to be thought of, and a female lodger must neither be so young as to have the slightest inclination towards flightiness, nor so aged as to be a possible liability in the way of attendance or nursing, a thing which Miss Pell was careful to explain you undertook for your own family—and she would be the last to shirk her duty to a relative—but she couldn't, no she really couldn't consider it in the case of a stranger. Doris's room was therefore still unoccupied.

The house was one of a row of cottages all joined together, so Miss Pell had no need to be nervous. If she were to knock upon the wall on the right as you looked to the front, old Mrs. Rennick would knock back and call out to know what she wanted. If she knocked on the left-hand wall, young Mrs. Masters would do the same. There were, of course, drawbacks to this state of things, because Mrs. Rennick disagreed a good deal with her daughter-in-law. They carried on long arguments from one room to another. And though the Masters baby was very good on the whole, it did sometimes cry. But then, as Miss Pell had often said, when you sit and sew all day it's nice to hear what's going on next door.

Miss Silver paid the visit, to which Randal March had raised no objection, at about half past three. Miss Pell admitted her to a narrow passage with a stair going up on one side and a half open door on the other. Everything was very clean, but the house had the peculiar smell inseparable from the profession of dressmaking. The room into which she was ushered had a goodsized bay window. It seemed improbable that it was ever opened.

Seen in the light, Miss Pell appeared to be about fifty years of age. She had sparse greyish hair brushed back from the forehead and pinned into a tight plait at the back. Her features were thin and sharp, her complexion sallow, and her eyelids reddened. She began to speak at once.

"If it's about some more work for Miss Renie, I'm afraid I couldn't undertake it—not at present. You are the lady who is staying with her, aren't you—Miss Silver?"

Miss Silver said, "Yes," adding with a friendly smile, "And you are too busy to take any more work?"

"I couldn't manage it—not for a long time," said Miss Pell. She spoke in a curious faltering way, running two words together, pausing as if she was short of breath, and then going on with a rush. She went on now. "I haven't really caught up, not since my poor niece— staying with Miss Renie, you will have heard about it, I daresay. And apart from missing her as I do, I was left with all the work the two of us had in hand, and I don't seem to be able to get it straightened out."

Miss Silver knew trouble when she saw it, and she saw it now. The reddened eyelids spoke of lack of sleep. She said in her kindest voice,

"I know that everyone has felt the deepest sympathy with you in your loss."

Miss Pell's lips trembled.

"Everyone has been very kind," she said. "But it doesn't bring her back. If it hadn't been for those letters—"

She didn't know what made her speak of the letters. She had been asked about them at the inquest, but ever since she had tried to keep them out of her mind. Wicked, that's what they were, and not fit language for a Christian woman to call to mind. And Doris always such a good girl. She felt her way to a chair and sat down because her legs were shaking. Her thought found its way into words.

"She was always such a good girl. None of the things in the letters were true. She was a good Christian girl."

Miss Silver had sat down too.

"I am sure she was, Miss Pell. If the person who wrote those letters could be found, it might save some other poor girl the same experience."

Miss Pell stared at her.

"Anyone that was wicked enough to write those letters would be wicked enough to know how to hide themselves."

"Do you think that your niece had any idea who had written them?"

Miss Pell's hands, which were lying in her lap, jerked and closed down, the right hand over the left.

"There wasn't anything to say who wrote them."

"If she had had any idea, in whom would she have been most likely to confide?"

"She hadn't any secrets from me."

"Sometimes a girl will talk to another girl. Had your niece any special friend? Was she, for instance, friendly with Connie Brooke?"

Miss Pell looked down at her own clasped hands.

"They had known each other from children," she said. "Miss Renie will have told you I was maid to Miss Valentine's mother, Mrs. Grey—and a sweet lady she was if ever there was one. When my brother died and I had to take Doris, Mrs. Grey let me bring her to the Manor. And just about then Mrs. Brooke and her little Connie came to Tilling Green, so there were two little girls very much of an age, and Miss Valentine was the baby."

"And they went on being friendly?"

"Really fond of each other, that's what they were. The very last bit of work Doris did was to alter a dress for Miss Connie. And she must have been one of the last people she spoke to too, because that was one of the things she went out for that afternoon, to go along to the school and let Miss Connie have her dress."

Miss Silver looked at her gravely.

"Miss Pell, you knew, did you not, that Connie Brooke was believed to have told Mr. Martin that she knew who had written those letters?"

"It wasn't Mr. Martin who said so."

"No, it was his housekeeper. It was all over the village that Connie Brooke knew about the letters, and that Mr. Martin had told her that it might be her duty to go to the police. Do you not think it would have been her duty?"

"I couldn't say."

Miss Silver waited for a moment. Then she said,

"Connie died next day, as suddenly as your niece did. If she had told Mr. Martin what she knew, I believe that she would be alive to-day. It was all over the village on Saturday that Colonel Repton had been heard to say that he knew who had written the letters. On Monday afternoon he was dead too. If he had told the police what he knew, he would not have died. Now, Miss Pell, I think that you know something, and I think it is of the first importance that you should tell what you know."

A little colour came up into the sallow face. The eyelids came down for a moment over the faded eyes, and then were raised again. In a changed voice Miss Pell said,

"It is the third sign—"

"Yes, Miss Pell?"

"Once by a dream," said Miss Pell, looking fixedly at her, "and once by the Bible text, and once by your mouth. If there was a third sign, I said that I would know what I had to do."

If the words were strange, her manner was perfectly composed. Her hands now held each other lightly and without straining. Miss Silver said,

"There is something you know and that you think you ought to tell?"

The answer she received was an indirect one.

"I will tell you about the signs. You won't understand unless I tell you about them. Because when Doris came home that day I promised her that I wouldn't speak of what she told me, and it isn't right to break a promise to the dead—not unless there is a sign, and I've had three. She said to me, 'You'll never tell, Aunt Emily, now will you?' And I said, 'Of course I won't.' Nor I wouldn't ever, if it hadn't been for the signs."

"What were they, Miss Pell?"

"The first was a dream that I had in the night. Last night it was, and as clear as if I was waking. I was here in this room and sewing on something black, and I was crying over the work, and I remember thinking that it would be spoiled, because nothing spots quicker than black. And then the door opened and Doris and Connie came in together, holding hands like they would when they were little girls. They had a big bunch of flowers between them, holding it—lilies, and roses, and all sorts. And there was a light all round them, so that they shone. Doris was on the right and Connie on the left. In my dream they came right up to me, and Doris said not to cry any more, because there was no need, and not to trouble about the promise I'd made, because it didn't matter. And I woke up in my bed upstairs with the alarm clock going."

Miss Silver said very kindly indeed,

"It was a comforting dream."

Miss Pell's eyes were full of tears.

"It ought to have been, but it wasn't. I'd heard about Colonel Repton, and I kept troubling in my mind about whether the dream meant that I was to break my promise and go to the police, and whether it was a sign, or whether it had just come up out of my troubling about what I had said to the police. I hadn't told any lies—I wouldn't do that—but when they asked me if I had told them all I knew, I just put my handkerchief up to my face and cried, and they thought that I had."

"I see."

"So I thought what I could do to make sure about the sign. And what I did, I took my Bible and I shut my eyes and opened it just where it fared to open and put my finger on a verse. And when I opened my eyes it was the sixteenth verse of the eighth chapter of Zechariah, and it said—'These are the things that ye shall do; Speak ye every man the truth to his neighbour; execute the judgment of truth and peace in your gates.' So I thought, 'If that isn't a sign, I don't know what is.' And then it come over me that I'd never broke a promise in my life, and that I'd got to be sure. And I thought, 'If the Lord wants me to speak, he can send me a third sign just as well as the other two, and if there is a third sign, I shall know that it's from the Lord and I shall know what I've got to do.' And then you come knocking at the door, a stranger, and the very words of the sign in your mouth, telling me that there was something I knew, and that I should tell it."

Miss Silver repeated the words.

"Yes, I think you should tell it."

Miss Pell brought out an old-fashioned linen handkerchief neatly folded and touched her eyes with it.

"It was that last day before Doris was drowned. She went out in the afternoon, and she'd got a mauve silk blouse she was taking to Miss Maggie at the Manor, and a dress she'd made for Miss Wayne, a blue wool that she had, coming out of mourning for her sister, and she said it was a little tight under the arms though I couldn't see it myself, so Doris had been letting it out. Quite a round she had, what with leaving the blouse, and the dress, and looking in to settle the pattern of a couple of nightdresses for Miss Eccles and finishing up with Miss Connie. She left the dress she had been altering for her to the end because of the children not coming out of school until four. Well, she went there, and she was properly upset, the same as she was when she came back home. And at first she wouldn't tell me anything at all, only that there was something not quite right about the neck of Miss Maggie's blouse and she'd promised to alter it quick and run up with it in the evening. 'Well,' I said, 'you're not letting yourself get upset about that, are you?' And she said, 'No, Aunt Emily, it isn't the blouse,' and she burst out crying. So then I went on at her to tell me what it was, and she said if she did, would I promise faithfully never to breathe it to a living soul—and I promised. So then she told me."

"What did she tell you?"

"She said it had come to her who had written those dreadful letters, and she said it was this way. There were the four houses she'd been in that day—up at the Manor with Miss Maggie's blouse, and at Willow Cottage with Miss Wayne's blue wool, and into Holly Cottage about Miss Mettie's nightgown. And last of all in at the Croft with Miss Connie. That's the only four houses she was in. And in one of them—and she didn't tell me which— she picked up a little bit of paper that was on the floor. You know how it is, if you see something lying about like that, it just comes natural to stoop down and pick it up. Well, that's what Doris did, and when she'd got it in her hand she could see it was a torn-off piece of one of the letters she'd had. A bottom left-hand piece it was, with the Til of Tilling on it. Torn right in half the word was on the letter when she got it, where it said everyone in Tilling Green knew that Doris went with men on the sly. Well, there was this piece and she'd picked it up, and she came over faint and had to sit down."

Miss Silver said quickly, "Which house was it?"

Miss Pell took a long sighing breath.

"She never told me. I told her she would have to, and

she said she didn't think she ought, and perhaps it would be better to tell the person she knew and make them promise solemn that they'd never do it again. I asked her if she'd told Connie, and she said, 'No more than I've told you, and she's promised the same as you have.' "

Miss Silver said slowly, "But Connie said that she knew who it was."

"There may have been something that she thought about afterwards. She came here to me on the Monday—that would be a couple of days before she died—and she said had Doris told me about the bit of paper? And I said whatever Doris told me, I'd promised I wouldn't say a word. So she said, 'Well, you don't need to, because I know what you know, and a bit more too.' I asked her what she meant, and she said it was something Doris had said that she remembered. 'Doris picked up a bit of paper, Miss Pell,' she said, 'and she didn't say where she picked it up, but she said how white it showed up against the carpet, and she said what colour the carpet was.' Connie said she didn't think about it at first, but it had come back to her, and now she couldn't get away from it because she knew the house that had a carpet that colour, and that would be the house where Doris had picked the paper up."

"She really did say that?"

Miss Pell put up her hand to her head for a moment.

"Oh, yes, she said it just like I'm telling you. I've wished she hadn't ever since, but once a thing's said it's said, and you can't take it back any more than you can forget it when it's been said to you."

"And Connie said the paper showed up white against this carpet, but she didn't tell you what the colour of the carpet was?"

Miss Pell shook her head.

"No, she didn't, nor what house it was in, nor anything more than what I've told you. She sat just there where you are sitting now, and she told me about the bit of paper, and she said, 'I wish Doris hadn't told me, for I don't know what I ought to do. You see, Miss Pell,' she said, 'if I tell, it will get round to the police, and even if it doesn't it's going to cause the most dreadful talk and the most dreadful trouble, and perhaps a case in court, and me having to go into the witness box and tell about someone that is a neighbour and would never get over it if I did. And what good will it do now Doris is dead? It won't bring her back again.' And I said, 'No it won't bring Doris back.' "

Miss Silver said gravely,

"It might have saved Connie's own life if she had spoken. Have you said anything about this to anyone except myself?"

She shook her head again.

"There's been enough talk. And Doris is dead, and Connie is dead. The way I see it there's been too much said already. And if anyone had told me I'd talk the way I have to a stranger, I wouldn't have believed them. And I wouldn't have done it if it hadn't been for my dream, and the verse in Zechariah, and what you said when you come in."

Miss Silver got up to go. But before she left the room she said very earnestly indeed,

"Do not tell anyone, not anyone at all, what you have just been telling me. If it comes to telling the police, I will be there, and I will make sure that you are adequately protected."

Miss Pell looked first surprised and then a good deal alarmed. She had risen from her chair, and now went back a step, her eyes widening and her face paling. The nervous hesitation with which she had begun the interview had returned upon her. She said with trembling lips,

"They say it's a sin to take your own life, but I say the sin is on them that drove poor Doris to it—and Connie too."

"Miss Pell, I do not believe that Connie Brooke took her own life, and I am beginning to have very grave doubts as to whether your niece did either."

Miss Pell's hand went up to her shaking lips and pressed them hard.

"You don't think—oh, you don't think there was anything done to them by somebody else?"

Miss Silver said, "Yes, I am afraid I do."

CHAPTER 31

Miss Silver woke next morning to the reflection that this was Wednesday, and that a week ago Connie Brooke was alive and Valentine Grey was still expecting to be married next day. Last Wednesday was, in fact, the day of the wedding rehearsal, and the Wednesday evening the evening of the party at the Manor from which Connie had walked home with Miss Eccles and said good-night to her at the gate of Holly Cottage. They were now on the eve of another inquest, and she was herself still staying with Miss Maggie, who appeared to derive a good deal of support from her presence.

"I can't say, I really can't say, how grateful I shall be if you could just stay on until after the inquest and the funeral. I don't feel that I ought to press you, for of course I have no claim and this is a house of mourning, but you don't know how much, how very much, I should appreciate it if you were to stay. The fact is—" she proceeded in a burst of confidence—"my sister-in-law—oh, dear it does seem so dreadful to call her that when, if it hadn't been for her, my dear brother might still be with us—the fact is, I really don't feel that I can meet her just as if nothing had happened. Because Roger was going to divorce her—you know that, don't you—but I never would have thought that he would do anything so dreadful as to take his own life, and in such a terrible way. Oh, Miss Silver, do you think he really did? Nora Mallet came in to see me yesterday afternoon when you were out, and when I said that to her—I hardly like to repeat it—but do you know what she said? Of course she is very downright and I have known her all my life, but she said, 'Of course he didn't, Maggie, and no one who knew him would believe it. That woman poisoned him.' Oh, Miss Silver, you don't think—do you? But it does make me feel so very nervous being here with her alone—and dear Valentine too. So if you could stay on for a little—because I keep hoping she will go away as soon as the funeral is over."

They did not actually have to see very much of Scilla Repton, since she only appeared at meals. She had rung up Gilbert Earle and found that he could hardly drop his end of the conversation quickly enough. And she had rung up her convenient friend Mamie Foster, who amongst a scattering of "Darlings" had advised her strongly to dig her toes in and stay where she was.

"Of course, darling, I'd simply love to have you and all that, but if there's been any awkwardness like you say, then if I were you I'd dig my toes in. Because even if he did change his will, as long as you're in you're in, and not all that easy for anyone to put you out without making the hell of a scandal. But once you're out, it mightn't be so easy to get back, darling, if you know what I mean."

Since she was just as well aware of this strategic fact as Mamie was, and as she had also received something rather stronger than a hint from the Chief Constable that the police would like her to be available for further questioning, Scilla made up her mind to stick it out. She went in to Ledlington and saw Mr. Morson, who informed her that she was right out of Roger's will, but that it was unlikely that Maggie Repton and Valentine Grey would do anything about upsetting the settlement, which raised her spirits considerably. She had really had no idea with whom the decision would rest, but if it was only old Maggie and Valentine, a little sob-stuff would get her by with them all right.

With this off her mind, she went into Ashleys' and bought a very smart black autumn model suit with the new skirt and a most becoming shoulder line. She liked colours herself, and the brighter the better, but when all was said and done nothing set a fair girl off like black, and men fell for it every time. She could wear it at the inquest and at the funeral, and it would be just the thing for town. She supposed she had better have a hat—just a twist of something—and some veiling. A veil could be very becoming, only it mustn't hide her hair.

She brought all the things home with her and tried them on again in her own room. Sometimes things were a ghastly disappointment when you did that, but these looked even better than they had in the shop. Good clothes gave you a pull when you were looking for a job, and with an off white blouse and something in the lapel there wouldn't be any need to look like a walking funeral. Meanwhile she didn't have to see anything much of either Maggie or Val—half an hour twice a day at lunch and dinner, and an occasional meeting on the stairs or in the hall. And for the rest, breakfast in bed and the struggle with being bored, which wasn't really anything new.

After Gilbert Earle had rung off in a hurry he sat down to compose a tactful and charming letter to Valentine Grey. It was going quite well, when he had a sudden urge to tear it up. Written words may be as charming as you please, but they take colour and warmth from the voice. He turned back to the telephone, was lucky enough to get Florrie, a devout admirer, and sent her to fetch Valentine. Actually, the romantic interest which Florrie was unable to disguise had more of a chilling than a softening effect. Valentine shut the door, took up the receiver and said, "Yes?" all in an extremely restrained manner. Yet after Gilbert's first few words there was no doubt that a thaw had set in. It was not so long since she had felt that it would be at any rate tolerable to marry him, and here was his voice, kind and warm and feeling.

"My dear, I suppose I ought not to be ringing you up, but I couldn't help it. Such a dreadful shock for you and for Miss Maggie. And I did think a lot of him, you know—I really did, Val. He was always extraordinarily nice to me. So I thought that in spite of everything you would just let me say how sorry I am. That's all, my dear. No need for you to say anything—I understand." He rang off.

As she hung up at her end, her first thought was, "He really meant it. It would have been much easier not to ring up at all." Then, quickly, "But that's just what he means me to think. He can't bear to be in the wrong, or to have anyone feel that he isn't as charming as one thought he was. He is counting now at this minute on my saying just what I did say to myself. Oh, yes, he's counting on it, but all the same I believe he did really mean that he was sorry." She didn't get farther than that.

The Chief Constable's car drove up just after lunch. He asked for Miss Silver, and when she came down to him in the study he greeted her with a smile.

"Well, I have one or two things I would like to ask Miss Maggie. I haven't liked to press her too hard, but she ought to be getting over some of the shock by now."

"She is a good deal better. I think she could answer anything you wish to ask her."

"I shall also want to see Mrs. Repton. You know, there is quite a *prima facie* case against her. I've been in communication with the Public Prosecutor, and her arrest is being considered."

She did not speak, but she looked away. With all the affection and respect which he had for her, there were moments when he could have shaken her, and this was one of them. He did not ask her to bow to his opinion any more than he was prepared to accept hers, either by force or by favour, but this standing aside from the issue, this silent impenetrable resistance, was exasperating in the extreme. He said with more sarcasm in his voice than he was aware of,

"I suppose you have nothing very epoch-making to report?"

She looked at him gravely, and spoke gravely too.

"It is often the very little things that count. I am sure I do not need to tell you that. As Lord Tennyson so rightly says:

'strong in will
To strive, to seek, to find, and not to yield.'

What we find may seem a little thing, but the smallest addition to knowledge is not to be despised."

"How true. Do I understand that you have a small addition to offer me?"

"I think so." She seated herself as before in the sofa corner, the flowered knitting-bag at her side. Having withdrawn from it little Josephine's now completed cardigan, she took out a crochet hook and proceeded to give it an edging of double tricot. A similar edging had already been added to the jumper. As she slipped the hook between two stitches she said,

"I think you had better sit down, Randal. What I have to tell you, though slight in itself, may prove to be important."

He complied with what was not so much a suggestion as a gracious permission, and reflected with a twinge of rueful humour that she had most perfectly contrived to put him in his place. Only just there he had to go back upon his own word. She didn't contrive these things, they were the result of an attitude of mind, an innate poise and dignity. He had seen her freeze a usually imperturbable Chief Inspector where he stood. He had seen her reduce the highly irreverent Frank Abbott to a very real reverence. And—he might just as well confess it—in his own case she could always with a look or an inflection waft him back to that long ago schoolroom over which she had presided with such efficiency. The smile he turned upon her had lost its sarcasm. He said simply and frankly,

"You went to see Miss Pell?"

"Yes, Randal."

"Did you get anything out of her?"

"I think so. You had better hear what it is."

"I should like to."

She told him accurately and succinctly about her interview with Miss Pell. As always, he admired her faculty for remembering and repeating a conversation. When it was done he sat silent and frowning for a while before he said,

"Well, it's true enough about a corner having been torn off the last letter which Doris got, but that appears to be the only point upon which there is any confirmation. It was, of course, that letter which pushed her right over the edge, and it was a filthy piece of work. But a girl who is wrought up to the point of drowning herself isn't what you would call a reliable witness, and what she said is hearsay at that."

Miss Silver sat mildly,

"I have no doubt that Miss Pell was repeating just what she had been told, both in the interview with Doris and in that with Connie Brooke. If you were to question her, you would find that she would repeat everything exactly as she repeated it to me. I doubt whether there would be the smallest variation."

He nodded.

"I don't doubt her accuracy, but a girl who is on the brink of suicide—"

Miss Silver laid her hands down upon the blue cardigan and said in a tone of astonishment and reproof,

"My dear Randal, are you still able to believe that Doris Pell took her own life?"

"My dear Miss Silver!"

She said earnestly,

"Consider for a moment. She has received a letter with a corner torn off. She visits four houses, and in one of them she picks up the missing piece of paper. She has no doubt of the importance of her discovery, and she comes home very much upset. She now knows who has written the slandering letters. Do you for one moment suppose that she was able to conceal all traces of her emotion at the time? She stoops down without thinking, she picks up the scrap of paper, and at once receives a severe shock. The effect of such a shock would be in most cases to paralyse action. She would keep the paper in her hand, stare at it, and become obviously confused and distressed. It is most unlikely that she was alone when she made the discovery, and she was a simple country girl not versed in concealment. We know, in fact, that something of this sort is what happened, since Miss Pell mentioned that she had 'come over faint' and had to sit down. Do you think it possible that her agitation was not noticed? And if Doris could recognise the torn-off corner as a piece of damning evidence, would not the person whom it would certainly have ruined be quick to do so?"

His attention had become fixed. He said,

"Go on."

"What would be your course of action if you were placed in such a predicament, and if, like this detected criminal, you were without moral sense and already actuated by feelings of bitterness and spite?"

He said with praiseworthy gravity,

"You are asking too much of my powers of imagination."

She shook her head slightly and proceeded.

"It would be absolutely necessary to silence Doris Pell. Three ways of doing so might suggest themselves. She might be bound by a promise, she might be offered a bribe, or there was the third and darker course which was, I believe, adopted."

"You know, this is pure supposition."

"Not entirely, Randal. Where a cause proceeds to its logical effect and where all the circumstances combine in a reasonable possibility, there is at least a case for very careful scrutiny. Consider the events of that afternoon. Doris Pell goes up to the Manor with a blouse which she had made for Miss Repton. Some trifling alteration is necessary, and she agrees to make it and bring the blouse back in the evening. She then crossed the Green to Willow Cottage, where she tries on the dress she has been altering for Miss Wayne, and afterwards goes in next door to settle the pattern of a couple of nightdresses for Miss Mettie Eccles. Now it was in one of those three houses that she picked up that scrap of paper, because by the time she arrived at Connie Brooke's, which was her last call, she was already in a state of distress and in a position to tell Connie what she had seen. What she told Connie was, except for the colour of the carpet, just what she afterwards told Miss Pell. She did not tell either of them in which house she had picked the paper up. I think this points to her having given some kind of a promise not to do so. You will remember that she told her aunt that she did not think she ought to tell her who it was that had written the letters, and that perhaps it would be better if she made the person give a solemn promise never to do it again. Does this not look to you as if she was planning some explanation with this person?"

She waited for him to speak, but as he said nothing, she continued.

"If the scrap of paper was picked up at the Manor, the letter from which it had been torn could have been written by Miss Maggie Repton, by Mrs. Repton, by Valentine Grey, by Colonel Repton, or—just possibly but not at all probably—by Florrie or by one of the other daily maids. I asked Miss Maggie where she tried on the purple blouse which Doris had made for her, and she said at once and without any sign of embarrassment that it was up in her bedroom."

March said quickly, "You really can't suspect Miss Maggie."

Miss Silver coughed faintly.

"In arguing a case it is better that there should be no exception, but I was about to remind you that Connie Brooke in telling Miss Pell of her conversation with Doris reported her as saying that the scrap of paper had shown up so white against the carpet, and that she had told her what the colour of the carpet was."

"And what was it?"

"Unfortunately, Connie did not say. But with regard to a piece of paper showing up well upon it, the carpet in Miss Maggie's room would not answer such a purpose at all well, since it is of Indian manufacture and there is a good deal of white in the groundwork."

He said with a smile, "Miss Maggie is exonerated."

A shade of severity just tinged Miss Silver's manner.

"With regard to the other people in the house, I find that Florrie let Doris in and took her up to Miss Maggie's room. She thinks that at this time Mrs. Repton was out and so was Valentine Grey, but she is not sure. Neither is she sure whether either of them returned before Doris left. Valentine Grey is not really a suspect, but this leaves us uncertain as to whether Mrs. Repton could have seen Doris pick up that scrap of paper. Colonel Repton we need not consider, since he was to be one of the victims. As for Florrie and the other maids, I feel sure they have nothing to do with the case."

"There I am able to agree with you."

She continued as if he had not spoken.

"To come to Willow Cottage where Miss Wayne tried on a dress, I think we may conclude that this would also take place in her bedroom. The carpet there is a plain Wilton in a faded shade of pink. That in the spare room, which I have been occupying but which would have been empty at the time of Doris' visit and might therefore have possibly been used for the trying on, is in a similar shade of blue. A piece of paper would certainly show up much better than on a carpet with a pattern. In the case of Miss Eccles there was no question of trying anything on. The interview with Doris for the purpose of selecting a nightdress pattern could have taken place wherever it suited Miss Eccles' convenience, but it would most likely have been held in the sitting-room. I have seen this carpet for myself, and it is darker in tone than the one in Miss Maggie's bedroom. Colonel Repton was for a number of years in the East and brought these carpets back with him as presents for his sister and his cousin. I have not seen the carpet in Miss Eccles' bedroom, but Mrs. Rodney informs me that it is a square of powder blue with a border in a darker tone. A piece of paper would show up very well on this, but no better than on either of the carpets at Miss Wayne's. I do not feel that any conclusion can be drawn from these particulars, but I thought it right to touch upon them."

"Do you really feel that any conclusions are to be drawn at all?"

"Some, I believe. You see, Randal, whether it can ever be proved or not, I am convinced that Doris Pell did not commit suicide. The account I received from her aunt does not warrant the theory. A girl who was so completely shattered by the allegations in an anonymous letter as to fly in the face of her upbringing and her religious training by taking her own life was not the girl who set out that afternoon on a round of errands and was prepared to go up to the Manor again in the evening. If she had been in the state of morbid despair which had been indicated, she would have shrunk from meeting people, shunned her friends, and implored her aunt to do the errands for her. In response to a question from me Miss Pell stated that Doris set off quite cheerfully. It is true that she was upset when she came home, but this was entirely natural, and the distress was not of the kind to drive her into suicide. She had discovered the writer of the anonymous letters, and she was profoundly shocked and on the whole disinclined to expose the person. Her mind was, in fact, fully occupied in considering what she ought to do. Could there be any moment when she would be less likely to take her own life? There is simply no motive for it at all."

He smiled.

"You build up a very good case."

"And you do not take it seriously, do you? Well, I have nearly finished, but I have just this to add. We shall probably never know whether the matter of Doris' discovery was mentioned between her and the person whom she suspected. There could have been fear and suspicion on both sides, with neither so sure of her ground as to risk putting suspicion into words. On the other hand it is possible that words were startled out of one of them, some interim pledge demanded and given, some appointment made. I incline to think that is how it happened, since Doris neither told Connie Brooke nor her aunt the identity of the person whom she suspected. Doris went home, and later on after supper she went back to the Manor with Miss Maggie's blouse. Is it assuming too much to suppose that she had talked of this errand in the other houses where she had been that afternoon? She could have been met in the Manor drive by someone either from Willow Cottage or from Holly Cottage. She could have been followed when she left the house by someone from the Manor. There is a point where the drive passes along the edge of the lake. You will remember the spot. A stream flows in there and is crossed by a bridge. Can you tell me just where Doris' body was found?"

He said,

"At the spot which you describe. It was considered that she had thrown herself from the bridge."

She said with great earnestness,

"Randal, can you really believe that she was not pushed?"

CHAPTER 32

March remained looking, not at her but past her into the small fire which burned on the study hearth. Actually, his mind had swung back to the recollection of other times when Miss Silver had used that earnest tone and when she had been right. Throughout his experience she had made a habit of being in the right. It might be, it frequently was, exasperating, but it had to be reckoned with. He felt himself obliged to reckon with it now. He could depend upon his own judgment to be intelligent, temperate, and fair, but he felt bound to recognise in Miss Silver something to which he could not lay a claim. And of course he could always save his pride by having recourse to the perfectly legitimate argument that she had the opportunity denied to the police of seeing the various suspects at their ease and without any consciousness that they were being watched. He found that he did not desire or intend to avail himself of this argument. His desire was, quite simply, to arrive at the truth. He turned an open look upon her and said,

"I wonder—"

He was aware of some added warmth in her regard.

The answer had pleased her. He was conscious of an absurd satisfaction. She said,

"I think, like myself, you must feel unable to push coincidence beyond a reasonable point. Doris Pell comes back to her aunt and says that she knows who wrote the anonymous letters. She is drowned the same evening. Connie Brooke is heard to say that she knows who wrote the letters. The story is all round the village within twenty-four hours, and only a few hours after that Connie is found dead in her bed from an overdose of sleeping-tablets. On Saturday Colonel Repton is heard asserting that he knows who wrote the letters. Once more the story is circulated. On the Monday afternoon he is found poisoned in this very room. Can you possibly believe that the case of Doris Pell has no connection with the other two cases, and that they are not all the work of the same hand?"

He nodded.

"It certainly looks that way. But as long as the first death stood alone and Miss Pell withheld her evidence, no other verdict than suicide could be expected in the case of Doris. There is now a presumption that these three deaths were caused by the same person. The question is, what person? And it seems to me that the additional evidence you have produced piles up at Scilla Repton's door. Doris could have picked up the compromising scrap of paper somewhere else than in Miss Maggie's room. We don't know in what circumstances it came to be on the floor at all. It could have spilled out of a drawer, a book, or a blotter. It could have been pulled out of a pocket with a handkerchief. It could have dropped from a waste-paper basket or a handbag. You say that Doris was shown up to Miss Maggie's room. What happened when she left?"

"Florrie took her up, but she found her own way down."

"Then she could have gone or been called into Scilla Repton's bedroom, or into her sitting-room which has a door into the hall as well as into the drawing-room. Was there anything to prevent that?"

"Not that I know of, Randal."

"Mrs. Repton may have wanted her to undertake some work for her. They could have been looking at patterns, and the piece of paper may have been caught up with them and fallen. Mrs. Repton would know that Doris was returning to the Manor after dark, and she is a strong, active young woman who could easily have pushed her off the bridge. If she did take that first step, the others would follow, with a strong additional money motive in Roger Repton's case. There is, of course, no evidence to connect her with Connie Brooke on the night of her death, but if it can be proved that she poisoned her husband, there would be no need to proceed with the other two cases."

Miss Silver shook her head.

"I cannot feel any assurance of Mrs. Repton's guilt."

"Would you like to tell me why?"

The crochet hook went in and out, drawing the blue wool into a trellised edging. She said,

"It is very difficult to put into words. If she is guilty, I should expect some indication of her guilt, some suggestion that she is vulnerable. But I could not discern that Mrs. Repton had the least awareness of danger. Fear is the hardest thing in the world to disguise. Had she been afraid, I do not believe that she could so entirely have concealed the fact. It did not seem to me she realized that she had any cause for fear."

"I should say she was fairly tough."

"Even the most hardened criminal has an instinct for

the approach of danger. Had Mrs. Repton been conscious when you were questioning her that she had committed three murders, and that she now stood on the brink of discovery, I feel sure that her reactions would have been other than they were. There was a kind of lack of awareness which impressed me. I do not know that I can get nearer to it than that."

"She is tough, and she was putting on an act. If these three people were murdered, I maintain that she is the most likely person to have murdered them."

Miss Silver shook her head.

"This case does not begin with the murders, Randal. It begins with the anonymous letters. They are quite fundamental. In looking for their author you are looking for a frustrated person with a secret passion for power."

He lifted his brows.

"I can imagine that Scilla Repton might feel frustrated in Tilling Green."

"Oh, no, Randal—not at the time when the letters began. Her affair with Gilbert Earle was going on, and her mind would have been occupied with the shifts and subterfuges which such an intrigue entails. Also I gravely doubt if she would have accused herself of infidelity, as the letters certainly did."

"Did any other letters accuse her besides the one to Colonel Repton?"

"I think it likely that Miss Grey's letter did so. According to Florrie, she received one. In fact she admitted as much to you, did she not?"

"Oh, yes—she said that she had burned it. I should say that you are probably right, and that it accused Scilla Repton and Gilbert Earle of an intrigue."

"And do you think that Mrs. Repton herself would have written such a letter?"

"I don't know. I think she might have done it if she

was out to smash Valentine Grey's marriage regardless of who got hurt. That was the motive suggested by her husband." He moved, got up. "This is all sheer speculation, you know, and I must get on. I think myself that we have enough evidence to warrant the arrest."

She put away her work and rose.

"Will you question her again?"

"I do not see that there is any other course open to me. She will have to be cautioned this time."

He left the room feeling a little as if he had not quite measured up to some indeterminable standard.

CHAPTER 33

Some little while later, lunch being over, Miss Silver was taking coffee in the drawing-room in the company of Miss Maggie Repton. Little Josephine's cardigan, now completed and needing only to be pressed, had been displayed and admired and Ethel Burkett and her family had been the subject of some desultory conversation, when Miss Maggie sighed and said,

"I have often thought how delightful it would be if Valentine were married and had a family. It is so interesting to see children growing up. But of course I oughtn't to be talking of anyting of the sort now that she isn't even engaged."

Miss Silver smiled.

"It may be too soon to call it an engagement, but surely she and Mr. Leigh—"

Miss Maggie said, "Oh dear—" and then, "Do you think that people have noticed anything?"

Miss Silver said indulgently,

"I do not see how they can help it."

Miss Maggie said "Oh dear—" again. She gave another sigh and followed it up with a hesitating, "If only there isn't another of those wicked letters—"

Miss Silver had been waiting for just such an opening. She said with a good deal of sympathy,

"Did you ever have one yourself?"

Miss Maggie looked over her shoulder in an apprehensive manner. The large room was empty of anything but its proper furnishings.

"Oh," she said—"Oh, Miss Silver, I never told anyone. . . . But yes, I did." She put down her coffee-cup because her hand had begun to shake. She really couldn't help it. Everything in her shook when she thought about those dreadful letters.

"It would have been better if you had shown it to the police."

A thin dull colour came up into Miss Maggie's cheeks.

"Oh, I couldn't—I really couldn't! It said such dreadful things!"

"About your sister-in-law?"

"Yes—you have no idea—"

"Did you keep it?"

Miss Maggie dropped her voice to a trembling whisper.

"Oh, yes, I did—in my jewel-case—locked up. Would you like me to show it to you? Since—since Roger died I have thought—I have wondered if I ought to show it to someone. You are such a help to me. If you would look at it—perhaps you could tell me—what I ought to do."

Miss Silver smiled in a reassuring manner.

"I will look at it when you go up to have your rest."

Miss Maggie's jewel-case was one of the large old-fashioned sort covered in black leather with a small gold pattern stamped round the edge and the initials M. B. upon the lid. The leather was shabby, especially at the corners, and the gold almost worn away. Miss Maggie explained the initials as being her grandmother's—"She was Lady Margaret Brayle"—and opened the box with a small round brass key. There were several trays inside lined with violet velvet and edged with the same gold pattern as the lid, only a good deal fresher. From the second tray she lifted a heavy bracelet and produced from beneath it a folded sheet of paper. Then, having taken it out, she stood with it in her hand and hesitated.

"I really don't like to show it to you."

"If it would ease your mind—"

"Oh, it *would*—it would *indeed!*"

Miss Silver extended her hand.

"Then I will look at it."

The paper was as described by Randal March, cheap and flimsy with lines upon it. But the writing made no attempt to follow the lines. It sprawled across the sheet in large ungainly letters which did not look as if they had been formed by a nib—the strokes were too thick and too smeared. It occurred to Miss Silver that if a matchstick were slightly pointed and dipped in the ink it might produce this kind of effect, and she thought it might be quite a good way to disguise one's writing.

The wording of the letter was even worse than she expected. Scilla Repton was accused in language of the coarsest kind. She turned the page and read to the end where the signature "Well-wisher" ran slanting down into the right-hand corner. The other corner was blank. Turning it over, she discovered that the space on the other side was empty too. An idea immediately presented itself to her mind. She said,

"Dear Miss Repton, I do think that this should be shown to the police."

Miss Maggie's eyes filled with tears.

"I should feel so ashamed."

"If you would like me to do so, I would show it to the Chief Constable."

Miss Maggie clasped her hands.

"Oh, if you only would! I have really laid awake at night wondering what I ought to do and feeling that perhaps I ought to have told Mr. March about it. I did try and answer all his questions, and he asked me about Roger getting one of these dreadful letters, and about Valentine getting one, but he never asked me whether I had had one myself—and I did feel so ashamed of showing it to anyone, especially to a man."

When she had tucked Miss Maggie up on her bed in a warm dressing-gown with an eiderdown to cover her and a hot water-bottle at her feet, Miss Silver went to the bedroom which had been allotted to her next door, a comfortable old-fashioned room with a good deal of dark mahogany furniture and a handsome purple bedspread which gave the bed rather the appearance of a catafalque. Not that this comparison would have occurred to Miss Silver. She considered the material to be sumptuous, and the colouring extremely rich. The fact that the room had a northern aspect had preserved it from fading, and both the spread and the curtains, which displayed a pattern of grapes and vine leaves in shades of brown and purple, were in a remarkable state of preservation. The carpet, of the best quality Brussels, had once possessed a small design in such dark colours as could be trusted to show no marks. They were all now gone away in a general gloom. The room had been furnished as a guest-room by that Lady Margaret whose initials lingered upon her jewel-case. She had considered herself very modern and advanced when, the year being 1840, she had done away with the tester which had until then surmounted the bed, and the heavy curtains which surrounded it.

Miss Silver went over to the dressing-table and sat down there. She spread out the letter which Miss Maggie had given her and looked at it for quite a long time.

CHAPTER 34

Jason Leigh lifted the latch of Mr. Barton's gate, walked up to the side door, and knocked upon it. The work on which he had been employed was of the nature to develop what is often called a sixth sense, though it may perhaps more properly be considered to be a heightening of the other five. As he stood knocking on the door of Gale's Cottage he felt tolerably sure that he was being watched. It was not really dark outside, but it was dark enough for there to be a light in the front sitting-room of Willow Cottage. All the rooms next door looked either to the front or to the back. Only a staircase window commanded a view of Mr. Barton's sideways-facing door. It is true that by leaning out of the nearer of the two front bedrooms such a view could be obtained, as Miss Silver had discovered on the night of Connie's death, when she had watched Mr. Barton come home with his cats. But while Jason stood on the doorstep knocking nobody leaned from any window, and the sensation of being watched connected itself in his mind with the stairway and the narrow pane of glass which lighted it. No one had leaned out, but he had a feeling that someone had drawn back in a hurry and then stood there watching him.

His mind gave an impatient jerk. The Miss Waynes had always been great collectors of gossip like Mettie Eccles and half a dozen more of their kind, and Miss Renie would be waiting to see whether he got in past Mr. Barton's guard. When he did, she would be disappointed. And with that the key turned, the door swung in, and he stepped across the threshold. There was enough light from the open kitchen door to pass him through.

James Barton locked the door behind him and took him to the lighted room with a friendly hand on his shoulder. The curtains were drawn, the lamp lit, and the cats laid out in front of the fire, but whereas they had not moved a whisker for the Chief Constable, they now rose, stretched, and came to rub themselves against Jason Leigh.

Jason had a name and a word for each of the seven— Achan—Abijah—Ahithophel—Agag—Abimelech—A- bner—Absalom. Mr. Barton came as near a smile as he ever did.

"They don't forget a friend. Animals don't mostly, and cats are the choosiest of the lot. If they like you they do, and if they don't like you they don't, and that's all there is about it."

The cats went and lay down again. The two men seated themselves. After a while Barton said,

"When do you go off again?"

Jason laughed.

"Probably I don't."

"Quitting?"

"Probably. I have an urge to farm. I trained and did a couple of years after the war, you'll remember, and I feel like taking it up again."

Barton had picked up his pipe and was filling it.

"Why?"

"I'm thinking of getting married."

"Then you're a damned fool."

"Not when it's Valentine."

Barton gave him a quick hard look.

"And what do you expect me to say to that?"

"If you're a fool you'll say all women are alike! But they're not, any more than all men are. If you say what I expect you to say, it will be that there's only one Valentine and I'm lucky to get her."

There was a long pause. Barton struck a match and lit up. When he had got the pipe going he said in his deep throaty voice,

"No, you can't expect me to say that—not when you know how I feel about women. But if there ever was one who was different from the rest, it was her mother."

Jason looked across at him with a spark in his eyes.

"And what did you know about Mrs. Grey?" he said.

James Barton met the look.

"Just what anyone couldn't help knowing. She was good, and something had broken her heart and she wasn't one that could live without it. And when I say she was good, I don't mean that she was what is commonly called a good woman, which is a way of speaking that can be stretched to cover all the pettiest and meanest of vices. So long as you don't borrow your neighbour's husband or step outside the bonds of your own marriage you may be mean, jealous, quarrelsome, deceitful, a spendthrift, a pinch-penny, a nagger, a doubter, and as vain as the devil, and yet be accounted a virtuous woman. Mrs. Grey had another kind of goodness than that. I didn't speak to her more than three times. Once when she came in upon us when I was in the study with the Colonel. He named me as an old friend, and she said 'How do you do, Mr. Barton?' and I said, 'How do you do?' And two other times, when she said it was a fine day—that was one of them. And she was afraid it was going to snow—that was the other. But there was something in her that was like a light shining in a window. When you see goodness like that, you can't blaspheme by saying it isn't there. The girl has a touch of it, I'll grant you that."

Jason was oddly moved. His friendship with James Barton went a long way back to a day when, at ten years old, he had plunged into single combat with a bull-terrier in defence of one of the current cats, an earlier Ahithophel, who would usually have been more than a match for any dog but had in this instance just been disabled by a stone thrown by one William Clodd. The stone broke Ahithophel's leg, and the bull-terrier got him by the scruff, after which several more boys and dogs joined in and the garden of Gale's Cottage became a pandemonium into the midst of which James Barton erupted with a broom in one hand and a poker in the other. Everyone having taken to flight except the bull-terrier, from whose jaws Ahithophel had to be prised, Jason was invited in for the stanching of wounds. He had two bites, but he won James Barton's heart by insisting that Ahithophel's need was greater than his own. After which he was more or less free of the cottage and Tommy Martin let him go there.

They talked now in a desultory manner, with frequent intervals of silence. It was during one of these, when Jason had strayed over to the bookshelves which covered the whole of one wall, that Barton said,

"I had the Chief Constable here to see me, but you'll have heard that, I suppose. Everyone knows everything in Tilling Green."

Jason made some sort of a sound, noncommittal and of an uninterested nature, following it up with,

"Where on earth did you pick this up?"

"What have you got there? Oh, the *Wonderful Magazine*. Picked it up on the stall at the corner of Catchpenny Lane in Ledlington. Full of nice examples of early nineteenth-century credulity, including a particular account of a case of spontaneous combustion."

Jason laughed.

"I don't know that credulity stopped in the early nineteenth century. If a thing is wonderful enough, somebody will believe it. Anything to escape being dull."

There was a pause, after which James Barton said,

"Tilling Green can't have been exactly dull for the last ten days."

"I suppose not."

"Do you know, as far as I'm concerned none of it had happened until this man March came to see me."

"How do you mean?"

"I don't go out in the daytime unless I have to. When I have to, I don't speak to anyone and nobody speaks to me except in the way of business across a counter, so I don't hear any of the scandals with which the Green enlivens the tedium of its days. I was not aware, for instance, that the police are more than half inclined to suspect that Connie Brooke was murdered, and that they are quite sure Roger Repton was. And that being that, I am only surprised they don't add in that other girl too, Doris Pell, and make a job of it. They can then tack the three of them on the anonymous letters that have been going around and lay the lot at my door."

Jason looked over his shoulder.

"Is that March's line, or did you think it up for yourself?"

James Barton said, "I was one of the last people to see Roger alive. He wanted to know what about it."

Jason pushed the *Wonderful Magazine* back into its

place on the shelf and came back to the table. He was frowning.

"His wife was the last to see him—no, Mettie Eccles when she brought him his tea."

"Fortunately for me. But I could still have put cyanide into the whisky."

"Why should you?"

"Oh, just an urge to kill my best friend, I suppose."

"March can't really think—"

Barton blew out a cloud of smoke.

"Perhaps not. Or—perhaps. I don't suppose he has made up his mind. And that being the case, what happens if I tell him something which might point the finger of suspicion at somebody else?"

Jason made a quick impatient movement.

"You mean Scilla—Scilla Repton. The finger is pretty firmly pointed in her direction already. He was going to divorce her, you know—or perhaps you don't."

Barton nodded.

"Yes, he told me. He was a fool to marry her. I could have told him so, but for that sort of folly nobody takes advice. It's like any other kind of poison, you must get it out of your system yourself. But sometimes it kills you first, or kills everything in you that has any interest in living."

Jason said quickly, "What do you know?"

Barton drew on his pipe.

"Oh, just something—something."

"What?"

"Nothing to do with Roger."

"With what? With whom?"

Barton blew out his smoke.

"Perhaps not with anyone at all."

"Are you going to tell me?"

"I don't know—I'm thinking about it. I'd like you to

do some talking first. Just tell me the whole thing right through as you know it—the letters, Doris Pell, that whey-faced Connie. Nothing to her one way or the other I always thought, but she gets herself mixed up in a murder! Now why did she want to do that?"

"I don't suppose she did want to."

James Barton nodded.

"Just a step in the dark and nothing there. Well, go on—let me have the whole thing so far as you know it."

"I wasn't here when Doris Pell was drowned, I've seen one of the letters and a nasty bit of work it was, and Tommy's Mrs. Needham has kept me well up to date with what the village is saying. So here goes."

He told the story as it had come to him, making a plain narrative out of the bits and pieces, and there emerged the basic fact of the anonymous letters. Doris Pell had drowned because of them. Connie Brooke had said she knew who wrote them, and she had died. Roger Repton had said he knew who wrote them, and he had died.

When Jason had finished, a silence fell between them. It went on for a long time. In the end of it James Barton spoke.

"This girl Connie—she came back across the Green on the Wednesday night, and Miss Eccles with her?"

"Yes."

"And said good-night at Holly Cottage and went on by herself to the Croft?"

"Miss Eccles says so."

"Meaning there's no proof that she did?"

"No, there's no proof."

"So she could have gone on with her to the Croft, and gone in with her and seen to it that she had enough of those sleeping-tablets in her cocoa to make sure she'd not wake up again."

Jason nodded.

"Yes, it could have happened that way."

"And it was Miss Eccles who took Roger his tea and was the last, the very last, to see him alive, and the first to find him dead. And then she cries out and accuses his wife. Quite a case to be built up against Miss Mettie Eccles, isn't there?"

Jason was watching him intently. He said,

"Quite a case. It's between her and Scilla, I should say, with the odds on Mettie Eccles in Connie's case, and on Scilla in Roger Repton's. Which I suppose is why there hasn't been an arrest. Logically, the whole thing ties up with the letters—Doris, and Connie, and Roger. And as far as Roger is concerned Scilla is heaven's gift to the police. It's Connie's case which is the snag. How in the world did Scilla Repton contrive to spirit Miss Maggie's sleeping-tablets into that bedtime cocoa? There doesn't seem to be any way she could have done it. And that goes for everyone else except Miss Mettie, who knew about the tablets though she says she particularly warned Connie not to take more than one, and could quite easily have gone the whole way home with her and drugged her cocoa. The alternative theory is, I gather, that the cocoa was drugged whilst Connie was at the party at the Manor, and that the drugging was quite irrespective of Miss Maggie's tablets. Which would be a bit of a coincidence, but not really anything to boggle at, because apparently everybody had been talking about Connie not sleeping, and that could have put the idea of how to silence her into the mind of the person who wrote the letters."

James Barton said in a slow, considering manner,

"Would you say it was about fifty-fifty as between Mrs. Repton and Miss Eccles?"

"I don't know. I suppose it would be. Just about, if it weren't for the fact that I can't for the life of me see how Scilla Repton could have drugged that cocoa. She was on show at the Manor from a quarter to eight when the dinner guests began to arrive until the party broke up. She couldn't have gone across the Green to the Croft during that time, and if it was done before that, Connie would have been in the house and the cocoa wouldn't have been made. Because, you see, Scilla would have had to dress, and I don't suppose that would be just a case of off with one thing and on with another. Make-up takes time, and Scilla's is quite an expert job, I should say. So if you were going to suggest that she nipped down one way whilst Connie and Miss Eccles were coming up by another, I can assure you that she wouldn't have had the time."

Barton said equably,

"I wasn't going to suggest that. If you would stop talking, I was going to tell you something."

Jason laughed.

"So you were! Or were you? I believe what you said was that you were thinking about it. Well, let's have whatever it was."

James Barton leaned forward across the line of the sleeping cats and knocked out his pipe against the open stove. Then he sat back again, cradling the briar in his hand. After a moment he said,

"I went for a walk. I do most nights. With the cats."

"What time?"

"Some time getting on for eleven. I didn't look at the clock. Abner wanted to go out, so then they all wanted to go. So we went round the Green."

"Were the cars coming away from the Manor?"

"Nary car—nary anyone at all. All the way till we came by the Croft. And then there was someone."

"Who?"

"Don't ask me—though I suppose I could make a guess if I tried."

"Who was it?"

James Barton shook his head.

"Abimelech crawled in under the gate. It was shut. I put my hand to the latch and I heard someone coming round from the back of the house, soft-foot and not making any more noise than one of the cats. I stepped back, and I can go soft-foot too. Someone went by me in the dark and Abimelech growled and spat. That's all."

"All!"

"As far as I am concerned."

"Was it a man or a woman?"

Barton said slowly, "It was a—shape. You might say it went too soft for a man. But some men can go soft—I can, and so can any poacher."

"Which way did it go?"

"Oh, back towards the village, the same as I did myself."

Jason said,

"You ought to tell the police, you know. A person who came round from the back of the Croft without showing a light wasn't likely to have been up to much good and could have been drugging Connie's cocoa. The police ought to know about it."

James Barton gave an odd half laugh.

"But you see, there isn't anything I can say about whoever this was that he or she couldn't say about me. I too lurked in the dark and showed no light. Also I was accompanied by the cats, always a sinister factor in midnight wanderings. You know, in spite of the cinema, the march of science, and the Education Authority, villages still have a lingering belief in witchcraft—and you can't have a witch without a cat, now can you?"

Disregarding this, Jason said abruptly,

"Why didn't you have a light?"

Barton shrugged.

"I don't need one."

"And yet when someone comes out of a gate right under your nose you can't tell whether it's a man or a woman!"

Barton laughed again.

"I suppose you think you've caught me."

"I think the word should have been won't, not can't."

"Perhaps. But that's how it is—I was there, and I can't say that I was there without laying myself open to any suspicion that is going."

Jason frowned.

"I think you know who it was."

Barton leaned forward.

"No one could swear to it by sight. It's very dark round by the Croft with all those trees."

"But?"

"Why should there be any but?"

"Oh, there's a but all right, and you might as well tell me what it is."

James Barton sat there with his pipe in his hand. He began to tap on the table with it. And then all at once he stopped and reached for his tobacco-pouch.

"There's only one person Abimelech growls at," he said.

"Well?"

"He growled."

CHAPTER 35

Miss Silver walked down across the Green between tea and the evening meal which the Manor still alluded to as dinner though the rest of Tilling Green was content to sup. Even in the war Miss Maggie had *dined,* in spite of being told to her face by Mettie Eccles that it was plain snobbery when it came to cutlets made with egg-powder or a sardine on toast. Miss Maggie had been a little perturbed by the imputation, but she continued to dine. She said Roger didn't like changes, and she didn't think Mrs. Glazier would like them either. To which Mettie replied that Maggie never did have a will of her own, and of course if you hadn't, she supposed you just had to prop yourself with conventions. There was quite a tiff, but Miss Maggie's obstinacy had prevailed. All this was now far in the past, but Miss Repton had recurred to it over the teacups that afternoon.

"Mettie has a very dominating character," she finished up by saying. "She is so efficient, you know, and if you don't do things her way, she tries to show you how. She means well, and I know it is wrong to get cross with her, but I am afraid I sometimes do. Only not now of course, because I am so very, very sorry for her. She and Roger and I were all really brought up together, and she truly loved him. Dear Eleanor was a good deal younger—Valentine's mother, you know. Oh dear, it does seem such a long time ago."

Miss Silver had begun upon the dark red wool she had bought at Ashley's to make a cardigan for her niece Ethel Burkett. It was to be a Christmas present. The first few rows made a line of rich colour upon the green plastic needles. She said in her kindest voice,

"You must have many happy memories."

Miss Maggie wiped away a tear.

"Oh, yes, I have. But poor Mettie—do you know, I am feeling so concerned about her, all alone in that cottage, and though she has Renie Wayne next door, I don't think—no, I really don't think she would find her any help. Renie always has so many grievances of her own—she wouldn't have time for anyone else's troubles. I did ask Mettie if she would come up here, but she says she can't whilst Scilla is in the house, and I'm afraid I don't feel equal to going down to her—not just yet. Now I suppose you would not feel inclined—it would do her so much good to see you—"

Since an interview with Mettie Eccles was a thing which Miss Silver greatly desired, she made no demur, replying with perfect truthfulness that she would be very glad to go down to Holly Cottage if Miss Eccles would not think her visit an intrusion, adding, "She may not care to see me. I am, after all, a stranger, and she has had a great shock."

"You have helped *me* so wonderfully." Miss Maggie's voice was full of gratitude. "You know, I am really anxious about Mettie, and I should be most grateful if you would go and see her. Valentine has already had too much strain, and I could make it all seem quite natural if you would just take her down a basket of James Grieves. Such a nice apple and she is so fond of them, but not a keeper so you can hardly ever buy them in the shops."

Miss Silver was half way across the Green with the basket of James Grieves upon her arm, when Jason Leigh loomed up out of the deepening dusk. A little to her surprise he stopped, spoke her name, and said,

"I should very much like to have a talk with you, Miss Silver."

From the equable tone of her reply no one would have guessed how unexpected this was.

"Why, certainly, Mr. Leigh."

Without directly pursuing the subject he said,

"You are on your way to Willow Cottage?"

"I shall be going there to fetch a few more of my things, but at the moment I am taking a basket of fruit to Miss Eccles from Miss Repton."

He stood before her on the path, blocking her way.

"Miss Silver, I think there is something that you ought to know. If you would turn and walk back with me to the edge of the Green and then allow me to walk with you as far as Holly Cottage, I think that would give me time to say what I want to, if you don't mind walking slowly."

Miss Silver turned and began to move back along the way by which she had come.

"What do you wish to say to me, Mr. Leigh?"

She had spoken to him before, because he had been often at the Manor in the last two days, but this was the first time that she had suspected him of having any interest in herself. She was not therefore prepared for his saying, "Well to begin with, I think I had better tell you that I know why you are here."

She gave her slight prim cough and said,

"Indeed?"

With this small encouragement, he continued.

"You see, I know Frank Abbott. I happened to see him on my way through town. He thought I had better know how you were placed. To be quite candid, he's got the wind up."

She said on a note between reproof and affection,

"Frank is not always prepared to allow other people to take what he considers to be a risk."

"Connie Brooke's death rattled him, you know, and last night he rang me up in what you might call a flap."

Miss Silver dissociated herself from this expression by saying, "He was apprehensive on my account?"

"He was."

"There is no need, Mr. Leigh. I hope the whole matter will soon be cleared up, and for the time being I feel it right to remain with Miss Repton. But there was something you wished to tell me?"

"Yes there was—there is. Does the name of James Barton mean anything to you?"

"Certainly, Mr. Leigh. He lives in Gale's Cottage next door to Miss Wayne. He is a woman-hater, a recluse. He has seven cats. They all have Bible names beginning with an A, and they accompany him on his nocturnal rambles."

There was something like a laugh beside her in the dusk.

"You have him taped! I want to tell you that he has been a friend of mine ever since I was ten, that he is a strictly truthful and honest person, and that he is quite incapable of injuring man, woman, child or beast. And when I say this I am talking of what I know."

"Yes, Mr. Leigh?"

Jason went on.

"I've just been seeing him. We were speaking about the anonymous letters and the three deaths associated with them."

They had reached the edge of the Green and turned again. Lights shone in the cottages which faced them on the farther side. There was some wind blowing and it was very nearly dark. They seemed to be the only people abroad. Jason said,

"He told me something—I think it may be important. He refuses to go to the police with it. Your position in the matter—it isn't official?"

"Not exactly. But I could not be a party to concealing anything which the police ought to know."

"That is what I thought you would say. I told Barton as much myself. The whole thing is too serious, too dangerous, for anyone to go about withholding evidence. But—and this is why I am talking to you—this isn't a matter for the Ledlington police station. It wants careful handling. In fact, to be perfectly frank, I am bringing it to you because you are in a position to take it to the Chief Constable. I told Barton that this was what I should do, and though he didn't say so, I think it was a relief to his mind. He wouldn't have told me what he did if he hadn't expected me to do something about it."

Miss Silver said in her quiet voice,

"And what did he tell you, Mr. Leigh?"

CHAPTER 36

Since Miss Eccles only had morning help, and that not every day, it was she herself who opened the door in reply to Miss Silver's knock. She had put on the hall light, and as she stood back under it Miss Silver was shocked to see how greatly she had changed in the two days that had passed since Roger Repton's death. She was, as always, carefully dressed, and she was not wearing black, but the navy blue skirt and cardigan seemed too loose. Her hair had lost its spring and the silver lustre which had set off the delicate complexion and the bright blue eyes. There was no colour anywhere now. Miss Silver was reminded of a doll that has been left out in the rain. There was compassion in her voice as she said,

"May I come in for a few minutes, Miss Eccles? Miss Repton has charged me with messages, and I have a basket of apples which she has sent you. I think she said the name was James Grieves. I hope that is right."

Social training is not lightly thrown aside. Whilst the last thing Mettie Eccles desired was to open the door to a stranger, she felt herself quite unable to close it in that stranger's face. Miss Silver, stepping into the passage, was conducted to a sitting-room with blue curtains, a few pieces of good furniture, and the oriental carpet which had been a present from Roger Repton. There was no white in the pattern, and the prevailing colours were a deep blue and some shades of rich old rose. Miss Silver reflected that a scrap of white paper would certainly be quite noticeable against it.

Miss Eccles took the basket of apples and emptied them out into a bowl of old *bleu de roi*. Returning the basket, she had intended to remain standing, but as Miss Silver had taken a seat, she could hardly refrain from doing so herself.

"Miss Repton hoped you would understand that she would have come down but she is not really quite up to it, and Dr. Taylor insists that she should not put any strain upon herself."

Mettie Eccles said in a dry voice,

"What a pity that doctors cannot give us a prescription against strain."

Miss Silver said,

"We have to find such a prescription for ourselves. Friendship and sympathy help, do you not think so? Miss Repton is reaching out for them. She asked me to say how very much she wanted to see you, and how glad she would be if you would come over."

Mettie Eccles did not look as if she had wept. Her eyelids had the brown, shrivelled appearance which comes from tearless grief. Momentarily between these dry lids her eyes took on colour—not their old bright blue, but the colder shade of steel. She said,

"Not whilst that woman is there." The words came short and sharp.

"You mean Mrs. Repton? Miss Maggie said—"

Mettie Eccles lifted a hand.

"I don't know what Maggie is made of. How can she eat or sleep or live under the same roof with Roger's murderess? You have come with messages to me. I would like you to take that back as my message to her. That woman murdered Roger, and Maggie and Valentine go on living in the same house with her, and the police don't arrest her!"

Miss Silver spoke with a sudden quiet air of authority.

"Miss Eccles, do you truly believe that Mrs. Repton poisoned her husband?"

Mettie Eccles gave a terrible little laugh.

"Doesn't everyone? Don't you?"

Miss Silver coughed in a manner which conveyed the impression that she was being discreet.

"Then you must believe that she wrote those anonymous letters."

Mettie Eccles stared.

"What has that got to do with it?"

"Everything, I think. Colonel Repton was killed because he had declared that he knew who had written them."

"He was killed because he was going to divorce that woman and cut her out of his will."

Miss Silver's air of authority became more noticeable. She said,

"I think not. He was killed because he knew who had written the letters, just as Connie Brooke and Doris Pell were killed because they knew."

Miss Eccles was accustomed to dominate an argument. She had a quick brain and a quick tongue. It was something new to her to find herself without words. She said almost in a whisper,

"I don't know what you mean."

Miss Silver went on speaking in that quiet voice,

"Only the person who wrote the letters had an interest in those three deaths. Did you ever see one of the letters?"

Mettie Eccles said, "No." And then, "Why should I?"

"You might have had one."

The sagging shoulders lifted in a gesture of pride.

"There hasn't ever been a reason for anyone to write me a letter like that. No one can say—no one—" Her voice shook and broke. "How dare you ask me that?"

Miss Silver went on calmly.

"Then you would not know what the letters looked like? You would not know whether this was a piece of one?"

She put out her hand with a small torn scrap of paper in it. A scrap of cheap white paper which looked like the corner torn from the bottom of a sheet. Mettie Eccles took it in her hand and looked at it. She saw scrawled on it the first part of the name Tilling—just three letters, and then the jagged edge of the tear. Miss Silver said,

"You wouldn't have seen this scrap of paper before? You would not be interested to know where it had been found?"

She was watching Mettie Eccles intently. What she saw interested her very much. She had come with an open mind, and with great experience in reading the motives and the thoughts of others. She had come without fear or bias, and she saw what she had hoped to see, an answer to the problem on which she was engaged.

Miss Eccles' reaction was in line with the most salient of her characteristics. Even in her present condition of shock and grief a lively curiosity had its way. She exclaimed and said,

"Good gracious—you don't mean to say you've had one!"

"No."

"Not poor Maggie! What a shame! It's too bad!"

Miss Silver said soberly,

"I would like to tell you a story. On the day that Doris Pell was drowned she paid a call in connection with her work as a needlewoman. In that house, and during that call, she picked up a scrap of cheap white paper torn from the corner of one of those anonymous letters. It had the first three letters of the word Tilling written upon it. She knew it at once for what it was, because she had herself received the letter from which this corner had been torn. By the way, may I have my piece of paper back?"

Miss Eccles handed it over. A little colour had come into her face. She said with almost her old energy of voice and manner,

"What a perfectly horrid thing! What house was it?"

"I cannot tell you that."

Miss Eccles' brows drew together in a frown.

"Good gracious—but you must! Don't you see how important it might be? Why, she was here that afternoon. I was going to have some nightgowns made—poor Doris! Now, let me see, where else had she been? I know she was up at the Manor because Maggie was in a way about her blouse not being right, and Doris had been there and fitted it and was going to run up again with it in the evening, and it was when she was coming back from there that she was drowned. That all came out at the inquest, only the more I think about it—I haven't been able to help thinking about it—the more I just don't believe that she did it on purpose. She was here that afternoon and I was talking to her, and if she had had that in her mind, don't you think it would have shown?"

Miss Silver said, "You interest me extremely. Will you tell me just how Doris was that afternoon? Was she just as usual?"

"No—no—she wasn't—I can't say that. But she wasn't depressed or gloomy. Not the way a girl would have to be before she made up her mind to commit suicide. And you know, the Pells weren't Church people, but they were very religious. Doris was a good girl and she would have known how wrong it was. I just thought perhaps something had upset her. As a matter of fact I wondered whether Maggie had been a little sharp with her about the blouse, and I thought it wouldn't be like her if she had. Maggie is a muddler, but she has always been easygoing." She paused, as if considering, and then shook her head. "No, I can't get nearer to it than that about Doris. I thought something had upset her, and I thought she was jumpy. But I don't believe she drowned herself."

CHAPTER 37

Miss Silver left Holly Cottage with the consciousness of a task accomplished. Actually two tasks. The scrap of paper which she had detached from the letter received by Miss Maggie and upon which she had herself scrawled the letters TIL with the sharpened end of a match dipped in ink had successfully served a part of its purpose. She also had the satisfaction of leaving Miss Eccles in a roused and stimulated state. She walked down a flagged path and out of a rustic gate, only to lift the latch of a similar gate and to walk up a twin path to the door of Willow Cottage.

Miss Wayne opened to her in an even more tentative manner than Miss Eccles had done. She had her door upon the chain and peered through the gap, to become profuse in apologies when she discovered that it was Miss Silver who was waiting on the step.

"Oh dear, I am so sorry. It's so disagreeable to be kept waiting in the dark, but I'm afraid I'm apt to be nervous when I'm here alone. My dear sister was always so strong-minded, and Joyce is too. But do come in—do please come in."

As Miss Silver stepped across the threshold she became aware of a very decided smell of gas. She remarked upon it.

"Do you think that one of the burners has blown out on your gas stove?"

Miss Wayne appeared flustered.

"I was putting on a kettle and I dropped the match before the gas had caught. I have opened the kitchen window and the smell will soon be gone. I always think there is nothing so handy as gas to cook by, but it does smell. We used to have it all over the house, you know, but Esther was nervous about it, so when the Grid came through the village we went on to electricity. It cost quite a lot, but it is much cleaner and safer—only I don't care about it for cooking, so we didn't have the gas cut off."

They had arrived in the sitting-room. Miss Silver made her way towards a chair.

"Oh—" Miss Wayne appeared to be surprised. "I thought perhaps you had come for some more of your things."

"And for a little talk with you," said Miss Silver.

There was a small fire on the hearth. Miss Wayne came over to it and sat down in her usual chair.

"Oh, *yes*," she said. "And there is so much to talk about, isn't there? Poor Maggie—how is she? And Valentine—it's a terrible thing for a girl to be jilted like that at the last minute. You know, I thought something had gone wrong when he didn't turn up for the wedding rehearsal. That story of an accident! I suppose he just felt he couldn't go through with it—and if he was only marrying her for her money, it was much better for it to be broken off. Her mother's marriage was a most unhappy one, you know. One wouldn't wish poor Valentine to have the same experience."

Miss Silver said, "No."

Renie Wayne got out her handkerchief and rubbed her nose with it.

"Now you think I am gossiping. My dear sister was so very strict about anything like that, but when you are *fond* of people, how can you help being interested in what is happening to them? It isn't as if one wanted to say anything *unkind!*" She emphasized the word strongly and went on. "Especially now that there has been this dreadful tragedy about Colonel Repton. And to happen as it did, with all of us there in the next room! It's really too terrible for words!"

"Yes, it is terrible."

Renie Wayne flowed on.

"And poor Mettie Eccles had just taken him in his tea! I've been round of course, but she doesn't seem to want to see anyone. She should think how it *looks*—giving way like that! Of course we all know she was devoted to him, but he was a married man and people will talk if she goes on shutting herself up. Somebody really ought to tell her so!"

Miss Silver gave a faint reproving cough.

"I do not think that it would be advisable."

Miss Wayne sniffed and rubbed briskly at her nose.

"We can all see what comes of shutting oneself up. One hasn't to look any farther than next door for that! That dreadful Mr. Barton and his cats—I have really often thought that I would go to the police about them. The one that he calls Abimelech is positively *unsafe!* Do you know, Miss Silver, the wretched creature actually growls at me! Only this afternoon—" She broke off with an effect of suddenness and dabbed at her nose. "But really, Mettie Eccles would do well to be *warned!* Naturally, poor Colonel Repton's death has been a terrible shock to us all."

Suspicion is one thing, certainty is another. For a moment Miss Silver was aware of Jason Leigh saying as they crossed the Green, "Someone came round from the back of the Croft in the dark, and the cat growled. Barton says there's only one person that he growls at. He wouldn't tell me who it was." And now here, in Miss Wayne's sitting-room, the information which Mr. Barton had withheld was being presented to her. She said,

"Murder is a terrible thing, Miss Wayne."

Renie Wayne gave a small exaggerated start.

"Murder? Oh, no, it was suicide. Because his wife—surely you must have heard that his wife—"

Miss Silver repeated the offending word.

"Colonel Repton was murdered."

"Oh, no—"

Miss Silver went on firmly.

"He was murdered because he had said that he knew who had written those anonymous letters. It is not possible to say whether he really knew or not, but he was overheard to say that he did. What he said was repeated, and because of it he was murdered, just as Doris Pell was murdered because she knew, and Connie Brooke because she too said that she knew."

The hand with the cambric handkerchief fell into Miss Wayne's lap. She said in a fluttering voice.

"Oh—oh—how dreadful! Are you sure?"

Miss Silver said, "Yes, I am sure." She opened her shabby handbag and took out of it the small torn scrap of paper which she had shown to Mettie Eccles. She held it out now to Irene Wayne. "Would you like to know where and in what circumstances this was found?"

The small eyes became focussed upon the hand and what it held, the voice sharpened.

"No—no. What is it? I haven't the least idea—"

Miss Silver said,

"I think that you have. I think that you have seen something very like it before. I think it was because of a scrap of paper like this that Doris Pell came to her death. I think you saw it in her hand, as you are seeing it in mine."

Quite suddenly, as if she were looking at a dissolving picture, Miss Silver saw before her not Irene Wayne, not in fact a human creature at all, but a ferret with small fierce eyes and a twitching nose. It was a ferret that had been muzzled and caged, and then all at once had found itself free to nose about and sniff out its prey, to lurk, and bite in secret. There was a spasm of something like terror, and then what was almost a snarl.

"Who gave you that? Who gave it to you?"

Miss Silver said,

"It came to me, Miss Wayne."

The small face was distorted by fury, by fear, and then by fury again.

"What do you think you are going to do with it?"

"There is only one thing that I can do."

"But you won't do it!" said Renie Wayne in a small sharp voice. "You won't do it, because I can stop you! You think yourself very clever, don't you, coming down here and spying into things that don't concern you! But I can be clever too! You didn't think of that, did you, but you had better think about it now! None of these stupid people thought about it! I was just Miss Renie whom they didn't have to bother about! Esther could be put on their committees, and Mettie Eccles, and that interfering Nora Mallett, and if it wasn't one of them who would be chairman it would be one of the others! But nobody ever thought about asking me! I was the one who could be left out! Why, Maggie didn't even ask me to the party the other night! I didn't let them see that I minded—I was too clever for that! But I found a way to punish them all right!" Her voice trailed down into a gasping whisper. "Long ago—oh, long ago—at Little Poynton— that's when it began—and it was all quite easy to do. But Esther found out and she stopped me. She said some very cruel things and she stopped me. But when she was dead I could do as I liked!" Her tone changed on the words. There came into it an extraordinary and dreadful gaiety, a smile stretched the dry lips. She tossed the wisp of a handkerchief in the air and caught it again. "You don't know how I enjoyed myself!" she said. "Nobody knew! I put on a black dress, and I cried when people were there, but I laughed when I was alone! There was a woman who called me a little dried-up faggot—I heard her! Well, I knew something she had done—oh, years ago! I put it in one of the letters, and next time I saw her in church she didn't look nearly so pleased with herself—oh dear, no! That was what was such fun, you know—sending off the letters and then watching the people to see how they looked when they had had them!"

Miss Silver had been looking at her gravely. The balance of a mind which had been long disturbed had now, and perhaps finally, slipped. For the moment at any rate, fear of discovery with its accompaniment of disgrace and retribution were lost in the egotism and self-adulation of the criminal. She began to consider how this interview could be ended.

Irene Wayne went on talking.

"Doris Pell was a very stupid girl. When people are as stupid as that, it is amusing to try and stir them up. She didn't like me, you know. I could tell when she was trying on that blue dress I had when I came out of mourning for Esther—she didn't like touching me! I sent her two letters saying that everyone knew she was an immoral girl." She gave a small shrill twitter. "Well, she didn't like *that!* And I suppose she thought herself *very* clever when she came here to fit me on and she picked up the piece of paper which had got torn off her letter. I don't know how you got hold of it, but I suppose you think you are very clever too! You had better take care not to be too clever, because—what happened to Doris?"

Miss Silver said gravely,

"You pushed her off the bridge and she was drowned."

Irene Wayne laughed—a dreadful sound.

"She hit her head against one of those big stones and she was drowned. It isn't at all a good thing to make me angry, you know. I can punish people. I punished Connie Brooke. She was going about saying that she knew who had written the letters, so I punished her. Esther was having sleeping-tablets before she died. I told the doctor that I had thrown them away, but I hadn't—I kept them. Did you know that my back door key fitted the lock at the Croft? I found it out quite by accident, because Connie forgot her key one night when I was with her, and I said, 'Oh, well, we'll try mine,' and it fitted. So all I had to do was to let myself in by Connie's back door whilst she was up at the party they hadn't asked me to, and there was her cocoa, left all ready on the stove! I had crushed up my dear Esther's tablets— there were quite a lot of them—and I stirred them in and came away. Of course I was very careful to see that they were quite dissolved. She shouldn't have made me angry—she really shouldn't. Colonel Repton was very foolish that way too. I punished him. I was very clever about that, you know. Sleeping-tablets wouldn't have done for him, but I remembered the stuff Esther got in for the wasps' nest in the pear-tree two years ago. She couldn't bear wasps. She said the stuff was very strong, and any that was left must be destroyed, but I hid it away. You never know when something like that will come in useful, do you? I put some of it in a bottle mixed up with a little whisky, and I slipped it into my bag when I went up to the Work Party at the Manor. That girl Florrie tattles, you know—very wrong of her, but girls always do—so everyone in the village knew that Colonel Repton had taken to keeping a decanter of whisky in the study. It was clever of me to remember that, wasn't it? Well, then of course I had to find an opportunity of putting my stuff into the decanter. I slipped out of the drawing-room—I was doing white work, so of course my hands had to be very clean, and I said I had a smudge on my finger. And do you know, just as I got into the hall Colonel Repton came out of the study and went into the cloakroom." She gave a little tittering laugh. "So I didn't wash my hands after all! Do you know what I did instead? I went into the study, and there was the decanter on the writing-table. Not at all the thing—oh, not at all! I only had to take out the stopper, pop in the stuff out of my bottle, and put the stopper back again. The room positively reeked of smoke. There was a most dreadful foul old pipe lying on the table. Quite disgusting—I was thankful to get back to the drawing room! I was very clever, wasn't I? So now you see how foolish you would be to make me angry."

Miss Silver rose to her feet. She had kept her eyes upon Miss Wayne in the blue dress which Doris Pell had made, but she was not prepared for the sudden movement which took her from the sofa to the door. There was in it a suggestion, a highly unpleasant suggestion, of a springing animal. Renie Wayne stood there against the panels, a little crouched, a little as if she might spring again. Then she said,

"I suppose you think you are going to go away and tell a lot of lies about me! But you don't suppose I shall let you do that, do you?"

Miss Silver said in her quiet voice,

"You cannot stop me."

There was that horrid laugh again.

"Can't I? Well, we shall see! You know, you were very stupid to come here this evening, because I was in the middle of some really rather important business. You noticed the smell of gas when you came into the house—"

Miss Silver had a moment of grave apprehension, but her voice was steady as she said,

"Yes?"

Miss Wayne bridled.

"Oh, yes, *indeed!* But it wasn't an escape from the gas stove—you were quite wrong about that. You see that nice big cupboard where the water cistern is—we had to put it there when we had the plumbing altered—

well, there is a gas-bracket there. Not incandescent, you know—just the ordinary old-fashioned burner. Well, we left it alone because it was useful in very cold weather to keep the pipes from freezing. Esther was always nervous about it—she would get up two or three times in the night when we had it on. But as I said to her, 'If there was any escape, you would smell it at once, your room being next door,' so she left it alone. And now it's being very useful indeed, because that's where the gas is escaping. The tap is turned on and the door is shut, and there isn't any window because it is only a cupboard."

Miss Silver used the strongest expression which she permitted herself. She said, "Dear me!" And then, "You had better turn it off, or there will be an explosion."

The smell was, in fact, in the room with them and quite strong. As she spoke she was already at the window, drawing back the curtains and throwing the casement wide. The night air came in with a rush.

Chapter 38

Jason Leigh went on up to the Manor. As he came through the hall he saw Scilla Repton. She had put off her scarlet and green tartan and wore a dark skirt and a sweater of greyish blue. The effect was of a light that had been dimmed. Even her hair seemed to have lost some of its brightness. She half passed him, and then turned back again.

"You don't lose much time!" she said. "I suppose you think you're going to marry Valentine. And settle down here and let the dullness just soak into you until you die of boredom."

He laughed.

"The country bores you because you don't do any of the country things. I shan't have time to be bored."

She said, "Oh, well—" And then, "I can't get out of it quick enough for me." She went towards the stairs, got as far as the first step, and turned to say over her shoulder, "Are you one of the charming people who think that I poisoned Roger? I didn't, you know. Foul minds the police have, don't they?" She shrugged and went on up the stairs, drooping a little.

He went along to the drawing-room, where he found Valentine. They talked about themselves. It was too soon to make plans, but they found that they were making them. Miss Maggie must go on living at the Manor. Impossible to uproot her—impossible and unkind. But she could have her own sitting-room. Once the funeral was over, Scilla wouldn't want to linger. Coming even closer to him and speaking very low indeed, Valentine said,

"Jason, they don't really think—they can't really—"

He said, "I'm afraid they do."

She caught her breath.

"You don't mean—they'll arrest her—"

"I think they may."

"Jason, do *you* think—Oh, she couldn't—not Roger!"

He found himself saying, "No, somehow I don't. I don't quite know why. There could be quite a case against her."

Looking back on it afterwards, that was where a chill discomfort began to invade his mind. It was like sitting in a room with a draught—you didn't feel it much at first, but you kept on feeling it more and more. It reached the point when he got suddenly to his feet.

"Look here, I've got to go. I'll be back again."

Valentine hadn't known him all her life without becoming inured to his being abrupt. She didn't even say, "Where are you going?" and was rewarded by having the information flung at her as he made for the door.

"I'll just pick up Miss Silver and walk home with her."

He ran down the drive, over the bridge from which poor Doris had fallen to her death, and out through the open gates. When he came to the path across the Green he didn't run but he hurried. It was as he came through the small rustic gate of Willow Cottage that the curtains of Miss Wayne's sitting-room were run back and the casement window thrown wide. He stepped off the path and looked into the room. Miss Silver, who had opened the window, now had her back to it. Renie Wayne stood in front of the door, her face contorted with fury and her voice shrill. The smell of gas came floating out to meet him. Miss Wayne was saying,

"The gas is turned on in that cupboard and the door is locked. And do you know who I've got in there? Do you know who is going to die in there unless you shut that window and draw the curtains and put your hand on the Bible and swear solemnly that you will go away tomorrow and never breathe a word, a single word, about all the stupid, senseless lies you have been making up! It's no use your looking at me like that, and it's no use your thinking you can unlock the cupboard and get him out, because I've hidden the key, and the door is very strong—you would never get it broken down in time to save him!"

Miss Silver took an almost imperceptible step towards the door. She said in her grave, calm voice,

"To save whom?"

Miss Wayne tittered.

"Why, who should it be except David? Joyce brought

him over to see me, and she left him here whilst she went to meet Penny Marsh at the Croft—this stupid idea about taking Connie's place in the school, when she ought to be grateful to me for a home and doing her best to look after me and make me comfortable! I haven't been pleased with Joyce for some time and I wanted to punish her, so I turned on the gas and locked David in. But I'll give you the key to let him out if you'll promise not to tell about the letters, or Connie, or anything."

Jason came in through the window on a flying leap. Renie Wayne screamed and went back against the door. When his hands came down upon her shoulders she fought like a cornered rat.

Miss Silver went past them and up the narrow stair. Since Renie Wayne had been alone in the house, what reason would she have to hide the key of any door that she had locked? She hoped and prayed that it would be sticking in the keyhole.

The smell of gas became overpowering as she came up on to the dark landing and switched on the small electric bulb which lighted it. There was a window looking towards Holly Cottage, and she set it wide, her head swimming and her breath catching in her throat. When she had taken a couple of long, deep breaths she turned round with the wind blowing past her. There on the right was the cupboard door, and the key was sticking in the lock. Up to this moment there had been no time to think. She had set herself to come through the gas to the window and to open the cupboard door. She had not let herself think what she might find there.

She opened the door now. It swung outwards.

The cupboard was a deep one, and it was full of shadows. Hardly any light came in from the bulb at the end of the passage. There was a water-cistern like a black rock rising up out of the dark and there was something lying up against it, but she couldn't see what it was. The gas made her head swim. She felt along the wall for the bracket and turned the tap. Then she went right in, holding her breath, and groping for the thing that was on the floor. Her hand touched something rough, and then the leather handles of a large old-fashioned carpet-bag. She pulled upon them with what seemed to be the last of her strength, and with an unwavering determination to get the bag and its contents into the draught by the open window. The air met her and she struggled towards it with a growing sense of thankfulness. The bag was heavy, but it was not heavy enough to contain the body of David Rodney. She struggled with the straps that fastened it and sank down by the sill. The wind blew round her and her head cleared. The open mouth of the bag disclosed the body of a large tabby cat.

Jason Leigh, taking the stairs three at a time, found her trying to lift Abimelech to meet the air.

CHAPTER 39

It was with more than her usual thankfulness that Miss Silver contemplated the familiar comfort of her own sitting-room in Montagu Mansions. Everything so cosy and so peaceful. So many blessings had been bestowed upon her, and she felt as if she could never be sufficiently grateful. The pieces of furniture with which she was surrounded bore mute testimony to the kindly thought of an earlier generation. The chairs had been the bequest of a great-aunt. The bookcase and two small tables had come to her from her grandparents. The silver teapot and milk-jug which Emma kept in such beautiful order had belonged to a godmother. And if the past provided food for affection remembrance, how full of kindness and of constantly increasing friendships was the present! She had just endeavoured to put something of this into words as she filled up Frank Abbott's cup for the second time and handed it to him.

"You will, I fear, accuse me, and with justice, of misquoting Lord Tennyson's so often quoted words, or at any rate of wresting them from their meaning, when I say that I cannot help being reminded of the line about broadening down 'from precedent to precedent.' "

He helped himself to another of Emma's excellent sandwiches. His eyes sparkled as he said,

"If anyone has the right to correct the great Alfred's words, it is a devout admirer like yourself."

She said soberly,

"No, I do not think that I have the right, but I feel that those words do express something of what is in my mind."

He looked at her with affection.

"You know, I never felt really happy about Tilling Green. You oughtn't to have gone there, and that is a fact. It seemed such a good idea to start with, but after that second death I began to get the wind up, and if I had had the least suspicion that Renie Wayne was the poison pen I should have got down there somehow, if I had had to forge a medical certificate to do it."

"My dear Frank!"

He laughed.

"It is you who turn my thoughts to crime. I can't think of anyone else who would make me contemplate forgery. All right, ma'am, don't bring up the big guns— I'm still on the right side of the law. Tell me, what made you pick on Renie as a suspect? Frankly, she never entered my head."

Miss Silver added a little more milk to her cup. Emma was always inclined to put too much tea in the pot when Frank was expected. Her thought turned back to her first impressions of Tilling Green.

"There was an association with the similar outbreak of anonymous letter writing at Little Poynton five years ago. An old aunt of the Miss Waynes was living there at the time, and they used to go over and see her. The post-mistress was under some suspicion—or at least that is what Miss Renie wished to convey. She also took care to tell me that this Mrs. Salt was a sister of Mrs. Gurney who has the post office at Tilling Green, and she used this fact to insinuate that it might be Mrs. Gurney who was responsible for the present crop of letters. When I asked her if there were any grounds for such a suspicion, she became a good deal agitated and said how much she disapproved of and how much her sister had dis-approved of it."

"And that made you suspect her?"

She did not reply for a moment. Then she said,

"I thought she was rather more agitated than she need have been, and there was the connection with Little Poynton. Then after Connie's death and Colonel Rep-ton's she was one of the four people who had to be very seriously considered—Mrs. Repton, Miss Eccles, Miss Wayne, and Mr. Barton. If it had only been Colonel Repton's death that was in question, Mrs. Repton must certainly have been arrested, but her connection with the other two deaths was slight, and in the case of Con-nie Brooke it is difficult to see what opportunity she could have had of drugging the cocoa. Miss Eccles, Miss Wayne, and Mr. Barton all had this opportunity, but I may say at once that I never really suspected Mr. Bar-ton. His only motive, as well as that of Miss Eccles and Miss Renie, must have been fear of being identified as the writer of the letters. But after my interview with Miss Pell it was clear that the scrap of paper which would have identified this person had been picked up in one of the houses visited by Doris Pell on the afternoon before she was drowned. Those houses were the Manor, Willow Cottage where she called on Miss Wayne, Holly Cottage where she saw Miss Eccles, and the Croft where she saw and to some extent confided in Connie Brooke who had been her childhood's playmate and companion. She certainly could not visit Mr. Barton whose door was never opened to a woman. I therefore dismissed him from my mind."

"And you did not really suspect Scilla Repton. Why?"

Again she was silent for a moment. She finished her cup of tea and set it back upon the tray.

"There was the question of the cocoa, and then— these things are difficult to put into words. There are impressions so slight, so indefinite, that one is scarcely aware of them, yet as one constantly succeeds another a picture is built up. Mrs. Repton struck me as unaware of being in any danger. She was conscious of having offended against the *moral* law, and aggressively impatient of that law and of the consequences which this breach was bringing down upon her. But she did not seem to me to be at all aware of any possible relation between herself and the criminal law, or of the consequences which it might have in store. She was brazening out the exposure of her intrigue with Mr. Earle, she was angry and resentful over the change in her husband's will, and she was a good deal more shocked at his death than she was willing to admit. She was in fact a vain, selfish, idle and undisciplined young woman who found herself in uncongenial surroundings and snatched at anything which would alleviate her boredom, but in my opinion she would not have gone out of her way to write the anonymous letters, and she would not have poisoned her husband. And, as everyone is now aware, she did not do so."

"And there was no one else at the Manor who could have filled the bill?"

"Oh, no. Miss Maggie is a gentle person, not very strong, not very efficient, but full of kindness, and Valentine Grey is a very charming girl. There is a good deal of sweetness in her character, and her principles are good."

He laughed.

"Well, she'll need the sweetness. Jason is an odd fish."

Miss Silver smiled indulgently.

"They have known one another from childhood and are very deeply attached."

"Well, so much for James Barton and the Manor. That left you with the occupants of three more houses."

She shook her head reprovingly.

"Oh, no—with only two. The third house would be the Croft, and Connie Brooke who lived alone there was herself a victim. I was left with two possible suspects, Miss Eccles and Miss Wayne. Either of them could have met Doris Pell and pushed her into the pond, since either could have known that she was going up to the Manor that evening with Miss Maggie's blouse. Either could have drugged Connie Brooke's cocoa, Miss Wayne by slipping round to the Croft while Connie was at the Manor, and Miss Eccles by seeing her the whole way home instead of saying good-night at the gate of Holly Cottage. Either could have introduced the cyanide into Colonel Repton's whisky, Miss Eccles when she took him in his tea, and Miss Wayne by slipping out of the drawing-room and making an opportunity of entering the study. As you probably know, she prides herself on how cleverly she managed this. Miss Maggie having handed over to me the anonymous letter which she herself had received, I tore off a corner of the page and produced what I hoped was a passable imitation of the scrap of paper picked up by Doris Pell. After some experimenting with a pointed match dipped in ink, my suspicion that the letters had been written in this manner was confirmed. I wrote the first part of the word Tilling upon my torn-off corner and took it with me when I went down to Holly Cottage with a basket of fruit from Miss Maggie. I believed that the sight of that piece of paper in my possession could hardly fail to produce a strong reaction in the person who had seen such a piece in the possession of Doris Pell, and who had, I was sure, committed murder in order to suppress this damning evidence. Miss Eccles' reaction was an open and natural one. She is a person with an extremely active and inquisitive mind. In spite of her state of grief she showed a very lively curiosity as to how I had come by this piece of evidence. Miss Wayne's behavior was very different. If she had not already betrayed herself by her complaint that she considered the cat Abimelech to be unsafe because he was in the habit of growling at her, the marked change which came over her when she saw my piece of paper would have done so. The shock, followed by my statement that I believed a piece of paper like this had brought Doris Pell to her death, and that Miss Wayne had seen it in her hand as she was now seeing it in mine, was sufficient to break her down. She could no longer control her fear, her anger, or the insensate pride which the criminal feels in his achievement. By the time that the police arrived her condition was plainly one of insanity. She must have been an anxiety to her sister for years. The elder Miss Wayne seems to have known that it was Miss Renie who was responsible for the affair of the anonymous letters at Little Poynton five years ago."

Frank Abbott said,

"There were two suicides then. Miss Wayne should have told what she knew."

Miss Silver had picked up her knitting. The rich red of Ethel Burkett's cardigan lay in her lap, the green needles moved briskly. She said,

"Three lives would have been saved had she done so, all good, all useful. But few people are prepared to subordinate their private feelings to their public duty."

Memorizing this as a vintage example of what he irreverently termed Maudie's Moralities, Frank brought a lighter tone to the conversation by enquiring after the health of the cat Abimelech.

"I don't know how many of his nine lives he had used up already, but the gas cupboard must have drawn pretty heavily on any that remained."

Miss Silver smiled.

"He is the youngest of the cats, which accounts for his having been so foolish as to be lured through the hedge by the offer of a piece of mackerel, a fish of which he is inordinately fond. Miss Renie is very proud of the manner in which she trapped him by placing the mackerel in an old carpet-bag which could be closed by pulling on a string. Those bags have quite gone out now, but they were very capacious and the opening was strongly reinforced by a metal bar. I have no doubt that Abimelech fought to free himself, but with Miss Renie on the watch he had no chance. But he is quite himself again now, and received me in a very friendly manner when I called on Mr. Barton before leaving Tilling Green."

"You called on Barton? My dear ma'am, you don't mean to say he let you in!"

Miss Silver smiled benignantly.

"He did indeed. He made me a most excellent cup of tea and introduced all the cats."

"Well, the case is over, and I suppose you have added Barton and half a dozen others to the list of your admirers."

She said with an accent of reproof.

"Of my *friends,* Frank. Miss Maggie has been most kind, and I must confess to feeling an interest in Valentine and Mr. Leigh. Joyce Rodney too. Do you know whether she has decided to stay on in Tilling Green?"

Frank nodded.

"I think so. If Miss Renie is certified, as she is bound to be, the administration of the estate falls to Joyce. She could live at the Cottage and carry on the school with Penelope Marsh as they had planned. It will really be much better if she does."

"You have seen her?"

"Well, no—she called me up."

It might have been his fancy, but he thought he detected a shade of benevolence in her expression. She said,

"I am afraid that I may have hurt her feelings by my decision that it would be inadvisable for me to call her Joyce, but now that the case is over—"

"There will hardly be any opportunity."

"You think not?"

He met her slightly disappointed gaze with a laughing one.

"It's no good, my dear ma'am, I am a hopeless case. You will just have to make do with Jason and Valentine!"

The Trouble with Thin Ice
by Camilla T. Crespi

A bride-to-be, is arrested for a very cold-blooded murder—the week of her wedding. Simona Griffo, a friend who likes to meddle in such matters, starts asking questions. As she puts the pieces together, however, she unwittingly pushes herself onto thin ice.

Hearing Faces by Dotty Sohl

Janet Campbell's neighbor has been brutally killed, and there's no apparent motive in sight. Yet Janet refuses to live in fear. When a second murder strikes the apartment complex , Janet's life turns upside-down. Seeking answers she discovers greedy alliances, deadly secrets, and a vicious killer much too close to home.